LOCAL HAUNTS

A HorrorTube Anthology

La Regina 2020

A Stone's Throw by Dane Cobain © 2020 Dane Cobain

The Gentleman by Ryan Stroud © 2020 Ryan Stroud

The Salt Hag by CJ Wright © 2020 CJ Wright

Crowthorne by Andrew Lyall © 2020 Andrew Lyall

Mount Gilead by R. Saint Claire © 2020 R. Saint Claire

Screen Eight by Michael Taylor © 2020 Michael Taylor

Drive Like Hell by Ken Poirier © 2020 Ken Poirier

The Mount of Death by Kevin David Anderson © 2020 Kevin David Anderson

The Drifter by James Flynn © 2020 James Flynn

The Blocked Cellar by Mihalis Georgostathis © 2020 Mihalis Georgostathis

The Night Watchman by Marie McWilliams © 2020 Marie McWilliams

Alone Among the Gum Trees by Cam Wolfe © 2020 Cam Wolfe

Highway to Hell by Nicholas Gray © 2020 Nicholas Gray

The Room Within by D.L. Tillery © 2020 D.L. Tillery

Fading Applause in Quintland by Lydia Peever © 2020 Lydia Peever

A Full Moon Over Black Star Canyon by Matt Wall © 2020 Matt Wall

Long Buried by E.D. Lewis © E.D. Lewis

Darkness Descends by Jason White © 2020 Jason White

At the End of the Rope by Cameron Chaney © Cameron Chaney

All proceeds from Local Haunts will be go to the literacy charity, First Book©.

Edited by R. Saint Claire

Cover art by Cameron Roubique.

Back cover image by Luke Aheran

Additional editing by Black Quill Editing.

*The stories in this volume contain variants of English spellings according to the authors' specific regions.

FOREWORD

A Letter to the Uninitiated

Do you work long, strange hours? I do. This leads me to sometimes find myself up late at night with nothing much to do but watch YouTube videos. My eyes are too tired to read, my brain too foggy to write, so why not? It was two years ago when I was doing this very thing and I came across a dude talking about books.

Wait a minute. There was somebody talking about books on YouTube?

I thought YouTube was for people doing idiotic things, trashing celebrities, and pirated music videos.

But books?

I know. I was shocked, too. It was a channel called Better Than Food, and I was immediately hooked. And thanks to the YouTube automated suggestions, I came across Matt Wall from Paperback Junkie. In each video, he would greet the viewer by saying, "Hello, BookTube."

This was an eye-opening event in my life. BookTube? What the hell was that? It suggested that there weren't just one or two or even ten people talking about books on YouTube, but a whole community discussing the act of reading. So, I decided to get adventurous and I typed in 'horror books' within YouTube's search bar. I was taken straight away to Cameron Chaney's channel (check Cameron's story, *At The End Of The Rope*).

I was hooked.

I then found Alex from Hey Little Thrifter; Dane from Dane Reads (check out Dane's story, *A Stone's Throw*); Rachel from Shades of Orange; Stephanie from That's What She Read; Leon from Paperback Mania; Lydia Peever (check out Lydia's story, *Fading Applause In Quintland*); and, of course, Regina from Regina's Haunted Library (check out Regina's story, *Mount Gilead*). There were so many of them I thought I had finally found my home. My people.

It's been well over two years and I still watch BookTube consistently, pending real-life busyness or, of course, reading. Even better, I'm still making my own videos.

What I found within BookTube is not only other creative people who love reading fiction, such as myself, but I also found a caring, compassionate community of readers who are very welcoming and who continue to strive for inclusiveness and diversity not only within the BookTube community itself but with which authors they are reading.

The book in your hands is no exception. *Local Haunts* has taken the horror BookTube community's global influence and shrunk it down into one village of horror and mayhem you'll not soon forget. Inside these pages are frightening stories from around the globe, telling tales of haunts, monsters, and other terrible things local to each author's place of residence. Within these pages you'll find terrifying tales from North America, my own included, joined by terrible happenings in the Australian bushlands, ghosts haunting an old Greek mansion, an abandoned Vietnamese hospital, and a creepy museum, among many other eldritch encounters.

So, I invite you to not only read the stories herein but to investigate each author's BookTube channel and check out what they think about the books they read. See which ones they found scary. What books they recommend versus what they feel you should distance yourself from. This new habit will come in handy when you're up late at night and find yourself too tired to read. If you love talking and listening to people talking about books, you'll find yourself hooked.

Jason White (Jason's Weird Reads)

August 16, 2020

CONTENTS

A STONE'S THROW

DANE COBAIN

I t was a dull October evening. Shrill winds blew over the Chilterns and a fine mist of rain flew in the faces of the patrons who'd braved the darkness to show their haggard faces in The George and Dragon public house. It was the year of our Lord 1780, and despite the foul weather, business was booming.

Suki, the teenage barmaid, wished it wasn't. The landlord didn't own her – he'd hired her from a pool of willing candidates because she had a beautiful singing voice and the kind of awkward confidence the job called for – but sometimes it felt like he did. It was always 'fill this' and 'empty that'. Sometimes he sent her down into the cellar to track down a special bottle for the well-off visitors who stopped in as they traversed the rugged landscape. She hated it down there. Sometimes she thought she heard voices.

On this particular night, The George and Dragon was short-staffed because Tom Woodynge had fallen from his horse and broken his ankle. Old Tom was the pub's owner, a member of the gentry who'd fallen on hard times and established himself in that peaceful corner of Buckinghamshire.

Unable to walk, and ordered by the physician to take to his bed until the bones started to fuse back together, he'd left Suki, and her brother Thomas, in charge of the place.

But Thomas was as much use to Suki as a chastity belt would be to Molly Forde, the wretched whore who plied her wares and her body under the eaves of the stables when the Dragon's drinkers went out to check on their horses. She wasn't allowed inside the pub, a respectable establishment, unless she was invited inside by one of the patrons and led into one of the private rooms that travellers called home when they were passing through.

'More ale, wench!'

Suki sighed, adjusted her dress, and carried a flagon across to the three young men who'd been sitting by the fire since the sun had gone down.

'I'll have none of that, George Barber,' she said, filling the young man's cup while avoiding his eyes. 'I knew your mother, you know. She wouldn't stand for this.'

'Aye,' George replied. 'Perhaps it's a good thing she's with the Lord.'

'Oh, damn the Lord,' said the lad to his right. His name was Harry Baker. 'It's not the Sabbath. The Lord can wait.'

'The only Lord around here is old Lord Dashwood,' said the third.

Suki turned to face him, a scarlet flush stealing its way onto her face.

'And I'll have none of your blasphemy, either, James Smith,' Suki said. 'I know your mother, too. Need I—'

But she was interrupted as Jim scowled and reached around to pinch her on the backside. Suki flinched, spilling ale onto the table and into his lap.

'I hope you're going to clean that up,' Barber said.

'Oh, go hang,' Suki said. 'I have other customers to serve.'

And she did, too. Despite the inclement weather and the

fact that there were a couple of competing inns in the village, The George and Dragon was ever-popular. It was where the labourers went to relax after a hard day's work on the fields. Suki preferred to listen than to speak; it meant she got to hear most of the gossip in the village. The George and Dragon was the closest thing the village had to a newspaper, which was a good thing for Suki because, like most women, she couldn't read.

There was a sudden gust of wind and the squall of a small-scale tempest as the door opened and a stranger walked into the pub. The punters paused their conversations and looked up appraisingly before turning their eyes away from the door and back to the faces of their drinking buddies or the playing cards on the booze-stained tables. The breeze caught the candles and blew a third of them out.

'Can a man get a bite to eat in this God-forsaken village?' the stranger's voice was well-educated with a hint of something almost foreign and exotic. He was young, though not as young as the three boys from the village, and he had a short mess of unruly brown hair and piercing blue eyes that shone with a fierce intensity. He had a good-natured smile on his face and was dressed well in the luxurious vestments of the wealthy. His eyes alighted on the various tables in the semi-gloom before settling on little Suki, better known by her elders as Susan Keane, the daughter of one of Lord Dashwood's liverymen.

'You there,' he said. 'Oh, my dear, what brings you to a place like this? No, no, never mind that. What have you got in your pantry?'

Suki readjusted her dress again and forced the biggest smile she could muster onto her tired, duty-worn face. She spoke to the man as she walked over to the fire, lit a piece of kindling, and used it to re-illuminate the snuffed candles. It was a job she did so often that she wasn't even aware she was doing it.

'If it pleases you, sir,' she said, 'we've got bread, mutton, and cheese. We may also have some pigeon, some eggs, and some veal.'

'If it pleases me?" he repeated, with mock politeness. 'And is it good?'

'I do say, it's the best eating this side of the Wye.'

Someone laughed into his pint, and someone else was talking loudly about a highwayman who was rumoured to be working in the roads over by Aylesbury. Around them, the drinkers were still drinking and the talkers were still talking, but he was a stranger to these parts and the locals couldn't help stealing the occasional glance.

'I'll take a plate of whatever you can give me,' the stranger said. 'And brandy. Bring me brandy.'

'As you wish.'

Thomas Keane, Suki's older brother, had been at the bar, sipping on a drink of his own and observing the situation. It was he who descended the steps to the cellar to bring out the brandy. He had no fear of the darkness. Suki was left to busy herself in the pantry, and then in the kitchen. She emerged several minutes later with a platter for the visitor who'd seated himself in a corner and was already smoking shag tobacco from an ornate pipe.

'Here you are, kind sir,' Suki said. 'Forgive me for prying, but do you have good coin?'

'Aye,' the man said. 'I have coin enough. Tell me, what do they call you?'

Suki adjusted her dress again, for the fortieth time that evening, and said, 'They call me Suki.'

'Suki?' the man repeated, thoughtfully. "tis a beautiful name for sure.' He paused for a moment to take another lungful of the tobacco plant. Then, he said, 'You've no cause to ask for my name, but I shall tell you anyway. I am Charles Dashwood. Perhaps you've heard of my uncle, Francis.'

'Lord Dashwood,' Suki murmured.

'Aye. The very same. See how I sign my name.' He reached into the pockets of his long coat and drew out an old, stained-looking letter. The signature was scrawled in black ink in a large, untidy hand.

'Please, sir,' Suki said. 'I can't read.'

Dashwood paused for a moment and then starting laughing, gulping huge lungfuls of the inn's stale air.

'My dear,' he said. 'I might have known. Then you must keep that piece of paper, and you must one day learn to read it so you can see that my name is what I say it is. I say it again: I am Charles Dashwood, and my uncle is Lord Francis.'

Suki had heard of Lord Francis Dashwood, of course. He owned the whole village, though he hadn't been seen in public since before she'd reached womanhood. That didn't matter. Suki had heard the tales.

It was an open secret throughout the village that Lord Dashwood was the leader of the Hell-Fire Club. Dashwood, along with a number of other preeminent men from Buckinghamshire and nearby Berkshire, used to meet at Medmenham Abbey, on the banks of the River Thames, for nights of drunkenness, debauchery, and devil-worship. Their motto was 'Fay ce que voudras', which meant 'do as you please'. It was said that Sir Dashwood himself was the most blasphemous of all. He'd administered the sacrament to his tame baboon. Later, he'd created work for the people of the village by having them hollow out the Hell-Fire Caves, barely a stone's throw away from The George and Dragon.

And then the Hell-Fire Caves became the new home of the Hell-Fire Club, and that's when things became very strange indeed. They – the same "they" who drank themselves into stupors in the front room of The George and Dragon –

said the caves were a breeding ground of moral turpitude. The men who'd helped to build it said that devils and demons were carved into the walls and that they moved around when no one was looking. There was a stream somewhere, far beneath the surface, which they called The Styx. And deep down, there in the darkness was a temple, located directly beneath the church. Its golden ball graced the hilltop and dominated the skyline.

'I've been down there, you know,' Dashwood said, as though he'd read her thoughts. 'The temple. It's hell, quite literally. Heaven above, hell below. They worshipped Christ on high and the devil in the temple beyond The Styx.'

'You barely look old enough, sir,' Suki replied.

'Oh, no, no,' he said waving a hand dismissively and coming dangerously close to sending his drink tumbling to the floor. 'Not to one of the ceremonies.'

There were rumours about the ceremonies, too. The members of the Hell-Fire Club were said to have taken young girls down there to "sacrifice" their virginity. That's what had happened to Molly Forde. Suki shivered.

'I shouldn't like to think of such things.'

'Then you won't want to hear about the ghost of Paul Whitehead,' Dashwood said. 'More's the pity.'

'Sir, I've heard tell of Mr. Whitehead,' Suki said.

'And pray tell me what you've heard.'

'They say he was a poet,' Suki replied.

'That he was,' Dashwood said. 'And like all poets, he was a madman and a lecher. He was also the steward of the Hell-Fire Club. He interrogated the new recruits and scored them on their ability to swallow port and claret. He was also my uncle's lover.'

Suki made the sign of the cross and darted her eyes nervously around searching for her brother and alighting only on the three boys from the village who were watching the conversation and quaffing their ale in near-silence.

'It's been six years since Whitehead passed,' Dashwood continued. 'And my uncle's health has been deteriorating ever since. Did you know he left my uncle his heart?'

'His heart?'

'His heart,' Dashwood repeated. 'He left it to my uncle in his will. His body was buried in Teddingham, but his heart . . . his heart was buried in the depths of the mausoleum.'

Suki shivered again. Then she took herself – and Charles Dashwood – by surprise. She started to sing.

'My lodging it is on the cold ground,' she began, her voice wavering as she strained to hit the higher notes. 'And oh! Very hard is my fare. But that which troubles me most is the unkindness of my dear. Yet still, I cry, "Oh, turn, love". And prithee, love turn to me, for thou art the man that I long for, and alack! What remedy?'

Her face flushed and she readjusted her dress, clearly uncomfortable on the receiving end of Dashwood's intense blue eyes. Dashwood smiled at her and said, 'I beg of you, please continue.'

Suki paused for a moment and took in a lungful of breath before continuing, 'I'll crown thee with a garland of straw then,' she sang, 'and I'll marry thee with a rush ring. My frozen hopes shall thaw, then, and merrily will we sing. Oh, turn to me, my dear love, and prithee turn to me. For thou art the man that alone canst procure my liberty.'

'I believe there's one more verse, my girl.'

'Aye, you speak the truth,' Suki said. She raised her voice a little and continued, 'But if thou wilt harden thy heart still and be deaf to my pitiful moan, then I must endure the smart still and tumble in straw alone. Yet still, I cry, "Oh, turn love, and prithee, love, turn to me! For thou art the man that alone art the cause of my misery".'

When Suki finished, there was silence. Then Dashwood began to clap, breaking the silence, then suddenly everyone else in The George and Dragon was clapping too. It started slow, swelled then overflowed. It wasn't unusual for Suki to sing. But it was unusual for the punters to take an interest.

'Bravo!' Dashwood cried. 'Marvellous! Fantastic! Spectacular!'

'You're too kind, good sir.'

'Sir? Bah.'

By this time, Dashwood had finished his food and was towards the bottom of his second cup of brandy. Thomas Keane, Suki's brother, was watching on impatiently.

'The meal pleased me,' Dashwood said. 'But your company pleased me more. Alas! I must move on. I'm London-bound, and there are men in the city desirous of my company. Suki. Suki, Suki. I'm pleased to have made your acquaintance.'

And with that, Charles Dashwood quaffed the rest of his brandy, doffed his cap at the other drinkers, and took his leave of The George and Dragon. Suki was left to clean his table. Then her brother sent her down into the cellars to bring up more firewood. The fire was blazing and the hearth already held more wood than the fire needed. It wasn't a necessary task; it was a punishment.

While she was down there, the boys made their plan.

'Snooty Miss Suki,' said George Barber. 'Too good for the likes of us.'

'Says she,' Smith added.

'I say we teach her a lesson,' said Baker.

'Yes!' Barber said. 'But how?'

'We write her a letter,' Smith said. 'We send her a message from the kindly Charles Dashwood, inviting her first to the Hell-Fire Caves and from there, to London.'

'Nay,' Barber said. 'Your plan can never work. What know you of the world of letters?'

"tis true,' Smith replied, 'I'm not a scholar. But Baker is.'

James Smith and George Barber turned their troubled faces to Harry Baker who had a glint in his eye and was emptying the last of his ale into the ever-thirsty maw of his mouth.

'Bring me paper,' he said. 'Bring me a quill and some ink. Bring me ale and cheese and bread.'

'Not here, you fool,' Barber said. 'Let us away. We'll write the note at my house and have my sister deliver it.'

And so the plan was formed, and sure enough, less than an hour later, little Cathy Barber braved the winds and rain, under threat of a bruised arm from her brother, to deliver the letter. As instructed, she handed it over to Suki, who was mopping down one of the tables with a piece of rag.

'A letter?' Suki said, incredulously. 'For me? Pray tell me who it's from?'

But Cathy just shook her head and scuttled back out into the night.

Like most girls her age, Suki couldn't read, but there were others who could. An old man who'd sat quietly in the corner, smoking a pipe and drinking his mead while staring off into the distance, was kind enough to do the honours.

'Let me see now,' the man said, shifting his position to hold the letter up to the flickering light of the candles which Suki had re-lit after Cathy Barber had taken her leave. 'Ah, yes. I have it.'

'What does it say?'

'Patience, dear,' the man said. He cleared his throat, held the letter up to the light again, and began to read, 'It says, "Suki, my dear. I find your voice enchanting; it won't leave my mind. Your natural beauty is like a ray of light in the darkness. Your hands are as delicate as bone china and you smell more heaven-sent than the fragrances of foreign lands. I, myself, am no masterpiece, but I have wealth and status. I can show you the world, if you'll let me. I'm asking you, Suki, to become my wife. If your answer is positive, meet me at the mouth of the Hell-Fire Caves at midnight in your best dress. My coachman will bear us hence to London where we shall be married. Yours most affectionately, Charles Dashwood.'"

When the old man finished reading, Suki dropped to the floor in a dead faint.

She was woken by her brother who was applying a damp rag to her forehead and muttering a catechism beneath his breath. She sat bolt upright and her hand flew up to her mouth.

'What is the hour?' she demanded

'Why, it's an hour until midnight,' her brother replied.

'Only an hour!' Suki said. 'I must prepare at once!'

'I don't know about this, Suki,' her brother said. 'I have half a mind to stop you.'

'You just try.' She flashed him a look of such ferocity he backed away a half-step before he caught himself. He opened his mouth to say something then closed it again. 'That's what I thought. Nothing can stand in the way of love.'

And so Suki dashed away to the house she shared with her brother, their father, and their elderly aunt, a spinster who was already asleep and would remain unaware of her niece's fate until she woke up the following morning.

Suki washed her face in a pail of water, dragged a comb through her thick, unruly hair, then took her best dress out from where it lay in a wooden chest. It was a beautiful dress, one she'd inherited from her late mother and which her aunt had helped her to modify to suit her smaller stature. Sewn from fine white silks, the materials alone would have cost her several months' wages from The George and Dragon. Nobody in the family seemed to know exactly where the gown had originally come from, and that just made it the more magical.

At the appointed hour, little Suki headed back out into the cold and wandered along the lonely dirt path that led to the caves. The wind howled around her, and while the rain had stopped falling from the sky, it remained in great puddles she struggled to skirt around in the darkness. From somewhere in the distance, a dog barked. It was the top of the hour when she arrived, and there was no sign of anyone else in her immediate environment.

Suki waited. And then she waited some more. But Charles Dashwood never came.

Instead, three others did.

It was close to one o'clock in the morning when Harry Baker, James Smith, and George Barber arrived. They'd been further in their cups and had lost track of the time. When they talked, they overlapped each other and spoke with slurred voices.

'We fooled you, snooty Suki!'

'Not good enough for the likes of us?'

'Your knight in shining armour never loved you!'

'You're nothing but the next Molly Forde!'

'A pox on you and your good-for-nothing brother!'

The jeers continued, but Suki ceased hearing them. Instead, all she could hear was her own heartbeat as a cold, hard rage took over her. She stooped, bending her knees awkwardly to lower herself in her dress. She picked up a handful of stones; plucked one out, the sharpest, most jagged-looking one, then pitched it through the air, scoring a glancing blow across Jim Smith's neck. She threw another and then another until she'd depleted the ammo in her hand. She was stooping again to pick up more by the time the boys figured out what was happening.

'It's her!'

'Let's get her!'

'Throw them back at her!'

The boys needed no encouragement on that front. Harry Baker was already on his knees, scooping up a handful of stones of his own. This being the ground outside the mouth of the Hell-Fire Caves, there wasn't exactly a shortage. The other two boys were beside him, and soon the air was thick with stones falling down around them in a hail of pain. Smith took the brunt of the blows, partly because he was the taller of the three and partly because the other two were using him for cover.

There was a shrill cry, a heavy thud, then sudden silence. The three boys looked at each other uneasily and ran in the direction of the sound. Little Suki Keane was lying face down amongst the rocks. She wasn't moving.

'What happened?'

'What do you think?'

'Is she breathing?'

Baker kneeled by her side and gave her a brief once over, but he didn't know what he was looking for. He found the cause, though. One of the rocks had caught her a good one on the side of the head, rending a gash across her temple and sending her tumbling to the ground. It looked as though she'd hit the other side of her head when she reached it.

'Well, is she breathing?'

'Give the man some space!'

'I have no idea,' Baker said. 'But I don't think so. We need to get out of here.'

'What about Suki?'

'What about her?'

'Should we take her back with us?'

'No,' Baker said. 'It's too risky. Someone might see us. We'll leave her here, at the mouth of the cave. If she comes to, she can walk home. If she doesn't . . . well, no one need know we were here.'

And so the plan was formed. Baker removed a knife from his pocket and cut each of them on the palms of their hands. They pressed their hands together in turn to seal their oath and to promise silence. Then they went home.

In the morning, a sad sun dawned over West Wycombe and the rains came down like the rage of a vengeful God. Little Suki wasn't found until the afternoon when a couple of children found her body during a game of hide-and-seek. She was soaked through to the bone, her china white skin and her best dress making her look more like a ghost than a physical being. The children raced into the village and screamed for help. Within half an hour, the bells were ringing and the whole community had poured out into what passed for a village square.

When it was discovered that little Suki had sustained an injury to the side of her head, the atmosphere turned sour and the violence threatened to spill over into an outright lynch mob. To begin with, there was only one suspect on everyone's minds.

'It's that no-good Charles Dashwood,' Thomas Keane shouted, beside himself with grief. That afternoon, he'd been taken to see his sister's body, and the guilt and the rage had almost taken him to an early grave along with her. 'He lured my sister out there and then—'

But he couldn't finish the awful thought.

With suspicions on Charles Dashwood, Lord Francis Dashwood himself was summoned from his repose. He arrived as dusk was beginning to settle, borne to the village in the back of a cab. Suki's father, the liveryman to Lord Francis, had overcome his grief to fulfill his duty, bearing the elderly landowner into his village to dispense with justice. Lord Francis was wearing his formal robes, and they served to offset the sickness and the sallowness in his face. He might have been old, he might have been on the verge of death, but he was still in charge of the land on which they stood.

'Begin at the beginning,' Lord Francis said. He was reclining in the back of his cab, leaning out of the window to talk to the locals. 'I want to know everything.'

So, Thomas Keane started at the beginning, and Lord Francis listened to the boy with rapt attention as he recounted the events of the night before. When he got to the arrival of Charles Dashwood, his voice cracked and he couldn't continue. But that didn't matter. Lord Francis held his hand up for silence.

'Charles Dashwood?' he murmured. 'There's no such man.'

'But he said he was your nephew.'

'Then he lied,' Lord Francis said. 'I have no heir. I have no family capable of producing one. Tell me, lad, what did this man look like?'

Thomas Keane wasn't one for stories and so his description of the man was fairly rudimentary and could have matched half of the men in the village. It was augmented by a few words from the pub's drinkers, but their memories were hazy at best. Not to be trusted in the sober light of day.

'This man could have been anyone,' Lord Francis said. 'Have you any other clues to his identity?'

'No,' Thomas said, but then he seemed to remember something and collected himself. 'Wait! There is one thing . . .'

'Go on?'

'He produced a note with his signature on it,' Thomas said. 'It's amongst my sister's belongings. No, hold! There was a second note, too. The one that summoned my sister to her death.'

'Bring me these notes,' said Lord Francis.

Thomas Keane departed at once and returned with the

two notes of which he'd spoken. He handed them in through the coach's window and Lord Francis buried his nose amongst the papers.

'Hmm,' he said, at length. 'It seems we have a problem. These two letters were written by two different hands. This one, the newer one which summoned your sister to the caves, was written by a younger hand, a steady hand. This other . . . well, I seem to recognise it. It may be signed in the name of Charles Dashwood, but this is the hand of someone else entirely. This is the hand of Paul Whitehead. But Paul has been dead these six years. How is it possible?'

'Perhaps he wrote the note before he passed.'

'Perhaps,' Lord Francis said. 'But why, then, did he sign with a fictitious name?'

'I have no answer for you, sir.'

'This vexes me,' Lord Francis said. He looked paler than he had when he'd first arrived. He rubbed a handkerchief across his forehead to mop the sweat off. 'I must consider this in private. This news is troubling.'

He looked troubled, too. In fact, he looked as though he'd seen a ghost.

The next witness to be called was little Cathy Barber, but her brother had already put the fear of God into her and instructed her about the lie she was to tell. By now, Cathy had figured out the truth, but she both loved and feared her brother and was willing to perjure herself to save his neck. When they asked who'd given her the letter, she answered that a tall, distinguished gentleman had handed it to her from a cab window and asked her to deliver it with all haste.

And there, with no further evidence available, the investigation stalled.

Unfortunately for little Suki, justice was difficult in the shadow of the Chiltern Hills. While efforts were made to track down Charles Dashwood, or whoever he was, they came to nothing. There was no report of him in the other inns, nor had he appeared in London's society. Stranger still, Molly Forde swore blind she'd been standing in the stables all night, plying her wares so to speak, and that she'd seen the man neither enter nor leave The George and Dragon.

Meanwhile, life in the village seemed to get back to normal, at least for most people. For James Smith, however, life was anything but. The day after Suki's body was discovered, he came down with a fever which left him sweating despite the chill. Even with his bed placed close to the fire, the chill refused to die. Before another twenty-four hours had passed, it had taken over the rest of his body. It looked like he was losing the battle.

There was no doctor in the village, so one was brought in from Great Missenden. It didn't take him long to make his diagnosis.

'The boy has an infection,' the doctor said. 'A bad one, a malady of the blood. Tell me, what caused this cut on the boy's neck?'

But no one in George's family could answer, and the two boys who shared his secret weren't permitted to stand at his bedside.

Jim's condition continued to deteriorate, even with all of the medicine the doctor gave him. The passage of a couple of days was enough to seal his fate. He died on a Tuesday, less than a week after little Suki passed, and he was buried on that Friday. His family couldn't afford to pay for the burial, but the undertaker agreed to do it for free. He said that he couldn't remember the last time he'd had to build two child-sized coffins in the same week.

George Barber was the next to die. He'd heard about what happened to Jim and thought he could outrun death by stealing a horse and riding it at full speed for the capital. Instead, he'd been captured along the way, brought back to

West Wycombe, and stood before a judge. His family had hoped for leniency, especially because it was his first offence. He was out of luck and ended up in front of old Justice Stonehouse known by the unpleasant sobriquet of 'The Noose Judge', a nickname he'd earned by his unremitting habit of passing down the harshest of sentences.

For George Barber, no exception was made. He was sentenced to be hanged from the neck until he was dead, and the sentence was carried out forthwith. His final words, which were only heard by the hangman as he pulled the lever to open the trapdoor, were, 'We killed her.'

Harry Baker, the writer of the letter and the architect of little Suki's doom, lived a long and healthy life, but it was unclear whether he was even aware of it. The poor boy lost his mind and lived out the rest of his days in a sanatorium, where he was the subject of an endless stream of medical procedures that culminated in a botched lobotomy silencing his hand and his tongue for good. He grew old there and was eventually buried beneath the oaks out back after nobody claimed his body.

Lord Francis passed too, although he held on for another year as his health continued to decline. Little Suki's death seemed to have a harsh effect on him, for he retreated to his manor and rarely ventured forth onto the grounds. Stranger still, there were rumours in the village that an apparition, purported to be the ghost of Paul Whitehead, had been spotted wandering the grounds. Suki's father was one of the men who'd seen him, and it was said that the shock combined with the grief to push him over the edge. He was found dead one morning in the stables with the horses he so loved. He reeked of cheap spirits, but there was no sign of whatever had killed him. It was written off as an accident, but the gossips called it a suicide. His meagre assets were quickly claimed by the crown and the church refused to bury his body in sacred ground. Instead, he was buried without ceremony at a crossroads so that if his spirit came back, it wouldn't know which direction to head in.

With time, life in the village went back to normal, although stories started to spread of the ghost of a teenage bride in a white dress who could be seen in the darkness of the Hell-Fire Caves by those brave enough to venture there after midnight. There were few who met that criteria.

Time passed, and the 18th century rolled into the 19th century then the 20th. Little Suki was forgotten about, first because of the slow march of time and later by the sheer number of young men from the village who gave their lives in the first and second world wars. Meanwhile, the country changed around them, and the horse-drawn carriages were replaced by motor vehicles. Television antennas sprung up on the sides of rural houses.

In the 1960s, an American called Jerry Pascale was visiting the area. Pascale had heard Suki's story from the lips of one of the perpetual old men who still drank themselves silly in The George and Dragon. The locals said that he braved the caves at midnight and returned to his hotel room disappointed, only to have a visitation in the night. He woke to feel clammy, ice-cold hands on his forehead. As he slowly rose to full consciousness, they passed along and reached his neck. He started to choke, and that was when movement came back to him. He was able to reach across to turn his bedside lamp on.

The feeling of the hands disappeared along with the darkness, and he sat upright in his bed for a while, turning it all over in his head and trying to figure out what was real and what was nightmare. Eventually, he turned the light off and tried to settle back in again. He'd been lying there for a couple of minutes when he spotted something by the door. It was a light, like the light from his lamp but at a fraction of the size. It grew bigger as he watched it. It was opaque and pearly, hovering in the air like a will-o-the-wisp.

Again, Pascale turned the lamp on, and the light vanished only to reappear once more when the room was plunged into darkness. By now, he was wide awake, and while he felt the fear of the devil at his heels, he picked up the courage to approach it. As he got closer, it grew brighter, until an eerie figure in white was illuminated. It looked like a teenage girl wearing an old-fashioned dress, something from the 1700s, perhaps.

As soon as he reached the girl, he was overtaken by a wave of cold that left him breathless. His limbs were heavy, too heavy for him to hold them up, and he felt himself collapse to his knees. The light grew brighter, and he crawled backwards like a crab towards the safety of his bedside lamp. When he switched the lamp back on, the apparition was gone. Pascale kept the light on for the rest of the night, but he didn't get back to sleep again. He left early in the morning and vowed never to return.

The room hasn't been slept in since, and even the staff at The George and Dragon don't like to go in there, especially at night. There are rumours of a ghost that haunts it. A ghost in a flowing white gown.

THE GENTLEMAN

RYAN STROUD

"Here, take them. I don't need them."

"Oh, sir, thank you but I can't."

"Nonsense. Take them, please. I have plenty of pairs in my luggage. I won't even miss these at all." The clean-cut Gentleman in a nice gray suit was holding a pair of socks he had just pulled out of his bag and handing them over to a bare-footed homeless man.

"Sir, really, I ain't gonna trouble you," the homeless man sheepishly replied in a rich southern accent.

The Gentleman was becoming accustomed to the accent as he traveled further south and it was beginning to grow on him.

The Gentleman, standing with the homeless man outside a small-town gas station in rural Georgia, closed his travel bag and placed his leather attaché case on top. Locking his car door, he then looked up at the homeless man. The Gentleman could read the pain and shame written all over the downtrodden man's face. The homeless man looked down at his feet once the Gentleman's gaze met his eyes. "Look, we've all hit hard times in our lives."

The homeless man nodded in response but still looked ashamed.

"Take my socks. Let's go inside the gas station and get you some food and water. And if you'd like, we can run to another store and pick you up some shoes."

"Bless you, sir. Bless you. The socks and food are enough. I . . . I cannot thank you enough. God bless you." A small tear ran down the homeless man's face. He wiped it away quickly.

The Gentleman pretended he didn't notice.

"It's nothing," the Gentleman said with a sympathetic smile.

The homeless man sat on the ground and quickly placed the socks on his blistered and bloody feet. Once finished, the two entered the gas station together.

"Hey! Hey, you two!" shouted an old man standing behind the gas station counter. "He can't come in without shoes on. No service for him. I want him out!"

"It's okay, just relax," assured the Gentleman. He looked over at the attendant, who was currently wearing a southern cross rebel hat and matching shirt, and wondered to himself if it was really about the homeless man's lack of footwear or something else. "We're gonna grab some food and then be out of your way. There's no need for any trouble."

"I don't like this," grumbled the old attendant. "I've got my eye on both of you," he said under his breath.

"Smile," the Gentleman genuinely replied. "It's gonna be a good day. I can feel it."

After the two men finished picking out food and soap, the Gentleman said his goodbyes to the homeless man. He walked to his car, beeped the alarm off, and entered the luxury automobile. He proceeded down the old southern road deep into South Georgia, where the street was lined with grassy fields crossed with deserted farmhouses and barns.

Roughly twenty miles past the gas station, the Gentleman's car approached a blue four-door sedan pulled over on the side of the road. As the Gentleman's car drew closer to the sidelined blue sedan, an elderly man, roughly around his late seventies, came around the front of the stranded vehicle, waving his hands in the air wildly. The Gentleman, always looking out for those around him, quickly pulled his luxury automobile over to the side of the road, parking directly behind the broken-down blue sedan.

An elderly woman exited the passenger side of the blue sedan and swiftly walked toward the lowering window of the Gentleman's car. Looking like a pleasant grandmother in an oversized pink cardigan, she yelled, "Oh my word! Thank you for stopping! Elvis and I were starting to believe we were going to die out here." She gripped the edge of the Gentleman's car window and leaned in a bit.

The Gentleman shifted backward as much as he could in his seat, trying to still look pleasant.

"Get a grip, Pricilla," the old man snapped from behind his wife. "We weren't going to die." The old man's face was rough with hard lines, forming a permanent scorned look. He was dressed neatly, wearing a tucked-in polo shirt, and moccasins with no socks.

"Yes, we were, but not now. Because of this handsome young man," the elderly woman said as she gently stroked the Gentleman's arm.

The Gentleman smiled at the woman as the old man approached and leaned in the car the same as his wife had done.

"Your names are Elvis and Pricilla? Just like the Presley's?" the Gentleman joked with the couple.

"Just like who?" the old man answered. His eyes were gazing around the car as if he was looking for a lost item.

"Never mind," the Gentleman said. "How can I help you two?"

The woman smiled, clasping her old hands together over her heart. "Would you mind taking a look at our car? It seems Elvis isn't good for much anymore." Pricilla slapped at the old man's arm as he grumbled under his breath.

"Sure I can," the Gentleman said with a smile as he exited his car.

"Oh, how nice. Such a good Samaritan, you are." She patted the Gentleman on the back as they walked over to the blue sedan. "You think he's a good Samaritan, don't you Elvis?"

"The very best, Pricilla."

"Yes, such a good Samaritan. Elvis, would you pop the hood for this good Samaritan?"

The old man slowly reached past the open blue sedan's door, pulling a lever and releasing the car's hood.

The Gentleman lifted the hood and peered at the immaculately clean engine. He took a closer look, puzzled by the way everything seemed in place. "Everything seems to look good under here. You sure you just didn't run outta gas or something."

"The car's fine, sweety," came the old woman's voice from behind the Gentleman's back. "But we'll be needing your wallet and your keys."

"What?" the Gentleman asked while turning around to face the older couple, but instead, the Gentleman came face-to-face with the barrel of a Colt .45 and Elvis' ragged smiling face.

"What the . . . " was all the Gentleman could say before Elvis squeezed the trigger of the Colt, putting a bullet square between the Gentleman's eyes.

THE SALT HAG

CJ WRIGHT

I

As the rhythm of the tracks slowed down, Cole Phillips opened his eyes and blinked the blurriness away, the brightness of the train carriage lights above him slowly coming into focus.

It had been a long day, what with working in the office, staring at a computer screen for nearly eight whole hours, except for the half-hour break he had managed to get for lunch. Then, with ten minutes to go until the end of his shift, just when he thought he could breathe a sigh of relief and head home to relax, Craig, the office party animal, invited him out to the pub around the corner for drinks after work with a few of the others as it was Friday.

He had to agree to go, didn't he? How would it look for him to say no?

Even though Cole was a spritely twenty-two years old, it had all taken its toll. He hadn't slept well the night before; thanks to the nightmare from his past rearing its head for the first time in years.

Now he was on his way home there were a few people in the train carriage with him, all dotted around, sitting on their own, except for the young couple in the back, acting as if they were the only people in the world. Just a couple of levels away from putting on a live sex show. The pair had been the same at the station as they all waited for the 11.32 p.m. train from Worcester to Birmingham. There, on their own on one of the benches, the girl had pretty much mounted her boyfriend, if that was indeed who he was, and her moans of excitement had caused the station guard to come over and kindly ask them to stop what they were doing. Reluctantly, they did so, but Cole could hear the girl cursing the interrupter of her fun as the guard walked down the other end of the platform. The couple then continued where they had left off the moment the train had pulled out of the station. This was one of the reasons Cole had closed his eyes, even though the journey to his destination was only a ten-minute ride away.

Cole couldn't resist looking over at them now his eyes were open, though only for a second; he didn't want to be caught staring at them and being thought of as some sort of voyeur or pervert. As he glanced away from the couple, he caught the eye of the pretty young woman sat opposite him. She had also been looking at the amorous pair, and with a sense of being caught in some kind of forbidden act, she smiled at Cole. Her face flushed slightly with embarrassment, she diverted her eyes towards the phone in her hand. Pulling his own phone out of his coat pocket, Cole checked the time and saw that the next station, his station, was only a minute away. It was then that the announcement came over the train-wide tannoy.

"The next station stop shall be Droitwich Spa. Droitwich Spa, next station stop. Thank you."

Getting to his feet, Cole moved to the door on the

correct side of the train for the platform and waited as they slowed down. He could see the streets through the window as they passed thanks to the bright streetlights illuminating the darkness. They passed a group of houses, and then the Middle School, before going under the bridge and arriving at the station platform. The doors opened, and the name 'Droitwich Spa' appeared on the station sign in front of him. The night had gotten colder than it had been when he had got on the train, and Cole hoped he could get one of the taxis that were sat in the car park back to his house, but even as he pulled the last of his money from his pocket, he knew he had nowhere near enough to get a ride home. Resigning to having to walk, Cole zipped his coat up to the top, shoved his hands in his pockets, and walked out through the station gates.

As he got to the bridge over the tracks at the end of the path next to the station his phone rang. Cursing as he struggled to pull it out of his pocket, he saw the smiling face of this mother on the screen.

'Hi mum,' Cole said as cheerfully as he could fake.

'Where are you, Nicholas?' she almost screeched into his ear.

He grimaced, more at the sound of his name than her voice, though that was bad enough. She was still the only person who called him Nicholas and would scowl at anyone who called him by his preferred name of Cole. If I wanted you to be named after a dirty, black lump I would have, was her usual refrain whenever Cole stood up to her about this issue. He had stopped correcting her of the different spelling of Cole and Coal when he realised she was just doing it to annoy him.

'I'm on my way home, mum,' Cole replied. 'I told you I was going for a drink after work.'

'But that was hours ago. I've stayed up, expecting you in.

You know I don't like to go to bed before I know you are safe at home.'

'Mum, I'm twenty-two for f . . . God's sake,' he had been about to swear at her but, thankfully, managed to catch himself before he did so. That was another thing his mother hated; when he swore, though blasphemy he could just about get away with — she wasn't religious in the slightest. 'I've just got off the train, I'll be home in about fifteen minutes. Don't worry.'

'Fine,' she snapped, reluctantly accepting that there was nothing else she could complain at. 'I'll wait up for you, but don't you dare be one minute late, you hear me?'

'Yes mum, bye,' Cole ended the call quickly and returned his phone to his pocket.

Turning left at the brick Boy Scouts and Girl Guides huts next to the station, Cole felt his heart pick up speed as he took the path towards the road he would have to cross to head home. The path was too dark for comfort, what with it being shielded from any illumination on one side by a thick line of trees and an eight-foot hedge on the other. He hated having to walk down it, but it wasn't long before there was a gap in the hedge and he could take the short path to the right which was bathed in the familiar orange glow of the street-lamps. That took him to where he could cross and be surrounded by streetlights and houses the rest of the way home.

Once he had come out into the open, Cole felt a shiver go down his back and he let out the deep breath he had been holding. He would be safe now, he was sure of it.

At the curb, he checked up and down the road for any cars, even though he already could tell that there was nothing coming, and jogged across the street to the path on the other side. Walking down the path, passing the back garden fences of the houses on his left, Cole chided himself for the feeling of fear he had had when he'd left the train station.

Living in the Worcestershire town of Droitwich Spa all his life, however, he had grown up on the chilling stories that filled the town that had stood since even before the Romans came in the first century A.D., laying their claim to the area because of its rich salt reserves in the salt mine under the ground. Being built on top of the natural brine spa and salt mine had caused some of the roads and buildings to gradually sink as more and more people walked the streets. This was most telling along the town's high street, where the road down the centre dipped and the high street shops leaned slightly. A few years ago this had caused disaster when, due to flooding of the nearby River Severn, the canal system off it that ran through the centre of Droitwich burst its banks. The water filled the high street like it was a soup bowl. It caused almost every shop along the street to flood, including the pet shop, where all the pets inside failed to escape their watery fate. There were also tales of ghosts aplenty that had been shared around by Cole's friends in the school playground when they were just kids.

Some of the stories were so "true" that you could even look up information about the hauntings on the town's own website. Ghosts, like the one of Captain Sir Richard Carbury at Priory House, the Tudor-period building opposite the town fire station, where Sir Richard was stabbed to death by his fiancée back in the seventeenth century. The ghost of the White Lady of Norbury House Theatre, who was supposed to bring good luck to anyone who saw her; though Cole would rather go without the good luck if he could help it. Along with ghostly visions of a horse and rider at Chapel Bridge.

Then there were the ghost stories that weren't found on the internet, though were just as prevalent in the haunting accounts of the town. One of Cole's friends, Jaime Crump, told him excitedly about the headless monk in the graveyard of St Augustine's church, which Jamie's older brother had reported seeing one weekend. Cole could believe it, as not only had the church been standing since the 1200s and had historically had monks living there, but he had heard his parents talk about the ghost of the headless monk on more than one occasion to their friends when they thought he was not around. Then there were the other stories of the many ghosts of English Civil War soldiers seen riding through the cellar of the Old Cock Inn.

All these stories flowed through his mind, the more he willed himself not to think about them, the more they came. But the one story out of them all that frightened Cole the most was the one about the Salt Hag, because his nightmare, the one that still kept him up at night, revolved around this terrifying old woman.

Though the origin of the Salt Hag had been lost to history, her legend prevailed more than any other of the town's terrifying tales thanks to the parents of unruly children warning their offspring to behave or The Salt Hag would take them away. These threats being helped by the occasional report of a missing child or teen in the local newspapers, and older children telling their younger siblings that this was proof the Salt Hag was real. Every so often, the teachers at the local primary and middle schools would hear the children talk about the Salt Hag in the playground. There was even a period of time when the children would play a game of tag where the child who was 'it' would pretend to be the Salt Hag, running with their hands outstretched like a zombie and letting out a low, guttural groan. Though this was stopped when the younger sister of a teenage girl who had disappeared one year hysterically broke down during the middle of a lunchtime break. The deputy headmistress had been called from her office as the girl stood in the centre of the play-ground, screaming so loud and with so much terror in her voice that every other child in the school stood and stared at her. As the deputy headmistress reached the girl, her voice broke and the screaming stopped, then the girl vomited the fish fingers and mash potato she'd had for lunch all over the deputy head's shoes. From then on the game was banned in every school in the town, and anyone caught pretending to be the Salt Hag was given various weeks' worth of detentions.

Cole had heard all these tales growing up, though then he hadn't really believed them. Not until the summer when one of his own friends, Anton Riley, disappeared one day. With the missing boy's parents frantic, and search parties having been called off after three days of looking, the rest of the friend group that Cole belonged to decided they would continue the search by hunting the Salt Hag and rescuing him from her.

They didn't get very far.

2

'Are you coming Cole, or what?' cried Jamie Crump, looking back as the others, except him and Cole, ran down the grass slope onto the playing field.

'Why did we have to come this way?' Cole moaned as he caught Jamie up, a little out of breath. 'We should have gone around and along the underpass.'

'Because Paul said that this way was quicker,' replied Jamie. 'Now, come on.'

Cursing under his breath as Jamie followed the others down the grass slope, Cole took a deep breath and followed. Slipping slightly on a patch of mud in the sea of green that was the shin-high grass, Cole was thankful he had made it onto the field on his feet, thus escaping the embarrassment of being laughed at by the others. Twelve-year-old boys could be cruel when they wanted to be, even with their friends.

'Which way now?' Jamie asked Paul Tramwell, the leader of their little gang, and the one who had organised this hunt to find out what had happened to their friend Anton.

The final two making up their hunting quintet were the twins, Mark and Mike Lane; a pair of big lads who looked in their mid-teens rather than only twelve, almost thirteen. They had been the ones who gathered up the weapons they were going to use against the Salt Hag when they found her, Mike carrying them all in the rucksack on his back.

'We follow the canal until we get under the bridge where the road goes over,' said Paul. 'We'll be out of sight of anyone else then and we can hand out the weapons. You did double-check everything before you left your house, didn't ya?'

'Of course I did,' replied Mike, a little sheepishly.

'I did too, Paul. We've got a couple of our dad's penknives, and the combat knife he brought over from his Europe trip last year. He'd kept it locked in the back of his desk drawer so mum didn't see it.'

'But luckily he left the key on the hooks in the hall with the rest of the house keys so it wasn't hard swiping it,' finished Mike. 'I think he's forgotten he's even got it.'

'We'll still have to return it after this in case he discovers we've taken it,' commented Mark. 'The penknives aren't a problem as he's always leaving them lying around in his workshop.'

Mr Lane's workshop was, in fact, a large shed he kept at the bottom of his garden where he did a lot of woodwork and D.I.Y. projects his wife wanted doing around the house.

'Well, one of you two can have the combat knife,' said Paul. 'I don't want to be on the receiving end of your pissed off dad if he finds it gone or damaged. What else you got?'

'We made a few wooden stakes, you know, to stake the Hag through the heart.'

'That's for vampires,' said Jamie incredulously.

'It'd still work,' replied Mike. 'You stick anything with a pointy bit of wood and it'll go down.'

'I suppose,' Jaime reluctantly agreed.

'And we've got a couple of our old cricket bats and our dad's mallet,' said Mark.

'And they're all really heavy,' moaned Mike, though no one paid him attention.

'Good,' said Paul, 'so, we've all at least got something we can use against the Salt Hag.'

'Do you really think this Salt Hag exists?' asked Jamie.

'Of course she bloody exists,' snapped Paul. 'People have seen her ain't they? Stories have gone back years.'

'But . . .' said Jamie. 'I thought the Salt Hag was a ghost. None of those things work on a ghost.'

'You don't know what she is,' Paul snapped again, a hint of fear in his words. 'We need to be ready for anything.'

'And you're sure she's got Anton?'

'Maybe, Jamie.' Paul smiled. 'But there's only one way to find out.'

'And you know she lives along the canal?'

'Look,' Paul snapped again at Jamie for the last time. 'Further along the canal, past the road bridge, the path gets all overgrown before you reach the bridge that carries the train tracks over it. No one goes along there to do any fishing like they do the rest of the canal. I've heard that those who have tried get scared off by something.'

'By what?' asked Mark.

'No one knows for sure, but I've heard that it's because the Salt Hag lives there somewhere, in between the train track bridge and outside the Railway Inn pub.'

'That's where we're going?' asked Jamie, his voice getting a little higher.

'Yeah, it's the only area no one's looked for Anton. No one believes the Salt Hag's got him. They don't want to believe. You scared?' Paul asked.

'No,' replied Jamie, a little too quickly.

'Good. Come on then.'

As Paul led the way, the others followed. Cole was glad he hadn't said anything, he didn't trust his voice not to give away how much of a bad idea he suddenly thought all this was. Yes their friend Anton had disappeared from his home three days ago, and so far the police and the formal search parties hadn't found hide nor hair of him, but where they were going was dangerous, Salt Hag or no Salt Hag.

As they reached the entrance to the bridge that carried the road over their heads, Paul unzipped the rucksack on Mike's back and handed out the weapons. He handed Cole one of the cricket bats, which Cole was glad of. He hadn't been too keen on getting one of the pen knives or the mallet; using anything belonging to Mr Lane was asking for trouble.

'Look, there's no one about,' Paul said to them as they cautiously walked under the bridge.

They were halfway along the path next to the canal when a loud noise overhead startled them.

'What was that?' Jaime asked, gripping the handle of the other cricket bat tight.

'It was just a lorry going along the road, or something,' snapped Paul. 'Jesus H. Christ, Jamie. I'm starting to regret bringing you along. I knew you were a wimp, but for f . . .'

'What's that? said Mark, pointing to something hidden in the long grass next to the canal path on the other side of the bridge.

'Not you as well,' said Paul.

'No, honest,' replied Mark. 'There's something near the canal bank up ahead.'

'I can't see anything," said Paul, looking in the direction Mark was pointing.

Mark, his father's combat knife in his hand, ran up near to where the thing was and pointed it out.

As the others got closer, Cole noticed that the colour had drained from Mark's face, and for a moment Cole thought his friend was about to throw up. However, Jaime did throw up, getting to Mark first, and seeing exactly what he had found.

It was a dead body.

As she, the body easily recognisable as female, lay next to the canal edge in a large, green anorak jacket, Cole understood why she had been hard to see as they had walked along the path, being well hidden by the long grass and weeds in between the path and the water. She was definitely an adult, despite her small frame and pallid features. She had quite long, varnished fingernails, in a pink colour that gave the impression she was trying to look younger, though her lined face and hair greying slightly at the temples, impressed to Cole at least that she was more likely in her late forties, early fifties, if he was being generous. Under her anorak they could see she was wearing a short, dark blue dress, torn black stockings, and a pair of high heels, one of which was nearly off her foot. The other had an almost-snapped-in-half heel.

'What do you think she was doing down here?' whispered Mike.

'She was probably a prozzy,' said Paul, using the slang word for prostitute.

'Or maybe she was out in town and someone killed her and dumped her here,' offered Mark.

'Either way, we'd better leg it,' said Paul. 'We don't want to be caught down here with a dead body and all these weapons. The coppers will think we'd done her in.'

'But we can't just leave her,' said Cole.

'Yes we bloody can,' replied Paul.

'And what about looking for Anton and the Salt Hag?' asked Mike.

'Things have changed,' Paul told them. 'We'd better just get out of here.'

'I'm not leaving,' said Cole, a lot braver than he felt.

'Fine, you can stay here then,' said Paul before beginning to walk off back the way they came.

'Don't be a dick about this, Paul,' said Mark, blocking Paul's path.

'Fine,' spat Paul. 'We'll call the police, but we need to get rid of these weapons. Mike, you take them all back to yours. And, Mark, you'd better go too. If your dad finds out you two were down here on this side of the playing fields he'll go ballistic.'

Mark nodded. Though they weren't technically out of bounds of where their dad said they could or couldn't go when they played out, it wouldn't look good if it got out that they were involved with finding a dead body next to the canal.

After each of them returned the weapon they had taken back to the rucksack on Mike's back, the twins headed off towards their home as quickly as they could.

'Either of you two got a phone on you?' Paul then asked Jamie and Cole.

Cole shook his head, there was no way his mum could afford to get him a mobile phone even if she didn't think he was too young to have one anyway. Jamie pulled his phone out of his jacket pocket.

'Good,' Paul continued. 'Jamie, you call for the police and an ambulance, and the three of us will wait for them to get here. Though I think one of us should stay down here with the body while the other two wait up by the road for them.'

'Who's going to be the one to stay with the body?' asked

Cole, knowing deep down that however they decided who that would be he would be the unlucky one. The other two knew this, too, and looked at Cole with telling expressions on their faces. 'All right, I'll do it.'

'Great.' Paul smiled, patting Cole on the shoulder. Jamie headed up the grass bank next to the bridge up to the road over the canal.

As Jamie called the emergency services, with Paul relaying to him everything he needed to say, Cole stood a few feet from the corpse, not looking at it directly, but keeping the sight of it in the corner of his eye.

The sound of a train going over the canal bridge as it picked up speed from the station drew Cole's eyes. He watched as the five carriages went past, wondering if any of the passengers who happened to be looking out of the windows could see him and his friends and their horrifying find. As the back of the last carriage disappeared from view, Cole reluctantly moved his eyes slowly back towards the corpse near his feet. He didn't get very far, as something else stood out in the shadow under the bridge the train tracks went over. For a moment he couldn't make out what it was, its movements were odd, out of place for a person to make, but the shadowy figure was definitely humanoid, with long arms and legs coming out of the shapeless rags it was wearing. With the distance between them, the figure was far enough away that its blurred appearance seemed natural to Cole, and though, for a second he wondered if it was due to either smears on the lens of his glasses or a need to get his eyes tested. He did have an appointment for one coming up in a few weeks, he could see that everything else that stood the same distance, or even further away from the figure, was in perfect focus. Just as the figure began to leave the shade of the bridge and come into the light it seemed to merge into the shadows and disappear, as if it couldn't be seen in the rays of the sun. A feeling of ice enveloped Cole for a moment, causing him to visibly shiver, and then it was gone. That seemed to answer the question Jamie had earlier, at least in Cole's mind; the Salt Hag must be some kind of spirit or ghost, unable to exist in the bright light of the sun.

Cole looked back at Jamie and Paul to see if they had noticed anything strange from their higher vantage point, but they were looking the other way, a police car just pulling up in front of them. As the two police officers got out of the car, Paul pointed over to where Cole was standing and was explaining what they had found. Along with the larger of the two officers, Jamie and Paul made their way back down the embankment to the path along the canal bank and approached Cole.

'This is how we found her,' Paul said as they reached the body.

'All right then, boys,' said the officer in a stern but kindly voice. 'You said that you asked for an ambulance as well?'

'Yes,' replied Paul.

'Good,' the police officer smiled. 'Now, go back up to officer Hampton, and he'll take your names and addresses so we can come over, later on, to take a formal statement from each of you.'

Though the officer didn't say, 'So we can make sure all your stories match up', Cole knew that was what he meant. As such, Paul made sure they went over their story again and again as they walked back to their homes, making certain to leave out Mark and Mike Lane's part in it all. Cole never got around to telling either him or Jamie what he had seen in the shadows of the bridge.

As the memory of all those years ago came to its climax, Cole realised he was now standing exactly on the spot where he, Jamie, and Paul had given their details to the other police officer.

Anton hadn't been taken by the Salt Hag, or anyone else, as it turned out. He had been found a couple of days later hitchhiking along the south lane of the M5 motorway just past Gloucester. Where he was trying to get to he never told anyone. Why he had run away was due to an argument with his father that he didn't go into with Cole and the others later on.

Looking down over the side of the bridge at the canal now, a shiver went through Cole just like the one he had felt all those years ago. A strange smell entered his nostrils, like damp sea air and rotten fish, coming from the canal. The water started to bubble, and indistinct white objects came up to the surface. It took a few seconds to realise what they were, but as he took a closer look, Cole could see the fish that lived in the canal were all floating on their sides, dead.

Puzzled by what he was seeing, a compulsion came over him to go down to the canal bank and take a closer look. Having to go back across the road to get to the path along the canal due to a steel fence constructed a few years ago, which ran along the top of the embankment next to the canal path, Cole carefully went down the steps to the mouth of the road bridge. On this side of the bridge, the canal seemed normal. There was no brine smell in the air, nor any dead fish, but as he took careful steps under the bridge things began to change. Once he reached the other side, he was shocked by what he saw.

Now he was down on the path next to the canal not only could he see there was an even larger number of fish floating dead in the water, but also a group of ducks and a few swans had succumbed to whatever was happening. Three of the beautiful, white-feathered birds lay in the water, their heads intertwined with the reeds next to the bank. The smell was so strong that it turned Cole's stomach, making him gag before he had control over himself once again.

It was then that Cole felt a familiar sensation, someone watching him from further up the canal. Looking towards the bridge that carried the train tracks, he saw the strange figure from all those years ago once again standing in the moonlight cast on the canal. No longer in shadow, no longer destroyed by the light of the day, Cole saw the Salt Hag in all her glory. Though she was still too far away to see the detail of her features, Cole could make out the long, skeletal arms and legs. Her skin looked a pale shade of green as if the colour of moss and algae had dyed her body. The tattered rags that covered her nakedness were a charcoal grey, and could have been some sort of thin dress once upon a time, but now looked like a sodden sackcloth that left her legs, from the knees down, and her arms, from her shoulders, exposed. Cole was thankful he could not see her face, her lank, long hair covering most of it, except for one of her eyes and part of her perpetually snarling mouth.

Jaggedly, the Salt Hag took a couple of steps towards Cole. With her clawed finger, she beckoned him to come to her. 'Come,' her voice played in his ears.

She hadn't shouted, and there was no way he could have heard her from that distance, but the word came to him as if she had been standing by his side. Instead of sounding harsh or croaky, her voice sounded seductive.

'Come here, Cole.'

I must be dreaming, he thought. None of this can be real. He believed he was still on the train he had taken from Worcester, fast asleep and dreaming. Any moment he would wake up to find he had missed his stop and would have to find a way to get back to Droitwich from whatever the next station was.

As he tried to take a step back, his foot slipped from underneath him and he landed hard on his back. Thankfully, it hadn't caused any real injury but he had knocked the wind out of himself. The pain in his chest as he gasped for breath told him that this was no way a dream. Managing to get to his feet, Cole wiped the dirt off his hands onto his trousers and took another look down towards where the Salt Hag had been standing, expecting to find himself once again alone. Unfortunately, he wasn't so lucky.

She was still there, standing exactly in the same spot continuing to beckon him to her. 'Come here, Cole,' her voice came again.

Before Cole realised what he was doing, he was walking towards her along the path. He wanted to scream at his feet to stop, to turn around and run away as fast as he could, but the rest of his body paid no attention. As he got within ten feet of her, the Salt Hag ordered him to stop, and once he had, she pointed to the middle of the canal, and the water once again bubbled up, revealing something that made Cole bite down on his tongue to stop from crying out.

For a moment, he hadn't registered what he was seeing. Along with the dead fish, the body of a person floated on top of the water. As the moonlight shone on the pale face, Cole thought it was the same woman he and his friends had found ten years ago, but on closer look, he realised that this girl, and it was most definitely a girl, was much younger than the dead woman had been. She could have been anything from early- to mid-teens, her eyes open wide, small white crystals forming on her eyelashes and the corners of her mouth. The glint of the train-track braces on her teeth just visible under her thin lips.

He looked over at where the Salt Hag had been standing to get instructions from her about what to do, but she was no longer there. Looking around to see where she had gone, he found himself alone.

Slipping off his coat and shoes, making sure his mobile phone was safe in his coat pocket, Cole knew what he had to do and stepped into the canal. He wondered if he would have to tread water or even swim over to the dead girl, but he was gratefully surprised to find the water only went up to just over his waist. Taking three careful steps, he made it over halfway to her, but on the fourth step, his foot slipped as the rock he trod on moved. Losing his balance, Cole's head almost went fully under the surface, his mouth filling with water. Thankfully, he didn't swallow any, as he now realised why the fish and birds had died, and probably also why the girl's body had floated to the surface: the canal, or at least this part of it, was filled with brine water. It tasted a hundred times saltier than the sea, and once he had reclaimed his footing, he spat it out as fast as he could.

As he reached her, Cole thought how pretty she looked. The cliché that she had the face of an angel passed through his mind, and he chided himself for it. As he put his arm around her neck he expected her to move, to reach up and put her arms around his shoulders as he pulled her to the bank of the canal and up onto the path, but she stayed frozen, blankly staring at the stars above her. Getting himself out of the canal first, he dragged the girl from the water. Once she was fully out, Cole sat for a second to catch his breath, not feeling the cold of the night to begin with, though as his heart rate settled back to its usual rhythm, he could feel his teeth start chattering together.

Despite being wet, Cole slipped his coat on to try and get some heat back into his body, then dug out his mobile phone. Looking at the screen he went through in his mind what he was going to say to the emergency services operator. How much of what had happened to him in the last few minutes wouldn't make him sound insane in the retelling?

They were bound to ask him if he knew her name, and as he turned his eyes to her, wondering if somehow he had seen her before, he caught sight of the bulge in her pocket. He hoped it might be something that could identify her. Managing to get his fingers to undo the button, Cole pulled out a sodden, purple, heart-shaped wallet and a couple of house keys attached to one of the wallet's zips with a rusted key ring. Going through the wallet, he found that most of the contents had been destroyed by the water except for some coins, a plastic library card, and a school I.D.

Unfortunately, her name on the I.D. card had been washed off, but the expiry date had been printed into the plastic so he could just about make it out. Cole was surprised to read that if the date was right then the girl had died nearly sixteen years ago, even though as he had fished her out of the water, she looked like she had only been dead for mere moments.

Looking down at the dead girl, Cole wondered if it had something to do with the salt as more crystalline deposits formed on her skin as the canal water dried. Crusting in the corners of her mouth, her eyes and under her nostrils, her skin drying and changing. Her once beautiful features appearing to melt with every second.

Not being able to stomach looking at the girl anymore, and knowing he couldn't put it off any longer, he took a few steps away from the body and called for an ambulance and the police, giving the operator his name and address, the bare minimum explanation of what had happened and his location.

'Someone will be with you in a few minutes, Mr Phillips,' said the operator.

'Thank you,' he replied, not adding the plea for them to

hurry that almost came to his lips as he hung up the call, now realising that he wasn't actually alone.

Looking around into the dark corners of the canal bridge he was standing near, Cole could sense something was looking out at him. A chill came over him that had nothing to do with his wet clothes, and as the smell of rancid breath hit the back of his neck, his mobile phone slipped from his fingers, the screen cracking as it hit the path. Just as a strong clawed-hand gripped his shoulder to turn him around, he screamed into the dark.

CROWTHORNE

ANDREW LYALL

C rowthorne had been on my mind for some time, so I wasn't surprised to find I'd been drifting closer towards the village I'd known as a girl. The notion that I could go back began as an idle daydream, but once the thought took root, it became inevitable that I would return to those childhood haunts of mine.

I don't think I've ever properly spoken about the place to anyone from outside. I always suspected that talking about growing up in a village would invite all kinds of assumptions. I mean, yes, there is a Carnival every couple of years. A young girl is chosen to be the Carnival Princess. There's a procession of floats and people in costumes which moves through the village, down the High Street, towards a fete on the recreation ground; but it's hardly 'Midsommar' or 'The Wicker Man'. The truth is that growing up in a village like that is mainly just the same rounds of home, then school, friends, then family, that most everyone knows from their early years. There were trips into town for the cinema or McDonalds; there was the same worry about being liked and the same hatred of homework that all kids have.

We did have the surrounding woodland, which I suppose not everyone gets when they're young. I've spent so much time since then in bricked-up places that I think the built-up world became normal to me. So, perhaps it was the sight of plentiful trees which made me realize I'd been drifting back. Maybe the trees had set my mind to returning.

Some of us kids had the woods on our doorsteps. We could leave the house, cross the street, and run into the green. We'd hear tell of older boys and girls taking their bikes out after dark and cycling the Devil's Highway, and of course, we found evidence of their fires and under-aged drinking when we played there in the daytime. But we were children and our concerns were childish. The High Street didn't hold much appeal (save the sweet shops and the video store), but out among the trees we built dens, we hollered, chased, screamed.

It was August and the chill of Autumn hadn't quite started to bite, but even so, the High Street was leaden and grey. I looked down that stretch of road with an uneasy feeling brought on by the strange marriage of the unfamiliar new and recognisable old. I hadn't been in Crowthorne for a little over thirty-four years, and as I made my way down the street again – feeling obtrusively out of place – I was surprised by how many of the shops from my time had survived. They stood like implacable artefacts and I marveled that some of these small, niche businesses were still around. They also made me feel increasingly self-conscious. What was I doing here? Everything had moved on. I had moved on. Yet here were these shop fronts dotted up and down: stubborn remainders from decades ago that felt as if they'd been waiting all this time for me to come home. I caught my reflection in a shop window and was surprised when I didn't see the pale image of a little girl staring back. Instead, I looked like a ghost out of time, almost as if my spirit were trapped on the other side of the pane while the other shoppers passed me by without a glance. What would I do if someone called out my name? If someone recognised me? I think I quickened my pace. I wanted to get off the High Street. I hadn't come back for that anyway. That wasn't Crowthorne. Not my Crowthorne. Now that I was there I wanted to see Amy's house.

Amy Dooley was my best friend. When I think of Crowthorne I think of her. I wasn't returning to the village, I was coming back to Amy. People called us 'the sisters' and eventually, secretly, we agreed that we were sisters. She was shorter than me, slighter, but she had more presence in a group than I could ever muster. Funny though: in my mind's eye she's always taller than me. I was simply happy to follow her lead. Wherever she wanted to go and whatever she wanted to do was always fine with me.

Climbing halfway up the hill to her house brought back memories of coming home from school. I was getting a little out of breath but remembered how we used to fly up this road in our buckled shoes, knee-high white socks, and acrylic navy skirts after the final bell. I thought about Mrs Dooley with a tray of jam sandwiches and orange juice for the two of us – 'her girls' she sometimes called us – insisting that we eat something before we both inevitably scrambled outside again. It wasn't the same when I got to her house. I'm really not sure what I'd expected.

Strangers lived there now, so I wasn't going to knock on the front door and I could hardly lurk around on the pavement outside. Instead, I walked past on the opposite side of the road and snatched surreptitious glances up at her bedroom window. The curtains were different; an extension had been added to the side of the house; there was a new front door. It made me feel sad and angry. Then I thought of Mrs Dooley crying: that strange, strangled noise she'd made.

I don't want to talk about that.

I might have run then, I'm not sure. Along the path between houses and into the moist cold of Napier Woods. Muddy tracks were hardening after the first frosts of the year but even so, I left the well-trodden pathways and stole into a crunching carpet of dead, curled leaves.

The air was thicker there; damp. I felt it was insulating me from the outside world. I inhaled deeply and the sounds of my breath and the fall of my feet joined the quiet cacophony all around me. A shiver of bushes to my left as something fled from my approach. The chirping whistles of starlings and thrushes overhead. The background static "shush" of the canopy of leaves set in motion by a breeze that didn't quite reach down to me.

How many times had Amy and I run down this path and through these woods? How many of our games had I forgotten? Not the raucous, shrieking hide-and-seek in gangs, or that one game of kiss chase suggested by a boy who lived on Amy's street; but the games we'd made up together in our own little world. The pacts we'd made as secret sisters. The things we'd promised never to tell anybody. How much of that was lost to me now? My heart was racing so I looked up into the branches and leaves and slowed my breathing just like my doctor had shown me.

The treetops shimmered; smaller limbs waved with a languor I didn't share, but I thought of the interconnected roots beneath my feet and with a wave of calm, I realised that the green understood time differently. Unlike the High Street, it wasn't strange that Napier Woods still felt familiar. Unlike the High Street, this place felt welcoming. I wasn't out of place or out of time there, and for these trees, my decades away were just a yesterday. It was all still there. Waiting.

I remembered the time Amy found a circle of mushrooms, a fairy ring. I counted my breaths, in and calmly let them out as my lips spread into a smile at the image of her spinning in that circle. She'd twirled and said hello to the invisible fairy folk watching from the shrubs and bushes. I joined in then, and at her instruction, we curtsied to the king who lived beneath the large tree near that fairy ring. We returned to that tree so often it became our tree – 'the tree' as we soon called it.

I caught a flash of yellow up ahead on the path and ducked behind the nearest trunk. A dog walker's raincoat. They hadn't seen me, though, and they were moving away. The black dog marked me, however. It paused, extended its neck, and swiveled its ears towards me, but after a moment's consideration, it turned and followed its owner. I waited for a while, minding my breathing, before moving deeper into the woods. I wanted to find the tree.

Back within the dappled, dewy light, I could recall it perfectly: the thick roots like a hand splayed on the ground, its fingers digging into the earth; gnarled bark with an old man's beard of moss and creeping ivy. That first, lowest branch curving down towards the ground, beckoning, as if waiting to scoop us up, inviting us to climb.

With it so fixed in my mind I was sure I could find the tree again without any bother, but each time I was sure it was near – just around the next turn or over the next small rise – my memories proved false. My steps became clompy and impatient, sturdy boots snapping twigs and kicking up plumes of leaf litter. More than once I turned around and doubled back. Hadn't there been a song? Something for the Fairy King? Something Amy had made up to allow us to approach the tree? Everywhere looked familiar but the tree was nowhere. I got the notion that the birdsong was laughter. Laughter directed at me. I had the mad thought that the tree was toying with me. I mean, it had been magic after all, hadn't it?

What I mean is: Amy and I thought it was magic. We

pretended it was magic. This wasn't right. It should have been here. I set my steps up the incline towards Broadmoor Hospital even though I knew Amy and I had never played very close to the high red brick walls of that place. As children, we'd only had vague notions of it being a "bad place". What I understood now as a high-security psychiatric hospital filled our imaginations back then with notions of the "criminally insane" – those two words meaning as much to us as the idea of a bogeyman.

We never went near, but we all lived with the sirens. Thirteen of them, built to alert the people of Crowthorne and the surrounding area if ever one of the patients escaped. They were tested every Monday morning at 10 a.m.: a two-minute escape siren which slowly wound down to be replaced by the two-minute all-clear tone. It was just part of life in Crowthorne. To outsiders, I understand it sounds quite bizarre, but you can find videos on Youtube of the things being tested if you don't believe me. There was a story – I don't know if it's true – of the sirens being tested one time and they forgot to sound the all-clear. We heard that a little old lady had locked herself indoors for three days because she thought someone had escaped. I don't know, we thought it was funny at the time.

Another time, an older girl told Amy and I about the 'Yorkshire Ripper' who was locked up in there. That was enough for us to keep our distance, trust me. I think maybe I had some nightmares around that time. My bedroom looked out over our back garden, and even though I didn't really know who the 'Yorkshire Ripper' was back then, there were a few nights, I think, when I dreamt he was in our garden, looking up at my bedroom window.

How had that song of Amy's gone? Something to the Fairy King, asking his permission to approach the tree. One of the sing-songy tunes she was always humming distractedly to herself. Right then a very strong image came unbidden of her red Wellington boots skipping away from me through the undergrowth, me trailing, always happy to follow where she led. Those boots skipping towards the tree; singing her song; skipping uphill. It hit me so suddenly that I thought for a moment I actually was following her again. And then there was the tree right in front of me. It looked exactly as I'd remembered it.

I stopped in my tracks and for the life of me I thought I'd hear Amy's crunching footsteps tripping away and the melody of her tune drifting up into the branches. For a moment it felt strange not to see her sitting on that low branch, swinging her legs and yammering away.

This was closer to Broadmoor than I ever remembered us coming, but here the tree stood.

I drew nearer with my arm out, gingerly, the same way someone might approach a horse. I lay my palm against the cold, scratchy bark and began searching with my eyes all around the base, thinking that surely, after all this time . . . but remarkably, it was still there. I could just make out the top of the frame amongst the usual woodland detritus, behind the ivy: the fairy door we'd nailed to the trunk between two fat knuckles of root. I dropped to my knees and pulled the ivy away, scooping handfuls of dead leaves and twigs from between the roots. It was weathered and time-worn; set crooked against the bark and held with bent nails where our small hands had tried to hammer it in place. The door had been Amy's idea, but I knew where my Dad kept his tools so I'd brought the hammer and nails to fix it in place.

This was the Fairy King's home. Amy would always address him formally and I know that she sometimes wrote things on notes – wishes and secrets – and slipped them behind the miniature doorway. Other times, we'd leave bits of food: a corner of a chocolate bar or some crisp crumbs from the bottom of a packet. One time we left a piece of Amy's birthday cake. Now those tiny hinges were stiff with rust, the wood warped, but adult hands can be forceful and insistent. I wriggled my fingertips into the gap and pulled. I thought I might snap the tiny door off, but with a couple of short tugs, it creaked away from the tree. I lowered my head closer to the ground, but inside the hollow, there was only the dirty candy floss of a long-abandoned spider's web. I stared inside for a few moments and a woodlouse scuttled out and into the nearby shelter of some dead leaves.

Above the door was more chainmail ivy which I ripped away, noting how the pattern of vines remained in the moss underneath like arteries and veins. We'd carved our spells there, in the trunk: my name; hers; some spiral shapes and stars. There had been a penknife in my Dad's toolbox which we'd used. They'd been so bright when we carved them but now they were dark and green, almost indiscernible. I traced our names with a fingertip as if they were braille and then followed one of the spirals to its centre.

This was Crowthorne. This was where we had run and laughed and made our silly pledges to the Fairy King, but this was not the secret place. This was not the Green House. This was where we first played with Mr Twiggs, but soon after that we would all go to the Green House, and eventually, I learned that Amy used to go to the Green House alone to play with Mr Twiggs.

Later that Summer Amy Dooley disappeared.

Mrs Dooley had cried and made that strange noise in her throat which sounded like the Broadmoor sirens.

After that, it was nothing but questions for a long time. People came to my house and sat with my parents and me. Other times my Dad would take me to visit the police station to talk about Amy. I wasn't in trouble. They kept telling me that I wasn't in trouble, but I was scared nonetheless. Sometimes in the evening my Mum or my Dad would come to my room and talk to me gently. They would ask me the same questions as the police.

One evening, after I'd gone to bed, Mrs Dooley came to the house. I heard her downstairs asking to speak with me, getting louder. I didn't want my parents to let her up to my room.

"I just want to know where my baby is," she kept saying. "She must have said something. She must be able to tell me something. I just want to know."

But Amy hadn't come to call for me that day; the day she went missing. I told lots of different people again and again, and my Mum repeated it, down in our hallway with Mrs Dooley crying at the front door.

"Amy didn't come here. I was here all afternoon myself, I would have known."

"She told me she was going out to play. She told me that, and we both know that meant she was coming here. They were inseparable."

"She didn't. I'm sorry. I'm so, so sorry, but she didn't come here."

I told about Mr Twiggs. I had to. Even though it was one of our secrets. I told the police about Mr Twiggs and how we played with him in the woods and then in the Green House, and then I told them how Amy started playing with Mr Twiggs on her own. Their questions went round and round and sometimes I would be taken out to the woods to show them where we played. I showed them the tree. I showed them our tree and felt a stab of betrayal watching these grown-ups set up a ring of tape around it and go rooting through the leaves and sticks and dirt on their knees with their fingertips. They took pictures. They took pictures of the fairy door and of our carvings; our spells. Then they asked me again and again about Mr Twiggs and the Green House.

I told them what I could.

I told them that I didn't know how to get to the Green House even though they asked over and over about it.

They asked me to describe it. Was it a long way from the tree? Did you walk there? Did he take you in a car? Was there anything about the place that stuck in your mind? What colour was the door? Were there any tall buildings nearby? Any road signs you noticed? Did it have a distinctive smell?

They asked me to describe Mr Twiggs. They asked me about the games we'd played there. One of them even brought me some paper and colouring pencils and asked me to draw him. I made them a picture of Amy and me and Mr Twiggs together in the Green House but I've never been very good at drawing. They seemed disappointed with everything I told them and eventually I got used to the forced smiles and being told I was doing very well while understanding that I wasn't telling them what they wanted to hear. I even sang them Amy's song:

"In the wood

A little man stood

Playing in the Green House

Yeah, yeah, yeah!"

We'd sing that over and over, getting louder each time, spinning around until we were dizzy and would fall to the ground laughing. Then we'd get up and do it again, jabbing at the words, heads awhirl, twirling till we must have look frenzied. Trying to walk in straight lines and stumbling, falling; shuffling on all fours like tots, trying to catch our breath while the rhyme still span in our heads:

"In the wood

A little man stood

Playing in the Green House

Yeah, yeah, yeah!"

Thinking back to that, my head began to spin again. It

was a good job I was already down on my knees and leaning against the trunk because the blood suddenly left my head and dark flowers bloomed in my vision. Inkblots. I thought I was having a heart attack. It was probably a panic attack. Everything around me went fuzzy and a high-pitched whine filled my ears. The blotchy sunlight through the leaves became abstract patterns of pulsing black, white and green. The tone in my ears was the screaming of the tree and I slowly comprehended that when a tree screams its cry lasts for years; a communicated underground through its roots to the surrounding vegetation, the plants, moss, and fungi. I realised that if I died there, and was allowed to decompose into the compost beneath me, I would become a part of that scream.

My vision returned slowly; the whine in my ears subsided; my heart was pounding and I was slick with a cold sweat. I think I'd probably lost consciousness for a few seconds. I rolled gracelessly onto my front and pushed myself up onto wobbly legs. A robin sat on the lowest branch of the tree, it's bead-black eye regarding me from a tilted head. My mind was a tumble of words like the association exercises I used to do with my doctor: robin; bobbin; robbing; gobbling; goblin. The string of words was in Amy's voice, though. It was time to move on from there.

My childish drawing of Mr Twiggs is probably still in an old police file somewhere along with cassette tapes of my interviews. My wavering, high-pitched voice cracking and afraid, trying to explain as best I could.

'Secret sisters.'

I can hear us saying that in unison even now. We said it a lot, linking our little fingers in a promise. I can also still hear me breaking a promise – telling a secret – with a small voice in a small room with a policewoman:

"One afternoon, Amy found me in the woods playing with Mr Twiggs," I'd said.

After that their questions wriggled like fingers at a stubborn lock. They pried me open and winkled more and more out of me. It was the school holidays. One afternoon, Amy found me by the tree playing with Mr Twiggs. Soon we both went to the woods to play with him and then, later on, we used to go to the Green House together. I found out that Amy had started playing with Mr Twiggs alone in the Green House. I promised not to tell.

They wanted to know everything I could tell them about him.

'Mr Twiggs lived in the woods,' I said. 'He would only come out if Amy and I were around. He had long fingers like twigs and a smelly coat of moss and feathers. We went to the Green House together. It was a special place that only we knew about. Our secret place where the walls were green. It was damp and cold and there were no lights so you needed torches. There was an old cot bed with rusty springs and we could make as much noise as we liked because no one could hear us when we were there.'

We moved away that winter, but my parents didn't stop taking me to talk to people. In my head it seems like an endless procession of men and women who wanted to talk to me about how I was feeling, what I was thinking, what I was dreaming about; but I knew they all really just wanted to talk about Mr Twiggs. Oh, they'd act friendly and we'd talk about anything or nothing or whatever was on my mind, but eventually, they'd all come sidling up to the questions they really wanted to ask. Some would wait for weeks and weeks but always, eventually, in some roundabout way they would bend their questions towards him.

Eventually I stopped talking about him, and soon after that – after we'd moved a couple more times – I stopped talking about Crowthorne altogether. If people never knew, I reasoned, they could never ask.

But I would think of him.

I never really made any new friends in any of the schools I moved to. I missed Amy, of course, in a way words can't describe; but after a while, when I wanted to conjure a friend, more often than not, it was Mr Twiggs I thought of and not her. At first, I used to talk to him out loud, and looking back that's probably why Mum and Dad had me talking to so many people even after we'd moved away. So, we learned to keep our games secret. Most of the time he'd hide from the adults to make me giggle. He'd be amongst the bushes in our back garden when I was out playing or looking out through the slit in a postbox when we walked past. Other times he'd be angry at me for leaving him in Crowthorne.

I cried for a little while by the tree and then tried to clean myself up as best I could. I made my way back out of the woods and returned on shaky legs to the High Street. I was suddenly very hungry and remembered a nice looking coffee shop I'd spotted which hadn't been there in my day.

I sat at a table away from the window, had some coffee and cake, and watched the late afternoon darken outside. After that, I walked the streets some more, keeping my head down, not retracing the steps of my childhood but measuring out time until nightfall. I had to wait for dark before I went back to the Green House. That was the one secret I'd kept. The one promise to Amy that I never broke. 'No matter what,' she'd said – our little fingers locked – 'This is our secret place. No one can ever know about it.'

'No matter what,' I echoed, 'I'll never tell.'

It was getting cold. I could have killed some time in a pub but I was worried I'd stick out as an unfamiliar face, or even worse, be recognised. Instead, I walked in varying loops around the quieter streets, always circling back towards the

Green House like water around a drain. I never told anyone where it was, and after Amy disappeared I never went back there in case I was being watched. That's why I felt sick standing in the dark, closer to the Green House than I'd been for the best part of my life. That's why part of me wanted to leave all over again: because after Amy left me, I had left him – left Crowthorne – and I didn't know if he'd still be there waiting for me. I didn't know if he'd be angry.

'He's Mr Twiggs and he dances jigs

In an overcoat like a smelly goat

And his fingers snap like a crackerjack

While he spins you round in the underground.'

I was singing another one of our songs under my breath, just putting off the inevitable. It was dark enough now and quiet enough. No more waiting. No more delays.

The Green House was so close to a busy road that I'd spent every day of that Summer waiting for them to find it. Every time the police took me out into the woods I felt sure they were going to take me there and make me break my final promise.

I crept a little way up the Devil's Highway, past the hum of an electrical substation, and slipped into the wooded area there. This was how Amy and I had always approached the Green House. The trees deadened the Doppler hiss of the occasional passing car and mostly blocked their headlights. Still, I moved in darkness, not wanting to risk the torch on my phone being seen. Progress through the undergrowth was clumsy and each noise I made seemed amplified in the relative quiet of the night. Something fussed and flapped in a nearby tree and every footstep seemed to crunch or snap something.

As a child, the Green House had been a wonderful, secret hideaway. As an adult, I understood it was a Royal Observer Corps Monitoring Post. One of over a thousand all over the country, mostly abandoned now, built during the Cold War to report in the event of a nuclear burst. The way in had been overgrown when we were kids and the past three decades had only worked to hide it further. Even in the low light, though – even covered in nettles and vegetation – I recognised the squat, metre-high concrete entrance to the underground room.

It took time, and I worked methodically and patiently so as to reduce any noise, but eventually, I cleared enough undergrowth to get to the rusted metal hatch. It took more time and effort to finally lever the hatch open. Stale air plumed over me from out of the shaft, like a puff of mushroom spores, and I stared into the square, black hole. My eyes had grown accustomed to the gloom and I could make out the top of the iron ladder on one side of the shaft which led four or five metres down into what Amy and I had called the Green House.

I tested the top rung with a boot before committing my full body weight to the ladder; tentative at first but then with more force. A dull creak echoed around the chamber beneath me and, with one last look around, I swung myself over the edge and began to descend.

Once I was in the shaft my breathing and clambering sounded loud, reflecting off the close walls. I could smell the rust on the ice-cold rungs. After a few metres, I expected to feel the concrete floor beneath me each time I dropped my foot, but there was always one more rung. The thought of descending forever flitted through my mind so when my foot met the bottom it came as a mild surprise. I looked back up the stain-streaked, flakey painted shaft and the opening above looked smaller than I'd anticipated – just a square of darkish blue, with perhaps a whisp of cloud, a creaking climb away.

I could feel the space behind me. It smelt earthy. He was here. He'd been waiting all this time.

I turned slowly. Little pins of light flashed in my eyes – my vision trying to compensate in the pitch black – and I could hear shallow breathing from the shadows (or was it just the sound of my breath coming back at me?).

'Mr Twiggs?'

I fumbled in my pocket for my phone, squinting against the screen's glow as I turned on the torch. Sudden light caused shadows to rear and slide around the rectangular room as I swung my arm back and forth. Swirling particles filled the air, caught in the beam like footage of a shipwreck at the bottom of the ocean. Part of the far ceiling had collapsed inwards and roots and mould had got in and spread like a sickness. I could see the corroded springs of the cot at the far end behind the dirty, waist-high cabinet which still stood against the left-hand wall. And there, perched on top of the cabinet, Mr Twiggs was watching me through the gloom.

I could feel my pulse in my neck. My shaking hand made his shadow wobble and he looked as if he were moving. 'I'm sorry I left you,' I said in a voice which sounded louder in that confined place than I'd intended.

He sat, impassive, and for long beats of time, I didn't really believe that I'd come back, didn't believe that he was really there. My little stick man. My little poppet made of twigs and leaves, old doll's clothes and feathers, bound by string. Bound in parts by lengths of my own hair. My idea. Mine.

One afternoon, Amy found me in the woods playing with Mr Twiggs. After that, she wanted to play with him, too. She decided that Mr Twiggs should live in the woods and I'd agreed; happy to play along, happy to follow her lead. So, we hid him in the bushes near the tree and we'd go and play with him together.

I crossed the room and picked him up. His coat was mouldy now, the stuffing gone so that I could feel the two bundles of twigs tied into a cross making up his thin body and outstretched arms. He still had his neckerchief on; a piece of patterned cloth I'd taken from an old dress I'd outgrown.

Once Amy found the Green House we started playing there instead, and she determined that Mr Twiggs should move. So, we moved him. And for a while, we played with him here. Together.

I looked across at the mouldering cot. Amy was where I had left her.

It's funny: in my mind, she's always that little bit bigger than me, but she was really very small on those corroded, bent springs. She'd become shrunken and grey. Her skin looked like old paper, pulled in at the cheeks and eyes, and her fingers looked like they'd snap just like Mr Twiggs' did.

'You shouldn't have played with him without me,' I said.

Amy hadn't called for me that afternoon. She'd gone to the Green House without me. It had been easy enough to slip out of the house without my Mum noticing. I could still see the handle of my Dad's screwdriver poking out just under her armpit.

'He was my friend first.'

MOUNT GILEAD

R. SAINT CLAIRE

The night before they found the body, the heat rose off Mount Gilead as if red-hot magma lay beneath the tall field grass instead of the rich Pennsylvania farming soil. The crickets were at war with the fireflies, and the lilac and honeysuckle smelled so sweet the scent was nearly rotten, like that time Paula stumbled upon her old dog lying dead in the woods.

In the tiny, first-floor bedroom with one window facing the field and the little church and graveyard on the mountain peak beyond, Paula stirred fitfully beside her kid sister Bobbie.

Bobbie smelled of horse manure because she refused to bathe in the summer. Her filthy feet blackened the sheets Paula had so carefully sprinkled with baby powder to cool the July night's fire. But the worst part about sleeping with Bobbie in the summer was the heat radiating from her sunburnt body and puppy-dog breath. The winter months were different, of course. She had enjoyed cuddling up with her sister because the house was always freezing. "My little hot water bottle," she'd call her.

But Paula was younger then, not yet a woman. That life-changing event came three months ago. Despite her mother's reassuring words and a package of pink *sanitary supplies*, it was demoralizing. Bobbie had teased her mercilessly until Paula had turned it around on her the way only a woman can.

"You're next in line," she told eight-year-old Bobbie with a knowing smile. And when that happens, she explained, "Wayne Shields from down the road will stop teasing you and will wanna marry you instead. And you will have to have his kids and you won't wanna ride horses anymore."

This proclamation, spoken with such mature certainty by her older sister, had left Bobbie so stricken she had hopped on her pony, Mercy, and cantered bareback into the woods. She didn't return until hours later. During dinner that night, Paula noted with satisfaction Bobbie's tear-stained cheeks and grim mouth. Paula had used the sibling squabble to plead her case for womanly privacy. Her parents agreed to convert the attic into a bedroom for Paula. But her father was slow in the construction of her feminine sanctuary. Who wants to work in a hot attic during the summer months?

So, for the time being, Paula was stuck with Bobbie and her matted hair and funky, nocturnal smells.

A breeze wafting through the open window brought a sudden relief from the heat. Paula peeled her cotton night-gown away from her damp skin to catch the swirl of fresh air. It provided just enough comfort to allow her to doze off, but just as Paula's eyelids began to fall like morning dew off a leaf, screaming sounds, two of them—one high-pitched and sharp and the other falling in timbre to a long, drawn-out moan— pierced the thick wall of night.

Jarred awake, Paula sat up in bed, pulling the sheet out from under Bobbie, who rolled like a log without missing a beat in the rhythm of her snores.

Remaining very still, a ready maiden-sacrifice to a raving,

unseen beast, Paula felt the sensation of invisible fingers teasing the back of her neck beneath her damp hair. Straining to hear over the hum of night, she listened expectantly for more screams. But all she heard were the sounds of gunning engines and a few wild whoops fading to the incessant noise of insects knocking against the window screen begging, "let us in, let us in." Reflecting on how loud silence is if you took the time to listen to it, she lay awake most of the night and only pretended to be asleep when her dad, up before dawn to drive a laundry truck in the city, poked his head into the room to check on his girls.

By the time Paula awoke, sparkling sunlight had chased away the night's shadows, and happy birdsong filled the echoes of screams in the dark. Bobbie had already led Mercy to the paddock to graze in the shade, and her mother was downstairs doing whatever mothers did.

Paula claimed the bathroom for her one daily luxury, a bath using the Love's Baby Soft bubble bath she had gotten for her last birthday. While the bathwater cooled around her and the bubbles popped into oblivion, she closed her eyes against the faded, daisy-print wallpaper and dreamed of another life, one filled with romance and handsome men who wore turtlenecks and blazers and drove sports cars in exciting cities where it was always nighttime.

Her reverie ended when her mother banged on the door, reminding her of her summer job at the neighbor's house. She hated skimming the Ross's new in-ground pool for fifty cents an hour. But a job was a job she told herself as she toweled off with a quick peek in the mirror to see if her breasts had ripened any—they hadn't—and slipped on her summer uniform of shorts, t-shirt (training bra underneath), and flip-flops. She twisted her hair into a long, wet braid. It was too hot for anything more elaborate, and besides, she had no one to impress at the Ross's. She often suspected Mr. Ross of spying on her through the window of his home office, feeling his eyes on her as she bent over the pool to scoop up a leaf or a dragonfly.

"Someone was screaming up at the graveyard last night," Paula said as she sat in the kitchen scarfing down a bowl of Count Chocula.

"Must be those biker gangs again," her mother said with a scowl as she stood over the sink squirting pink dish soap onto a sponge.

"Yeah, I figured it was. But it was pretty scary."

Her mom switched on the small black and white TV before Paula could elaborate.

After breakfast, Paula walked up the drive to the neighbor's house, thinking about the biker gangs with scary names like Warlocks and Pagans, who partied in the graveyard on summer nights and left empty bottles of Schlitz and Michelob she and Bobbie would pick up on their way home from school.

Paula opened the gate to the Ross's property and immediately felt the keen sting of her own family's poverty.

From the shimmering blue swimming pool to the striped awning gracing the changing shed to the smooth carpet of green lawn beyond, the Ross's estate put her family's farmhouse and overgrown acreage to shame.

"Nouveau-riche," her mother had sneered on more than one occasion.

But I have beauty, Paul thought, gazing at her wavy reflection as she scooped up a drowning spider from the blue water, and depth of thought and. . .

An old, gray pick-up truck rattled down the mountain road; Paula paused mid-scoop to watch it go by. Passing cars were events on long, hot summer days in the country, on par with walking to the far side of the mountain to get the mail or watching *The Addams Family* reruns.

Must be in a hurry, she thought, absently.

She had just resumed her labor of catching a daddy longlegs in the net when the same truck began backing up the hill in a cloud of blue exhaust, gears grinding with the effort. The truck turned into the Ross's driveway with a slow crunch of gravel and stopped. The parking brake let out a wail.

Two men slowly got out of the truck. One was older in a standard farmer's uniform of denim overalls atop a sweat-stained t-shirt. The other man was young, a few years older than Paula. He wore green coveralls with a Shell Station patch on the chest. His eyes when they met Paula's held a hollow look of shock that made the pores on her skin flush with a cooling sweat.

Mr. Ross popped out of the screen door with a bang to see what's up.

Paula, swatting away a spiral of gnats, tried to hear the men's conversation over the hum of the pool filter. The older man waved his heavy arm at a spot up the hill, while the young man seemed to deflate suddenly. Sitting down on the back bumper of the truck, he dropped his head; the skin on his neck turned white beneath his farmer's tan.

As Mr. Ross and the older man headed up the drive to take a look, Paula stood there, dumbly frozen, until the young man glanced up at her and said in an up-county accent, "Someone better call the cops. There's a dead body thrown over the side of the road up there like a piece of trash."

Once "dead body" had registered in Paula's brain, she dropped the bug-skimmer and ran down the drive to her house, the sharp gravel biting her feet through the thin soles of her flip-flops. By the time she barreled through the kitchen door, she was a kid again screaming, "Mommy! Mommy!"

When she had at last calmed down, Paula begged her mother to let her go back up the road and see what was happening. They had already heard the distant sirens drifting through the trees and across the meadow. Even Bobbie, used to being outdoors from sunup to sunset, seemed to sense the subtle energy shift when she poked her messy face against the kitchen window screen to ask what's up. Their mother, perhaps understanding they would investigate with or without her permission, turned the dinner roast to warm, and led her girls up the long, gravel drive past the Ross's property and out to the narrow country road.

By then the sun was turning the treetops from green to yellow, and two police officers and a volunteer fireman had strung a rope from tree to tree to keep out any traffic or curious onlookers, not that there was much of either on Mount Gilead.

When the girls spotted their dad, already home from work and chatting with the fireman, they broke from their mother's grasp and ran to him. Paula hugged his sweat-stained khaki work shirt while Bobbie's arms circled him from the other side. He flicked his cigarette into the thick summer foliage and pulled them close, as if grateful it wasn't one of his own lying facedown on a carpet of black leaves.

From beneath her dad's arm, Paula gazed at what was happening on the other side of the rope. She wasn't surprised to see that Mrs. Ross, the tall, Maine-bred matriarch with her ever-present ramrod posture and hair in tight pin curls, had taken charge of the scene. Mrs. Ross pointed the flyswatter she carried with her at all times during the summer and barked directives at the men who scuffled down the steep ravine to reach the body.

Paula knew the spot in the road well. *Dead Man's Curve* they called it after Wayne Shields nearly broke his neck that time his go-cart brakes gave out. The ravine running parallel to the guardrail-less road was a notorious trash dump, a buggy, poison ivy-laden no man's land, where once, several summers ago someone had disposed of a dead donkey. Bobbie, flying down the mountain road on her spyder bike, had discovered it with its bloated belly and four legs stiff in the air. She had cried about it for days.

Paula's dad handed the girls back to their mother and ducked under the rope to give the men a hand. Even from a short distance, Paula could tell the dead girl was naked. Her skin was so white it looked bluish-green, like the bellies of the fish her dad would catch in the creek and then kill when they were unfortunate enough to swallow the hook. Two officers had the girl's feet and Paula's dad and the fireman her shoulders. The girl's head hung limply; curly brown hair obscured her face. Someone counted to three and the men flipped her over. Something, which Paula later realized was a flap of skin, fell back, revealing a gaping wound running down the length of the girl's body. Paula gasped at the flash of white ribs within the ravaged hollow darkness.

Suddenly there was screaming. Paula realized it was Bobbie. But by then their mother was already dragging them both away.

Later that night, Paula tiptoed barefoot down the back steps and huddled in the stairwell to listen to the grown-up talk trailing up from the kitchen along with the scent of cigarette smoke.

"Carved open like a deer," her father said. "Looked like her organs were cut out. "

Paula's heart pinged at the sound of her mother's quick intake of breath.

There was the sound of liquid pouring into glasses. Her mother cleared her throat and said, "It's a damn shame. Who would do such a thing?"

"Sounds like a sex maniac or a devil worshipper," Mr. Ross offered.

"One of the officers said maybe she was pregnant," Mrs.

Ross said, her Maine accent hushed and awestruck. "And someone cut that baby right out of her."

A quiet whimpering filled the silence hanging like a cloud of heat before a storm. Paula hadn't realized Bobbie was sitting on the stair above her, listening to every word. She was crying, her mouth opening in a great black O, a volcano about to erupt. A mother's instinct rose in Paula as she rushed Bobbie up the stairs and back to bed. The humidity broke with a clap of thunder, and a cool, grass-scented breeze wafted through the window, caressing Paula's skin. She listened to the patter of rain on the roof and held onto Bobbie long after her little sister's sobs had changed to soft snores.

A detective knocked on their door the next day. He showed Paula and her mother a Polaroid of the dead girl—her eyes closed like she was asleep—and asked if they recognized her. They didn't. Paula's mother prodded her daughter to speak up about the screams she had heard. "I think it was about three in the morning," she admitted shyly.

The detective, sweating through his tan polyester suit, said, "Looks like this girl was killed somewhere else and dumped here. But maybe the bikers saw something. I'll look into it."

For days afterward, Paula made sure she was the one to pick up the mail so she could follow the story in the newspaper. Sitting at the edge of the graveyard where the partying bikers had marked their presence with flattened grass and cigarette butts, she read about how the case had the county detectives flummoxed. The manner in which the girl was killed: blunt trauma to the back of the head and the horrible mutilation of the body—a surgically precise incision from stem to stern and the removal of several internal organs—was like nothing they had ever seen before. The Manson murders were still fresh in everyone's imaginations, and this had all the markings of a devil worshipping ritual. A local witch was consulted. The tarot reader and psychic from the next town over said in her newspaper interview that this was not connected in any way to the type of magic she practiced and cautioned people about jumping to those conclusions. She and her friends were "white witches." Peaceful, loving people, she asserted.

In the coming weeks, the investigation sputtered to a grinding halt. The victim had been identified as Tammy Reynolds, a twenty-year-old "party girl" from the lower county who was last seen leaving a bar with a "bushy-haired stranger."

"Well, what do you expect with a girl like that?" Mrs. Ross tsk-tsked to Paula's mother one morning when they were chatting over the property fence.

The late August sun browned the tips of the tall grass, the black-eyed Susans withered in the field, and eventually, cool winds brushed through the woods with the promise of an early fall.

Paula got a more dignified job as a babysitter for a new family who had just moved in. While cutting through the woods at dusk, she came upon something she recognized from an occult book she had checked out of the library. Carved in the dirt was a large circle and within it, a star made of fieldstones. Stubs of black candles punctuated each of it five points. As Paula gazed at the pentagram, a sudden gust of wind stirred the embers of memory, of a torrid, scream-filled night and the dead girl dumped on the side of the road whom everyone seemed to have forgotten about.

But by the time she had arrived home, one of her friends had called to chat excitedly about the start of seventh grade, and the scene in the woods scattered like the fall leaves.

Years passed. Paula went to college and moved to New York where she married a lawyer. They have two sons. Bobbie never married. She owns a small farm in the shadow of Mount Gilead. She still rides horses.

AUTHOR'S NOTE: THIS IS A FICTIONAL ACCOUNT OF A real murder that happened near my childhood home in the late 1970's. The case has haunted me ever since and remains unsolved till this day.

SCREEN EIGHT

MICHAEL TAYLOR

PROLOGUE

In a glass office cubicle, Chief Superintendent Alan Wye presides over a series of evidence bags scattered across a desk. Labelled, logged, returned from forensics; they are the possessions of one Lee Mark Matthews, twenty years of age. Deceased.

#oB3-LM01 – 1X iPhone (black, shattered)

#oB3-LM02 – 1X Earphones (black)

#oB3-LM03 – 1X Trainers (white, size nine, bloodstained)

#oB3-LM04 – 1X Cinema Uniform (med., bloodstained)

#oB3-LM05 – 1X Lanyard (black)

#oB3-LM06 – 3X Keys

#oB3-LM07 – 1X Keyring (metal cannabis leaf)

And one more item. #oB3-LM08. An empty pistol. Small. Cold and weighty in the hand. The last piece of evidence lay cold in a bed, awaiting formal identification.

"Mr Wye! Staying late again?" Alan hadn't noticed his colleague behind him.

"Looks like it. I'll go home soon." Alan hears his own

voice and rubs at his throat. Raw. Gruff. Strained. Beyond sore. It hurt to speak. He was overworked before the Matthews case. His hand moves from his throat to his ribs.

"Still sore?"

"A bit, yeah," Alan admitted. "D'you know the bullet only glanced me but it's as though I was properly shot."

"Lucky the kid had poor aim! And lucky for you and your team, you don't! I've buried one colleague this year, I never wanna do that again."

Alan thought of his wife who'd be cooking for his twin girls right about now as they finished up a night's revision.

"Any . . . regrets, Alan?"

"None."

TWENTY-FOUR HOURS EARLIER

7:12 p.m. The glass doors swung open and offered their usual mix of popcorn, hot dogs and sweets. Lee Matthews, due at 7 p.m., struggled to make his way to the clock-in machine through crowds queueing for tickets.

Lee had worked at the cinema for eighteen months. His experience during this time ranged from enjoying his place of work to disciplinary hearings and warnings. His misdemeanours never amounted to anything criminal. No. They'd be more suitably categorised as 'disruptive', 'disappointing', 'showing a lack of cooperation'. He knew he should do the decent thing and find a new job, make a fresh start, but he just could not muster up the motivation to do so. In fact, he wasn't sure he could muster up the motivation to cross the foyer.

'Excuse me, yep – coming through.' Many simply slid out of Lee's way. One mother, mouth open, already drafting a complaint in her head shuffled her children aside. A well-built man in his twenties would have stopped Lee were it not for his girlfriend distracting him with two buckets of popcorn to carry.

Lee dropped his rucksack into his locker with a weighty clunk, keeping his phone and earphones handy in his pocket. A cigarette behind his ear. He was caught descending the back stairs by his shift manager, Matt.

'Lee, a word?'

'Already?'

'Lee, - you've just got here. Late . . . again. And what was that in the foyer?'

'It's . . . I've had a rough day.'

'Lee. Just talk to me. You can't let whatever's going on outside this place affect your work.'

'Cut me some slack tonight, aye?'

'I'm bending over backwards for you almost every shift. I can't do it. You know that. I want you on screen-clean. Start in Three, okay? I'm not putting you in front of guests tonight.' Matt unclipped a radio from his belt. 'Check in every twenty minutes, okay?'

'Okay.'

'Anything you need – radio.'

Lee entered Screen Three as credits rolled. A couple in the back row remained seated while Lee started sweeping around them.

'So, is this like, you're whole job? Sweeping?' the kid asked.

Lee bristled. 'Just leave.'

The teen grinned and tipped the remainder of his popcorn on the floor. 'Oops. Missed a bit!'

Lee seethed as they left. At the door, the boyfriend turned, launched what was left of his drink at Lee, then kicked the exit open.

Lee gave chase but the couple had already left the building. He'd lost count of the number of times he had to bite his tongue while his blood boiled. He scanned the foyer: happy couples, date nights, first dates, fifth dates, anniversaries, and dads treating their sons or daughters. All smiling goofily and taking selfies, stealing a piece of popcorn on the way to screen. The whole charade made him sick.

Lee returned to the team area with his earphones blaring. He reopened his locker and took a swig from a can. He began rummaging through his rucksack and paused, rapping along, seemingly having located what he'd returned for. He palmed the item and stuffed it into his pocket. The rucksack, now more or less empty and considerably lighter, nestled back into his locker. No clunk.

Lee returned to Three and finished cleaning. He crossed the mezzanine to a fire exit at the rear of the building, pushed the metal bar and the door gave way as the wind outside took it. Lee launched the black sack at the already overflowing bin and wrestled the door shut. As it clanged closed, Lee and the cold concrete space around him was plunged into total darkness.

"Oh, fantastic!" Lee laughed to himself, thinking a power cut would see him sent home.

DARKNESS

Lee emerged from the fire escape to find no one and nothing. He paused on the mezzanine to look down at an empty foyer. Not just empty, deserted. No lights. No Guests. No staff. All gone. Lee blinked in disbelief at the front doors. Locked and barred.

'Hello? You can come out now!' He crossed the foyer and began banging on the office door.

'Oi! Open up. Not funny!' How long had he spent at his locker, Screen Three, the bins? He checked his phone: 7:44. Not possible.

He stood in the middle of a dark, colourless world. The neon signs were off. A derelict warehouse. The popcorn machine was quiet. It had the echo of an abandoned hangar. Had there been an evacuation? Lee brought the radio up to his chin.

'Matt. Matt, are you receiving?' Silence. 'Matt, come in.' Nothing. 'ANYONE?'

He scrolled frantically through his phonebook.

'Hey, you've reached Matt. Leave a message.'

'Matt, it's Lee. I'm locked in at work. I don't know what's going on but I've been left behind. Where is everyone? Can you let me out? I'm freaking out here, boss. Get back to me.'

Lee hated being alone. Empty auditoriums unnerved him. Lone train rides home unsettled him. He took a seat on a sofa where guests usually waited for their films to start. He stared up at the clock above the foyer wondering how long Matt would be. Lee's phone now showed NO SERVICE. He texted his mum to let her know he'd need a lift home should he miss the last train, trusting it'd be sent when signal returned.

8:30. 9 p.m. 9:40. No response. No movement.

At the front doors, he shifted slowly along them left to right, right to left, a caged animal. He looked out from what felt like a giant inkwell. No drunks, street-sweepers, deliveries, taxis. Nothing. He was utterly forgotten. Rescue seemed unlikely before daybreak. He gave up hope. Then, the radio on his belt crackled. Lee felt teased by it. Another crackle.

'Is someone there?' he asked into it.

Static.

'I swear, if someone's messing with me I'll–'

Lee? came a cold and quiet voice.

'Yeah?'

It's time to talk.

Lee had no choice but to engage, 'Who is this? I know you're nearby.'

Lee, you'll need to cooperate. You're going nowhere. Make peace with that fact.

'Make peace with–? Listen, if you can let me out, do it quick or–'

Or what? You're quick to make threats, Lee. Here's what we're going to do: You'll go into Screen One and we'll talk.

Determined to "confront" the owner of the voice, he burst into a pitch-black and empty Screen One.

'Where are you? You said we'd talk!'

Oh, we will.

'Show yourself. Who are you?'

We're here to get to know you, Lee.

'I know who I am. Listen, I just want to go home. I'm tired.'

Not possible. What I need to see, Lee, is change.

'Right – the cinema's unrecognisable. Is that change enough for you? The place is abandoned. I'm sat here being spoken to by a voice YET-TO-IDENTIFY-ITSELF . . . I think that represents change enough, no?'

Changes from you, Lee. And if you cannot make those changes of your own accord, I'll help you.

'How?'

By showing you the error of your ways.

The radio fell silent and the auditorium became dimly lit as Screen One flickered into life.

SCREEN ONE

Sunlight. Fuzzy home footage. A school field flooded with hundreds of children and parents. The camera panned to a familiar face. Twelve years younger but without the tired lines.

'That's my mum, you sick freak. What is this? How did you get this footage?'

You're asking the wrong question, Lee. You're asking "how". Try asking "why"?'

Lee's mother laughed into the camera. 'All right – I hope this is working! Good luck, Lee!'

She panned to the start line where a dozen eight-year-olds stretched and jittered nervously awaiting starter's orders. All except Lee who stood poised, deer-like, eyes fixed on the finish line, ears pricked awaiting the crack of the gun. Parents roared as the gun fired with a puff of blue smoke sending white polo-shirted children sprinting. Lee's red sash flapped fiercely as he galloped to victory sending his mum into jubilation, the footage now a series of blurry spins.

She steadied the camera at herself and squealed, "Go on, Lee!"

A crowd gathered around him at the finish. The footage froze as one of Lee's arms was held aloft.

'Sports Day . . . ten years ago? Why?'

Twelve years ago. I was hoping you'd explain why I've shown you this particular memory.

'I won my race. What do you want me to say?'

An empty victory, wasn't it? You should have had stiffer competition, should you not, Lee?

'What are you . . . who?'

Lee. Wake up! the Voice rose in pitch and volume. You're not eight anymore and I'm not some pre-school nurse you can fob off. Don't. Play. Dumb.

Lee knew what was about to be revealed but couldn't face it. He'd long buried it. He knew what was coming, what really happened.

'Yeah, there was . . . supposed to be another kid racing. Dean. Decent runner.'

And?

'And . . . he skipped school that day.'

Don't you dare.

'What?'

Lie!

'What do you want from me exactly? I won the race. I can't change that. Do you want me to dig out the medal and send it back? Get in touch with everyone there, apologise for being faster than them twelve years ago? This is outrageous.'

No, Lee. This was outrageous.

Grayscale CCTV footage of a sunlit school corridor. A suited man in his fifties came striding through the scene, tie characteristically hung over his shoulder, megaphone in hand. Lee knew he was looking at his head teacher on Sports Day twelve years ago. The Head stood at the double doors to let two boys through. The Head leaves, and the boys, Lee and Dean head into the cloakroom.

'Right, how have you got this footage?'

You had a chance to explain, admit . . . confess. You didn't. Now watch.

Lee watched nervously. He knew what was taking place on the other side of the wall. Minutes later, an eight-year-old Lee emerges from the cloakroom, heading straight out to the field via the double doors.

Anything you wish to add Lee?

'No.'

You're sure?

'Um . . . you don't . . . have footage from inside the cloak-room, do you?'

Do I need it?

'No. I just – Didn't want to see . . .'

Fast forward. Thirty minutes pass and a receptionist

attends. Audio would reveal she was attending cries of help. Dean's cries. She re-emerges and sprints to a phone. She returns with a blanket. Fast forward. An ambulance crew arrives. A stretcher is wheeled into view. Fast forward. Dean is wheeled out on it, leg in a splint.

'It was an accident.'

Try again.

'We were playing and . . .'

No.

'He climbed up on the coat rack, he jumped . . .'

Lie.

Lee hid his face in his hands.

'Okay. Okay. I never meant to hurt him. I kicked him. Not hard. He was bragging about how he was going to win.'

Go on.

'I couldn't take it. I remember him saying how my mum would watch me lose. He knew she had brought the camera. So, I kicked him.'

You didn't just kick him, did you? It wasn't a foot in the back. A toe in the shin.

An X-ray flickered up on the screen as though whoever was in the projection booth simply held the original in front of the light.

Lee, his knee was dislocated. Fibula: fractured. A targeted blow to the side of the knee. You wanted to incapacitate him.

'I never thought I'd hurt him like that. I thought I'd give him a dead leg and that'd be enough to win. I snapped.'

A school incident report flashed up ruling an accident. Dean climbed the lockers and fell, landing awkwardly. Lockers were to be removed immediately. The screen went dark and only the Voice filled the space.

An accident! Dean never mentioned you, Lee. He convinced the school, that after you left, he stuck around to warm up. He gave some story about how another boy had

79

thrown his football sticker collection up there and he tried to retrieve it but fell. All to protect you. Now, why would he do that?

'Because I threatened him.'

With . . . ?

'His other leg.'

Silence.

Lee was disgusted with himself. With the whole scene. He couldn't get the sound of Dean's knee cracking out of his mind. The silence of the auditorium amplified it.

'Where is he now? I'm assuming you know.'

Glad you asked. You never saw him again after Sports Day?

'No, there were rumours he moved abroad.'

Houston, Texas to be precise. Dean and his family now live on a ranch he bought.

An image from a property company appeared. A sprawling ranch, blue skies. Another website appeared. Under the word ROSTER were thirty or so portraits of footballers in orange jerseys. Lee spotted Dean instantly.

Following a summer of physio, Dean's father was offered work in Texas and relocated his family. Dean worked diligently through school and earned himself a full scholarship. He began playing first-team professional football and is a rising star in Major League Soccer. Dean and his wife Beth have just welcomed a daughter.

Dean's social media appeared corroborating all the voice had told.

'Am I . . . supposed to feel jealous?'

Do you feel jealous?

'Well, I . . .' Lee thought about his bank account. His bedroom. His grades and the look on his mother's face when he passed them to her. He thought about the fact he hadn't kicked a ball since he was thrown off the school team. 'Okay, big whoop, he's made something of himself. I can't change what I did.'

Anyone would think it was you on the receiving end of a vicious assault. Anyone would think you were the one held back by mental and physical childhood trauma.

Lee remained quiet thinking about his prospects. There was no shame in his current role. The shame lied in potentially throwing what little he did have, away. Colleagues were supportive but Lee insisted on closing doors or kicking them in. When thrown out of college, the cinema gig was a lifeline. He remembered kicking a ball about with Dean one Parent's Evening at school. Dean would hog the ball and outstrip him with pace time and time again. Then Lee thought of Dean with crutches being helped onto a plane to his new life. He'd never travel like that. If his mum threw him out of the family home, which looked increasingly likely. Well, Lee didn't want to meet the type of landlord who would take him on. The football career, the ranch, all incredible. But the image that stuck in Lee's mind was that of Dean, his wife, and their little girl. Happy. Healthy. Successful.

He slumped deeper into his chair, utterly miserable, and as he did so, something clicked behind him. The door to Screen One was open.

The radio crackled into life.

It's time for Screen Two, Lee.

SCREEN TWO

Not knowing what'd be shown on Screen Two, Lee sat towards the back.

Cast your mind back, Lee.

'No, I'll stop you there. I want out. You can't keep me here.'

Are you ready to leave, Lee? the voice paused for an

answer that didn't come. No, no you're not. Lee, you're here because you've ignored this stuff long enough. The rules are simple. You listen to what I have to say. You watch. You listen. You learn. And those doors behind you will continue to unlock all while you're changing. You know, admitting, repenting, acknowledging.

A local newspaper article flickered into life. An elderly woman standing proudly outside a grocery shop. 'Local widow vows to continue late husband's work – Popular convenience store reopens.'

Who's that, Lee?

'Read the article yourself.'

Lee. Who is it?

'Jean.'

Jean. That's all? Try, Nanny Jean, a woman who – in the absence of a father – helped your mother raise you. When your mother found herself homeless at eight months pregnant, Jean and her husband helped get you two housed when the rest of the street had doubts. She babysat you, put food on your table, treated you and your friends to ice lollies all summer. She helped your mother in ways you'll never understand. How did you repay her?

The article slid from the screen to reveal CCTV footage from a few summers back. Four teenage boys enter the store and the shopkeeper, Jean, is visibly alert. Phone footage now accompanies the CCTV. One lad helps himself to fruit and veg, juggling them to the amusement of his peers. A sixteen-year-old Lee films proudly as his friends clown around. The shopkeeper begs the boys to leave while her frail husband makes a call to the police. The tallest lad grabs a large bottle of milk from the fridge, smashes it and himself to the ground in his own version of a "stunt" popular at the time. The boy writhes in faux agony. Jean is distraught and seems caught between fearing for her safety and helping the boy who, to her, seems genuinely hurt.

'Arghhh, my back. I'M GONNA SUE! I'M GONNA SUE THIS PLACE!' All three boys were folding over laughing.

Lee I want you to listen in now to a call made just that evening from Jean to a solicitor.

'It was just a prank,' Lee pleaded.

'You've reached Hansen and Pender solicitors. We're currently closed. Leave a message and some details and we'll return your call when we reopen.' BEEP.

'Oh, hello. It's Jean Davies – I'm hoping to contact Stuart, he's worked with us before. I'm afraid someone's had an accident on my business premises and I'm terrified it's going to cost us. As you know, my husband's not well, and anyway, I'm rambling. I think I may need Stuart's advice. I've got a teenager threatening to sue us – it's all a bit much for us.'

'It was just a prank. She didn't need to . . .'

No. I'll stop you there. YOU don't get to decide how she should react. You had no right treating her, her husband, or her business like that. They're elderly, Lee. They've lived on the street all their lives. Only . . . it didn't stop there did it?

CCTV footage outside the store dated a week later showed four youths arrive on BMXs at night, slam them to the ground, and begin spray-painting obscenities on the glass front. Lee felt he had a way out.

'You can't prove that's me. Look, you can't even see who–'

An e-receipt popped up on the screen for four silver spray paint cans on Lee's mother's account. 'Art coursework,' he'd told her.

As you know, Lee, Jean's husband died of a heart attack. Do you remember the trouble leading up to his death? Jean and Norman reported your lot to the school. A campaign began on social media, NOT started or endorsed by the couple, exposing your actions. None of you were popular. And, someone – you, perhaps, or one of your friends – began to retaliate. Hate mail. Intimidation. Glares. The stress that man was under in his final days. Fifty years of marriage. Sixty years spent serving the local community. To be bullied into a coffin by a group of punk kids?

Lee had no response. He knew the Davies' were great people. Lee remembered being babysat by Jean. They would bake while his mother took extra cleaning shifts. Jean would only ever talk about one thing: Norman. When Lee's mother returned from work, there would be Norman ready to escort his wife home. She never charged one damned penny for looking after Lee. He wished he had those guiding lights in his life now. He pulled his hat down over his eyes to conceal a tear he hadn't anticipated and sent a message to the page set up in Norman's honour, hoping it'd send the moment signal resumed, and with that, the door opened.

SCREEN THREE

Haunted by past transgressions, Lee feared what'd be shown next. He glanced over his shoulder at the dark and cold space that was a bustling foyer only hours earlier. He'd take a busy shift right now! He'd take complaints, queues, any of it.

There's only one way you're getting out of here, Lee.

And with that, he pushed the door to Three open. Lee recognised a female voice immediately. The face of a teenage girl filled the screen, mascara smeared.

'I don't want to do this. I don't want to hear it!'

The Vlog showing on the screen paused.

The Voice mocked him, Oh . . . Is it inconvenient? Painful? It returned to its usual cold bark, Try telling that to Claire. Her family. Her therapist. Oh, you'll listen. And you'll learn. And hell, you may end up hating yourself just one ounce of the amount Claire did.

Lee leant against the wall.

Claire's voice was punctuated with sobs., 'It's just . . . he doesn't get it. It's like his sole purpose is to humiliate me. I try to ignore him – doesn't work. I try to reason with him. I try to befriend him, hate him, flatter him – doesn't work. Any approach I take just fuels him. I'm rambling. I'll probably never even post this. I just wish he'd see what it does. I hate school. We share nearly all our classes. I'm tired of asking for help because it always means me going into detail. Too much painful, embarrassing detail. I don't want them knowing the things he says and writes about me! We all know what he calls me, what he's called me since Year Seven. It's disgusting.' Claire adjusted the camera and wiped her cheeks. She repositioned the camera at her face, now redder. 'Whatever. I'm tired. I'm done with it all. Is anyone even gonna watch this?' And with this question, the camera cut off.

Seen her lately?

'No, no I haven't. Is she okay?'

Agoraphobic, Lee. This word won't exist in the bubble that is your vocabulary. She's housebound. Three years. Left school, struggled through a couple of failed job interviews, and never bounced back. She's terrified of leaving her own home, due in no small part to your treatment of her.

'Clair the Pair'. That's what he called her. She developed early, and sick as it was, an eleven-year-old Lee found humour in it. He knew Claire was mortified. He leaned back flush to the wall and looked up at the high ceiling.

'She was . . . beautiful. And NOT because of . . . you know – her body. She was pretty. I could never tell her then, didn't know how. I was terrified of my own feelings and took it out on her. It all just went on and on. And it became . . . a norm? Once it was a habit I didn't know how to break it.' He looked at the black Screen where Claire's tear-stained face had been.

'I swear to God, if I get the chance, I'll make it right. I'll get in touch. I'll apologise, I swear.'

You have to ask yourself, Lee, what difference it'd make. And whether you're too late.

Lee was terrified that awful news may be revealed. He backed himself as far into the wall as he could while considering the idea that he may never get a chance to put things right for Claire. Lee pictured her face in Year Seven as she sat quietly staring out a window of a maths classroom. He recalled the first time he'd seen her on the bus in First Year and the last time he saw her on the bus in Second Year before she started getting lifts. The first Disco. Claire helped organise it. She didn't attend the Disco itself, instead, she signed people in, but she did her make-up and wore a dress. Lee remembered being told to close his mouth by Jack Debbins. He made up a quick story that he stared because of how bad her make-up was. It wasn't. Of course it wasn't.

Nothing further was revealed, to his silent relief. He agreed first thing tomorrow morning, when all this had blown over, he'd try and reach out. With that, the door of Screen Three opened and Lee began filling his lungs with gulps of air.

SCREEN FOUR

It sounded like a trailer was playing as he entered Four. Dubstep, tyres squealing, engines revving. Phone footage revealed neon-lit, modified cars filling a car park, all quickly replaced by a news programme.

'Local residents reported hearing engines revving and backfiring long into the night. But the chaos didn't end there. CCTV footage from the carpark shows what appears to be a theft. Engines left running to show off sound systems and various other modifications were taken advantage of by a gang of four youths who led a number of car fanatics on a high-speed chase ending in a ditch on the outskirts of town and thousands of pounds of damage.'

'It wasn't my idea.'

Next screen, Lee.

'No, wait, I swear I wasn't–'

Next. Screen. Lee.

'Wait, aren't I supposed to think and reflect?'

The door behind him swung open.

SCREEN FIVE

All Lee could think about as he headed upstairs to the next trial was the joy-ride in that car. It was his idea. He hadn't personally stolen the car, but he'd planned it. He'd excited his friends by the prospect of it, the ease of it, the rush of it all. The blue lights of the police and the slap of helicopter blades above made him feel invincible. The crash was rough. His body ached for weeks, unsure what damage was done. Police never caught them but he still awaited a knock at the door any day now.

Lee, take a seat. Front and centre, please.

'I'll stand.'

It was an order, Lee.

Lee sat and began preparing excuses. 'Okay, so it all began when we were playing Xbox at mine.'

Lee, I don't want to hear it. Let's just look, shall we? the Voice fell silent as a slideshow that would cut Lee to the bone appeared.

He didn't need commentary.

He spotted his Mum's profile picture immediately. Now, her search history: 'Car, theft, law'. 'First offence taking without consent'. 'Likely sentence car theft'. 'Funeral expenses'. 'Help with funeral costs'.

Next, a bank statement with the following outgoings: Watts Pharmacy. Watts Pharmacy. H&P Solicitors. Watts Pharmacy. Acorn Therapy. Hyde Security Solutions. C&M Autos.

'Tell me she didn't pay for that car,'

Lee does nothing else there disturb you more? A single mother, YOUR Mother, medicating herself, convinced you'll be locked up or killed. She's installed CCTV around your house terrified of the repercussions of your actions. And yes, she paid for repairs. The money it cost her could have buried you in a modest ceremony, if you were wondering.

Lee had nothing to say. He opened his mouth and pulled the radio up to his chin to speak.

Screen Six, Lee. We don't have all night.

SCREEN SIX

No welcome came. Lee sat gingerly, front and centre. 'Am I good, here?' he asked out into the darkness. 'I do want to change, you know. Whatever you're doing, it's working. I need to speak to my Mum, a lot of people, actually. I really feel I can explain–'

Explain this, Lee.

The screen blinded Lee momentarily, from pitch black to bleached white. His eyes adjusted to two figures. Outlines. He knew this was coming and wished he'd got there first. A body map. Front and back. Female. Eighteen. He knew it was coming.

Explain yourself.

'I can't. It's awful. Please don't show me anything else, I can't bear it.'

You? You can't bear it?

'I know how that sounds. It's terrible, but you weren't there.'

Do I need to have been there, Lee?"

Lee glanced at distinct shaded marks covering the arms and wrists. One on the back of the neck.

'No, but . . . I just get so frustrated. She winds me up.'

And?

'And I just, snap. I have anger management issues.'

Said like a true victim. Lee, this is horrific.

'I've been attending therapy. I've been trying.'

The voice laughed. Therapy! Trying?

The body map was replaced by CCTV footage dated last week. Twelve or so people sat in a circle on plastic chairs.

Found yourself yet, Lee?

'No. I . . .'

Allow me to help.

The footage switched to that of a different camera angle focusing solely on Lee. His arrival. Slumping into the chair. Staring out the window. Fast forward. Playing with his trainers. On his phone. Occasionally looking up. Fast forward. Rolling cigarette. Phone. Fiddling with keys. Then, stood up, hood up, leaving.

Trying? Lee, you're a disgrace.

'Look, you're not giving me a chance to explain.'

We're done here. Next.

'No, wait, just going to those meetings is a big deal. And as for Laura, those marks, I . . .'

The door swung open with a bang and Lee's anger rose. Outside he stalked the dark corridor. He lunged at the wall and punched a fire alarm as hard as he could. A shrill screech emitted with an announcement to evacuate and Lee wasn't sure what his next move was. But time slowed. The alarms and the announcement distorted and Lee realised they were winding down, playing in reverse, until gone. Silent.

Tut tut. You know, I wonder, Lee, if paying more attention at group could have helped there.

SCREEN SEVEN

Lee charged into Screen Seven now feeling the end was in sight. Watch the screen. Say what needs to be said.

'Look, I've messed up. I get it,' he began.

Silence.

'I had a fight at school, Ben something. Never liked each other. Gonna show me that?'

'Stole a teacher's smokes once. Not proud, probably where my habit started.' Lee laughed awkwardly, feeling the need to build a rapport anew.

Silence.

'What's taking so long?'

Silence.

No Voice. No footage. Nothing. Lee was being given time to reflect on what had come, what had been. Process. Revelations had come thick and fast, and, with one more to come, Lee was being given time to prepare. Time to change.

So, how did Lee fill this time?

Shifting seats a few times. Shining his phone light towards the projection box to see who was behind the Voice. He made an unsuccessful attempt to access the crawl space behind the screen. He baited the Voice. He begged forgiveness. He built himself into a frenzy that ended with him launching his iPhone at the centre of the forty-foot screen. The phone fell, a shattered mess. The door behind Lee swung open as he retrieved his phone, glancing at the dent above him.

A chance missed, Lee.

A DETOUR

Lee needed only to exit Screen Seven and turn left for Eight but the lift beckoned. He decided he needed a break if he was going to get the last screen "right". He entered the lift, jammed his locker key into the panel, and pressed Four. Roof access. Lee knew he didn't need the actual key to get the lift up to Four, just a key.

The lift doors opened into a cold concrete corridor filled with scaffolding and ladders.

Wrong way, Lee.

'I just need a minute.'

It's always about what you want, the Voice mocked him.

'I need time. I don't want to see it.' Lee propped open the roof access with the foot of a ladder. There was no roof-to-floor access via the outside of the building and he'd need a way back down to Eight; he knew he'd have to face it sooner or later. Night air agitated him. He looked at the town below and shouted, but not into the radio. 'Who does he think he is? Trapping me here. Freak. Stalking me. Hacking my life left, right, and centre.'

The radio crackled in the night air. Lee. You're going about this all wrong.

'Wait. How can you hear me?' Lee checked the radio to make sure he hadn't accidentally pressed the button making himself heard. Lee launched the radio to the river below where it broke the surface of the water with a slap. 'Keep your words.'

The wind reminded Lee that he was too close to the edge. He stepped onto the ledge. He didn't want to jump but something inside him had to know what it felt like to stand on the edge. He could hear his own name being whispered in his ear, Lee. Leeeee!

He jolted. He'd lost focus. He stepped off the ledge and ran for the propped door and the safety of the concrete cocoon indoors.

His heart rate slowed and he heard his name again, louder, Lee. Leeeee.

Was it his mother? He couldn't quite make it out.

Leeee.

Was someone here to rescue him? Let him out. Release him from this torment?

Lee.

And there it was, the Voice. That familiar Voice.

Lee. It's time.

'Not possible. I chucked the radio.' He looked up for speakers.

Lee, you know what needs to be done. Screen Eight. Chop-chop.

Lee entered the lift, wondering if the Voice was coming through the control panel. He hit three and the doors closed. The Voice now clearer than ever.

You see, Lee. We've got to take care of this.

So clear.

Really confront it.

Like whoever it belonged to stood beside him.

You've a choice to make. You've changes to make.

The Voice deep within his ears now. No crackle.

Screen Eight, Lee. No more detours.

SCREEN EIGHT

This one's simple, Lee.

'Okay.

One bit of footage. One question.

'Okay.'

The screen revealed a CCTV shot of familiar carpet, burgundy walls, gold trim. The cinema interior. The time stamp: just after 7 p.m. A door with a gold plaque that read PRIVATE, a gold keypad. Lee appears in shot, rucksack in hand. Enters team area. Fast forward. Lee re-emerges, uniformed. Leaves the frame.

'Okay . . . it's me arriving at work earlier. If I could change that, I would. What's the question?'

Patience Lee.

The footage moves on. Lee reappears in shot, ear-phones in, re-enters team area.

'I came back for a drink.'

The footage moves on until Lee re-emerges.

'I went to get a drink.'

Lee pulls the door marked PRIVATE closed behind him. Leaves the frame.

'I went to get a drink. I didn't drink before the shift.'

The Voice filled his head, Lee. Come on.

'What? I'm not allowed to drink now?'

Lee.

'Fine. Look. Whoever you are, whoever put you up to this – it's worked. I've let everyone down. I'm a disgrace.'

Silence. Lee thought he was getting somewhere.

'And, and . . . I'll make it right. Anyone I've wronged, I'll fix it.

Silence.

'And I won't tell anyone. That guy you just showed me on screen. That's not me anymore. I'm not that person anymore. I'll take more shifts. Pay Mum back.'

The Voice was absent.

'I'll focus at therapy. You can open the door. I've watched the footage. I – Wait. You said there was a question.'

There is.

'What is it? What's the question?'

The Voice was deep within Lee's skull. The question is simple, Lee. But its answer, I'm afraid, will not be. And the answer you give will determine whether or not you walk out of here.

Lee swallowed. 'What's the question?'

Silence.

It's simple. What's in your pocket, Lee?

Lee grabbed at his hip instinctively as soon as his pocket was mentioned. 'Um, it's . . . my phone? Here. Smashed. Take it.' Lee offered his phone to the darkness.

What's in your pocket, Lee?

'I swear, it's . . .'

WHAT'S IN YOUR POCKET LEE?

'It's for my own protection, okay?'

Protection. No, no, Lee. The only thing you need protecting from is yourself. Bring a gun onto shift, yeah? What, threaten customers? Staff? Hold the building up? What was the plan?

'You said one question.'

What's the truth, Lee? What were you going to do with it?

'I DON'T KNOW!'

It's your job to know, Lee.

'No one else was going to come to harm, I swear.'

No-one else?

'No. I just . . . it was there as an option.'

An option?

'Yes. An option.'

Banging and shuffling could be heard lower in the building.

Explain.

'I can't. I don't really understand it myself.'

Lee, what was the plan?

'Didn't have one. Just wanted . . . options. Ways out.'

Is the gun the answer, Lee?

'It's an answer. I don't know if it's the answer.'

The banging came closer. Doors being kicked in. Footsteps in the dozen. Radio bleeps.

Lee, you're running out of time.

'What do you mean?'

Lee, make a choice.

'I can't think this fast.'

Lee, you seem to have convinced yourself you've changed, or that you're at least on the pathway to change . . . it's everyone else you need to convince.

'Well, how do I do that? Where do I even start?'

Lee, we're done here.

'No. Wait! What do I do next?'

Lee, my role in this is over.

The noise outside reached Lee's floor.

'Wait – who's outside? What do they want?'

Lee panicked. He stretched out his leg and removed the gun from his pocket. Small, weighty in his palm. He pointed it clumsily at the door.

'It's the police, right? What the hell do I do?

. . .

'How do I convince them, what do I even say?'

. . .

The Voice was gone. Try as he might, Lee couldn't hear it. In the seconds that followed he'd forgotten what it even sounded like.

The noise was right outside now. Manoeuvres being organised in hushed tones. Lee climbed on to the small stage at the foot of the screen and hid behind the curtain that hung at the side.

'Lee? Lee, we know you can hear us.'

. . .

'Lee, you'll need to cooperate. We need you to lay on the floor, face down.'

. . .

'Lee, we know you're armed. Toss the weapon, Lee.'

He tried to calm his breathing but kept the gun firmly in his grip, loaded.

Silence.

They were giving him time. His mind raced. Surrender? Shoot? Hide?

'Lee, we're coming in.'

And with that, the door slammed against the wall and many pairs of rubber-booted feet shuffled in. Searchlights flooded the auditorium as they got in position. Plastic shields bounced here and there.

'Lee. We see you. We know you're there. Toss the weapon and this'll all be over.' The policeman's voice was close now. Raw. Gruff. Strained. Beyond sore.

Do it, Lee, the Voice. It was back! Do it, Lee. What are you waiting for?

'Do what?' Lee asked.

'Come on, Lee. Throw the weapon. Show us you're cooperating.'

Now's the time, Lee. Get it over and done with.

Lee pointed the gun at himself. The searchlights were now trained at the curtain he hid behind.

Come on, Lee.

'Come on, Lee! Do the right thing. Just throw the weapon across the stage and we'll talk. We can work through this, we just need to know that—'

Now, Lee. Now. End it.

Lee was overwhelmed, barraged with commands.

'Work with us, Lee. We can help!'

Come on, Lee. Get it over and done with.

'Listen to us, Lee.'

Do it, Lee.

And with the Voice's final words rattling around his skull, Lee leapt from the curtain, screaming, gun raised.

One shot followed by four in quick succession. Five flashes. In the ensuing darkness, Lee slumped to the floor.

Chief Superintendent Wye lifted the visor on his helmet and clutched the radio mounted on his chest.

'Medics, urgent. Screen Eight. Area secure. Suspect down. Shots fired.'

Armed responders shuffled out. Medics worked on Lee for ten minutes before wheeling him through the foyer to an ambulance outside to the horror of his colleagues at a cordon. Upstairs, Wye sat on a bench outside Screen Eight. Downstairs, Matt stood speaking to officers by the front doors shaking his head. And all over the building, with the assistance of the police, staff and customers were being retrieved from hiding spaces – cupboards, stock rooms – and escorted to support, the words 'Active Shooter' having sent them scattering like mice earlier in the night.

Matt handed Lee's staff file over. The officer receiving gave a confused glance at the name printed in bold. 'Umm . . . Lee's surname here.' He pointed at the file. 'Lee Wye? I was told Matthews.'

'Oh, yeah, he's been using his mother's name of late. Wye was his father, apparently. He never knew him. Left before he was born.'

The officer took the file and headed up the three flights of stairs to the man sat on the bench outside Screen Eight.

DRIVE LIKE HELL

KEN POIRIER

Howdy, howdy! Nice day, ain't it? Going up to the lake to do some fishing? Good day for it.

Twenty dollars on pump number one? No problem. Just let me punch that into the machine here . . .

Stories? Down at the end of the aisle there, we got some audiobooks.

Oh . . . Urban legends . . . Who told you I knew anything about that?

Well, he's right. There was something that happened around here . . .

Hmm . . . Must have been about ten years ago.

That's right. Now I remember. It was the day of the solar eclipse . . .

BILLY AND ANNIE HAD FINALLY FOUND A DAY TO MAKE IT away from the big city. They had driven out to a quiet little lake in the middle of the hills, far from civilization. They set out a picnic lunch on the grassy beach of the lake. Not another house, car, or sign of human life to be seen anywhere. Only the sound of birds in the waving trees and the occasional plop of fish reaching out of the water to snag a dragonfly could be heard. It was total peace. Everything they had desperately needed.

They gorged themselves on apples, chicken, French bread, and wine until they laid nearly comatose against each other on the blanket. Billy took out a joint and lit it. They passed it back and forth looking at the clouds and the moon making its way toward the sun.

"This must be heaven," Billy said.

"As about as close as we can get, I think," said Annie. "I really didn't think your car was going to make it out here. That thing must be close to dead."

"Don't remind me," Billy said.

Living in the city, they didn't use Billy's old Ford Pinto very often. They only used it for grocery shopping and the occasional trip somewhere. The car had nearly two-hundred-thousand miles on it. It burned gas like it had a hole in the tank and was constantly breaking down. Quite frankly, the thing was a bit of an embarrassment to be seen in.

"How close are you to saving up for your new car?"

Billy rolled over and put out the joint in the grass.

"Not very," he said.

"What do you mean, not very?" Annie asked sitting up. "You've been saving up for months."

"I spent it."

"Spent it on what? We've barely left the apartment in forever. Every time I wanted to go somewhere, you said, 'We can't. I got to save money.'"

Billy reached into his backpack and took out a little box. He got down on one knee and opened it.

"I spent it on this," he said. "Annie, will you marry me?"

Her eyes teared up. "Yes! Of course, yes!"

She threw her arms around him. He slipped the ring on her finger. She kissed him. He kissed her back.

After a few text messages to friends and family and some pictures posted to Instagram and Twitter, they celebrated by making love under the eclipsing sun.

As they drove down the interstate home, Annie admired her new ring and Billy admired Annie admiring the ring. It had been such a good day, Billy hadn't noticed—

"Oh shit!" Billy smacked his hand against the steering wheel.

"What? What is it?"

"I forgot to get gas. The tank is nearly empty."

"How empty is empty?" Annie asked with concern. She knew Billy all too well. When it came to money, he was always thinking with his heart and not with his mind. It was just like the car. He should have gotten rid of it long ago, but he loved it. She was beginning to suspect that he bought her this engagement ring just so he wouldn't have to trade the old rust bucket in.

Sometimes she wished the car would just die already.

No sooner had she thought that the car began to shake violently from side to side.

"Oh my God!" she cried, clutching the roof strap to brace herself.

"That's weird," said Billy. "Running out of gas shouldn't make it do that. At least I don't think it should."

"Jesus Billy, pull over before we crash!"

"All right already! I'm pulling over. Look! There's a sign for gas at the next exit."

Billy steered the wobbling car off the highway. When they reached the next stop sign, the car stopped shaking.

"Well . . . Hmm." Billy stared at the dashboard as if trying to look through it with X-ray vision. "It can't be the engine. We haven't run out of gas and if it was the engine, we'd still be shaking. It has to be the transmission or maybe the steering column?" He twisted the wheel back and forth. "I think we should just keep going."

"Are you crazy? We need to go to that gas station!"

"What gas station?" Billy pointed down the gravel road that led into the woods. "There's nothing there!"

"There has to be," said Annie, "there was a sign. It's probably just around the corner."

"Or maybe it's just an old sign? I'm going to keep going." Billy pulled the car forward. It began to shake again.

"Billy! I'm not going to die on my engagement day! Go to the gas station!"

"Fine, but if we run out of gas in the middle of the woods, it'll be your fault." Billy turned the wheel and the car wobbled down the gravel road.

They drove one mile, then another with nothing to see but gravel and trees. All the while the needle moved closer to empty. Finally, another half mile down the road, the trees opened up into a clearing of farm fields. Up ahead, they could see an old 1950s style gas station near a little farmhouse with a few people sitting on the front porch.

They pulled the car up to the pump and got out. Billy looked at the old chrome-and-white plastic gas pump that was peppered with rust. The meter was one of those old flip cards from before digital readouts were invented.

"I don't think this thing takes credit cards," he said.

He stepped up to the door of the service station and gave it a tug. Nothing. He wiped the dust from the window and looked inside. Not only was there no one in there, no one had been in there for a long time. The entire building was filled to the brim with junk and scrap. A rusty stove was pushed up against the front door. It was the only door to the building.

How the hell did they manage that? Billy thought. It's

almost as if someone had barricaded themselves in. He turned to Annie.

"Babe, I don't think we're getting any gas here."

"Maybe those people know how to turn on the pumps." She pointed toward the farmhouse.

"I don't think these pumps do turn on."

"Well, maybe there's another gas station down the road. This is probably just the beginning of the town. I'm going to go ask those people." Annie took off across the field toward the farmhouse.

Billy followed after her.

As they walked across the field, they realized it was much larger than it seemed. They both were finding themselves out of breath. The ground was overgrown and treacherous. Annie waved her hands in the air.

"Hello!" she shouted. When she was about a hundred yards away she stopped abruptly and put her arms down.

Billy caught up to her, catching his breath. "What's up?" he asked.

"Those people," Annie said, "they're not moving."

Billy looked across the field. An old man and woman sat on the porch. They hadn't moved an inch since they first pulled up to the gas station. They were sitting still as statues. They looked like wax statues out of Ripley's Believe It or Not, sitting there on the porch. A fly landed on the old man's face and crawled in and out of his mouth.

A wave of fear flushed over Billy and Annie. They slowly started walking backward, keeping their eyes on the farmhouse. Still no motion. When they were at what felt like a safe distance, they turned, ran back to the car, and got in.

Billy started the engine and continued down the road past the farmhouse.

"You're going the wrong way," Annie said, "we need to go back to the highway."

"I don't think we'll have enough gas if we head back now. Maybe there's another gas station up the road. Like you said, it's probably just the beginning of town."

"Billy . . . Those people were . . . dead"

"Maybe they just looked dead," Billy reasoned more to himself than Annie, "sometimes old people just look like that."

"They were dead," Annie said again. "They sat on their porch until they died. What is this place? What if there's some kind of plague? What if we got exposed?"

"Well, then we have to find help, right? I really think going this way will be our best chance. Who knows? Maybe this road loops back to the highway up ahead."

The clearing turned back into woods.

"Or," Said Annie. "They have these things called cell phones." She took her phone out of her purse and unlocked the screen. "Damn, I can't get any bars. Maybe I should just call nine-one-one."

"And tell them what, exactly?" Billy asked. "Hello, we are in some weird town we don't know the name of and we think some old people might look like they're dead at some address we don't know?"

"We have to tell someone."

"We will," he said, "when we get to town. I'm sure someone will know who they are."

"What town?" cried Annie.

"I'm sure there is a town," said Billy. "There's got to be."

But there wasn't. Only more trees for the next five miles. Then, through the trees, they could make out a large building.

"See," said Billy, "there it is."

It was another half-mile of curving road before, in the thick of the trees, they came across a large barn with a parking lot full of tractor-trailer trucks. They could hear some kind of noise inside as they approached.

"Looks like some kind of Roadhouse," said Billy. "Maybe someone there knows where this gas station is?"

They turned into the parking lot, and there it was. Hidden between the other tractor-trailers was what could only be described as a Hell-truck.

"What, the fuck, is that?" Asked Annie.

Billy had no reply.

Before them was a rusted out tractor-trailer truck. No driver could be seen behind the jet black windows, but the cab of the truck was adorned with rusty iron chains and meat hooks that dangled severed human limbs.

"I don't think this is a good place to stop," said Billy.

The Hell-truck's engine roared to life and began revving. Annie hit Billy on the arm.

"Jesus fucking Christ! Get the hell out of here!" she cried.

Billy put the Ford Pinto in reverse and spun the car around. He floored it back toward the highway but driving at top speed was doing nothing to help the car-shaking problem. If he continued to drive like this on the twisty, gravel road, a crash was inevitable. When they were a good half-mile away from the truck barn, he slowed down.

"What are you doing?" Annie asked. "We've got to get out of here."

"I don't want to crash," he said. "That was probably some kind of prank or something. It's only like seven miles back to the highway. I'm just going to drive nice and easy."

They heard the blast of the truck's air horn and it soon emerged from the trees on the road behind them.

"Fuck that!" yelled Annie. "Drive like hell!"

Billy hit the gas while Annie tried to make an emergency phone call. Still, no signal. She unbuckled her seat belt and turned around in her chair, pointing the phone at the back window. Billy pulled the car hard to the right around the corner, sending Annie crashing into him.

"What are you doing?" Billy shouted.

"I'm trying to see if I can get a video of his license plate or something."

"Can you?"

"No," she said, "it's some kind of novelty plate."

The truck came crashing into them. Annie's cell phone went flying into the back seat.

The Pinto sped down the country road, kicking up dust in its wake. Billy pressed his foot down on the gas pedal as hard as it would go.

"Come on, come on!" he shouted at the speedometer.

Annie was on her feet in the passenger seat. She reached, trying to pick her phone up off the floor behind the seat, but it was just out of reach. She could feel the muscles in her arm pulling out of place as she nudged the phone around with her fingertips. Despite her effort, the phone was just sliding further into the narrow space under the seat. Her arm was cramping badly, so she gave up. On her way back into her seat, she looked out the back window.

"He's gaining on us!" she screamed.

"I know, I know!" yelled Billy, looking in the rearview mirror.

Behind them, the tractor-trailer shifted gears. Thick, black smoke spewed from the truck's exhaust pipes. Annie could see it now. The license plate bore a confederate flag and the words "See you in Hell!"

The truck once again barreled into the back of the Pinto. Annie flew backward out of the seat, hitting her head against the windshield. The glass spider-webbed with cracks but didn't break. A splash of blood painted the spot of impact.

"Jesus!" yelled Billy. "Are you okay?"

"Yeah," said Annie in a daze, sitting back in her seat. "I'm fine."

"Well, then put your seat belt on before you get killed, please," Billy said, trying to keep the car on the road as the killer truck smashed into the back of them for a third time.

Annie had said she was fine, but that wasn't the truth. There was a ringing in her ears like she had never heard before. As the truck rammed into the Pinto for the fourth time, the impact sent a shock wave of pain through her entire body. She turned to look for the seat belts and found she couldn't see out of her right eye. She reached her hands up and wiped blood from her eyelids until she could see again. She reached further up to her hairline and pull the sliver of glass out of her scalp.

She grabbed the seat belt with her right hand, pulled on the belt, but then let it go and screamed in pain. Tears ran down her face.

"What?" Billy asked. "What is it?"

"My fucking arm!" Annie screamed. "I think it's broken. Oh my God! I don't want to fucking die."

Billy tried to keep his eyes on the road as he reached across Annie to try and put her seat belt on. The car slowed just enough for the truck to collide a fifth time. Billy flew forward, hitting his head on the dashboard hard enough to crack the plastic over the radio, but managed to use his arm to keep Annie in her seat.

The car began to skid, Billy needed both hands on the wheel to keep the car on the road. The maneuver slowed the car enough for the truck to hit them again. Those other times had been love taps, however. This time, the truck bashed with full force.

Annie flew out of her seat and smashed the windshield. Glass sprayed the inside of the car. She had only caught herself by snagging the heels of her feet underneath the passenger seat and her thighs on the dashboard. The top half of her body slapped against the hood of the car.

Annie tried to lift herself up and back into the car, but her broken arm was making it difficult.

Billy shook himself to clear his head and saw Annie hanging out of the windshield. He slammed hard on the gas pedal and Annie fell back into her seat. Annie, on the verge of passing out, reached across her body with her left arm and grabbed the seat belt, pulled it down, and latched it into place.

"Billy... Billy..." Annie was slipping in and out of consciousness. "Drive faster, Billy..."

Billy wanted to do something for Annie, but now, with the wind cutting into his eyes, he was doing all he could to not crash the car into the side of the road.

While the Hell-truck was certainly faster than the Pinto, it had to slow down in the tight turns of the road through the woods. Billy had a good lead now, but when the road opened up into the fields near the abandoned gas station, that could all change. They were almost there.

"Stay sharp," Billy said to Annie, but she couldn't hear him.

Annie was dreaming. She was dreaming that they had never left their apartment in the city that day. The car had broken down, so they couldn't leave town. Billy was upset because he had bought a ring and he was going to propose to her by the lake under the solar eclipse. Annie tried to tell him it was okay because now the monster truck couldn't kill them, but Billy was insistent on fixing the car and going to the lake.

"Hang on tight!" Billy shouted into the wind. The last turn, onto the ramp of the highway, was a little too sharp even for the Pinto. Damn it, he thought, I'm going to have to slow down.

Billy drifted to the left side of the road, hit the brake, and then gassed it out while cranking the steering wheel to the right. It was a bold maneuver and it would have paid off, had the Pinto been just a slightly faster car.

The truck slammed into the back end of the Pinto, but this time, on the side, sending the car spinning out into the grass. Billy and Annie bounced around against each other in the car like a pinball machine in multi-ball action. The truck slowed for a moment, then drove under the underpass.

Billy was rattled. He knew he had to get moving before the truck managed to turn around and come back for them. He reached down and turned the keys, but the engine made a grinding noise because the car was still running. He hit the gas pedal. The wheels spun in the grass for a moment, then caught dirt and went lurching forward. Whatever condition the car was in before they pulled off the highway, it was a thousand times worse now. Nonetheless, the car drove forward.

Billy pulled on the highway.

"We made it, Annie! We made it!" he said, but Annie lay motionless, strapped into her seat. "Annie! Hey, Annie!" He grabbed her by the shoulder and gave her a shake. Nothing.

He put his fingers on her neck and then under her nose. She was still breathing. He reached across her lap and pulled the lever that made the seat lay back. "You go ahead and rest for a second," he said.

A second was all she had, for she woke to the sound of a blaring truck horn. She tried to sit up, but she was too weak and fell back down into the reclined seat. She gripped the shoulder strap of the seat belt with both hands.

Billy hit the gas.

But, when he turned to look, it wasn't the Hell-truck. It was just some regular tractor-trailer passing on the left. The driver was flipping them the bird and shouting at them to get off the road.

A FEW MILES DOWN THE ROAD, THEY PULLED INTO THIS GAS station right here. They began telling me their story and I didn't wait for them to finish before I called nine-one-one.

It was quite the scene. Everyone came out. Local police, the county sheriff, highway patrol, the fire department . . . You name it. Pretty sure even the department of transportation had a guy here.

Well, the EMTs did what they could, Billy and Annie needed to go to the hospital, but before they did, they had to tell their stories over and over again to all the different arms of the law that showed up. I heard it so many times, it felt like I was there in the car with them myself.

After they left for the hospital, the cops started going over their car. Bagged up a whole bunch of stuff: Annie's cell phone, a bag of weed, chunks of bloody glass. While they were doing that, highway patrol went out searching every exit, North and South. Every one of them came back and said they found nothing that matched the place Billy and Annie told them about. The video on Annie's cell phone turned out to be just black as if the phone had been in her pocket or something.

Then they all just left. Gave up or something. Left that Pinto, beat up, right here in the lot. I didn't know what to do with it until a few days later I got a call from the insurance company. They wanted me to look over the car and send them an estimate for the repairs.

I got in the car and the keys were still in there, so I started her up and drove her into the shop. The first thing I noticed was the belts in the tires had blown out. It was making the car wobble like a drunk when you drove her. Four new tires were about five-hundred bucks, so I put that down.

I popped the hood and took a look at the engine. It was certainly a bit weathered. Transmission, brakes, steering, everything seemed fine, though. There was the busted out windshield, which was an easy fix, three-hundred dollars, just pop the new one in. Then I went around to the back, where most of the damage was.

Most of it was bodywork. The taillights were a mess. She's going to need a new muffler, three-hundred-and-fifty bucks, and electrical kit, five-hundred bucks, and about two-grand in bodywork. All in all, it was going to cost four or five thousand dollars to fix that car.

Well, I told the insurance company and they said it was about two grand more than the car blue-booked for, so I should just go ahead and scrap her.

I had the phone in my hand and was about to go and call the tow truck when I thought about something. Instead of making the call, I went out to the shop and I tore the back end of the car off and took a look at the gas can. It was smashed up real good, but there was still at least a half-gallon of gas in it.

Now, when I was a kid, there was a rumor that if you rear-ended a Ford Pinto, its gas can would blow up. I know, for a fact, this car must have gotten smashed at least a dozen times and the gas can was just fine. So, that whole thing about Pintos blowing up when you rear-end 'em? Believe me when I say, that can't be anything more than an urban legend.

THE MOUNT OF DEATH

KEVIN DAVID ANDERSON

"**B**eer-me!"

Collin took a hand off the steering wheel, the one not holding his smartphone, and thrust it back toward Aaron.

Aaron shifted uncomfortably in the SUV's rear compartment, wedged between a cooler and sleeping bags. It was the only spot left since Collin and his girlfriend occupied the front, and Max and Carole took up the entire backseat.

"Not gonna happen. You're driving . . . and texting," Aaron replied. And a colossal douche, he wanted to add but didn't. Collin's sober driving on the heavily forested, treacherous Highway Thirty-nine through the San Gabriele Mountains was scary enough. There wasn't a chance in hell, Aaron would allow alcohol into the mix.

"Hey, I'm not going to spend the weekend in the woods with you people, sober," Collin said. "Now, beer-me."

Max leaned forward on the back of the driver's seat and slapped Collin's shoulder. "Love you too, buddy."

Collin rolled his entire head. "Ah, I didn't mean it like . . .

for the love of—Aaron, will you please just get me a damn beer."

Collin's new girlfriend, Aaron couldn't remember her name—Debbie, Donna . . . something—turned from the passenger seat window and smiled at Aaron. "I'll take a Coke."

Aaron narrowed his gaze at the young woman he felt answered the age-old question what would a Wookie look like if it lost all its hair, then started looking for a Coke.

Max reached back and put his hand on the cooler lid. "Got a Red Bull back there?"

Aaron furrowed his brow. "When did I become the bartender?"

Collin drummed his fingers impatiently on the roof. "When you volunteered to sit in the ass-end of the car."

Volunteered? Everyone had simply beaten him to the car. Aaron sighed. Who was he kidding? It made sense that he be tucked in with the luggage. He was the fifth wheel, Max's best friend. Collin had Debbie or Donna or whatever the hell Wookie-face's name was, and Max had Carole.

God, Carole was amazing. Beautiful, strong, intelligent. She had the brains of Dana Scully, the eyes of Deana Troy, and the tenacity of Katniss Everdeen. Her hair rested over the backseat right in front of Aaron, and he delighted in every breath he took filling his nostrils with her fragrance: clean, fresh, a hint of strawberry. He was well aware of how creepy it was, but it wasn't like he could move, or find some other air to breathe.

"Hey, you awake?" Collin shouted. "Look, I'm putting my phone down. Now, beer-me."

Max slapped Collin's hand down off the roof. "Crystal Lake Campgrounds is less than an hour away. Just wait."

Collin put his hand back up, wrist wresting against the soft top, fingers shaped as if cradling a beer. "I want to be well into my first buzz by then. Now, tell ComicCon back there to get me a beer."

"Collin!" Aaron sat up. "You vomit-spackled ninja-fart, I'm not getting you a beer. You can barely drive sober in the light of day, let alone in the dark. Jesus, man, it's pitch-black out."

Collin made a wide sweeping gesture over the dashboard. "Aaron, my little nerdy friend, there is nothing out there in the dark that ain't there in the daytime."

"That's some really brilliant fortune-cookie wisdom there, Buddha," Aaron shouted.

Max turned around. "Dude, that sounded kind of racist."

"What? No, that's not—"

"I could use a 7-Up or something like that," Carole said, turning around, temporarily paralyzing Aaron with the full power of her deep brown Diana-Troy-eyes.

"Yeah, I'll see what I can . . . uh . . ." Aaron looked away and plunged his attention into the cooler.

When he looked back up, Max was staring at him, uneasy. He seemed to be reading something on Aaron's face. Something Aaron had been trying to bury for months. Although he hadn't done anything disloyal to his friend, Aaron knew it was more from a lack of opportunity than an unwillingness to do so.

Max brought his arm up and slid it around Carole's shoulder, pulling her close.

Shit. Aaron turned away and continued rummaging through the cold cans. The weight of the guilt for something he hadn't even done yet crushed him. He and Max had been close since third grade when they'd discovered their mutual interest in all things geeky, especially Science Fiction. Truth be known, Max was a little more Star Wars than Star Trek, but Aaron felt that when it came to best friends certain things could be forgiven. They cosplayed at conventions together, they joined a quidditch league together, they even went to their prom together. Not with each other. There were girls involved. Point being, they were tight. At least until Max started playing lacrosse and hanging out with troglodytes like Collin and his Wookie-faced girlfriend. Aaron felt them drift apart over the past year, and now he was falling for Max's girlfriend, a circumstance guaranteed not to improve the situation.

Collin turned down the rap music he'd insisted on tormenting his passengers with since San Bernardino, then cleared his throat, clearly wanting everyone's attention.

"Allow me to demonstrate," Collin said.

Demonstrate what?

There was a soft click and the car plunged into darkness.

"What the . . . ?" Aaron let the cooler lid fall and turned forward, unable to see the curvy road or the surrounding trees.

In the driver's seat, Collin's hands, illuminated by the faint glow of dashboard lights, waved in the air like someone reaching the top of the big drop on a roller coaster.

Max slapped Collin on the back of the head. "Turn the headlights back on, asshole!"

Collin's hands lowered. There was a click and the lights came back on.

Aaron's hands were shaking. "Seriously! Is there any part of you that's not stupid?"

Collin's grin reflected in the rearview mirror. "Just conducting a little science experiment about the dark."

"Well, congratulations," Aaron said, "you proved you're a moron."

Collin raised his hand, once again thrusting it back toward Aaron, fingers cradling an invisible beer can. "I told ya there ain't nothing there in the dark that isn't there in the daylight.

"Now stop being a beer-nazi or I'll conduct another experiment."

Collin's girlfriend turned around. "Yeah, stop being a beer-nazi."

Aaron pointed a finger. "Nobody is talking to you, Donna."

"My name is, Deedee, you skid-mark."

"Whatever," Aaron said. "Collin, when we get to Crystal Lake you can drink yourself into a coma. But let's get there alive." Aaron raised his right hand. "All in favor?"

Carole and Max raised their hands.

Collin shook his head. "Well, this isn't a democracy."

Soft click.

Darkness swallowed the landscape and Aaron's entire body began to tremble. "You shit-head!"

In a casual tone, Collin said, "Beer-me."

"All right," Aaron said. "Just turn them on."

"Another successful experiment." Collin flicked the head-lights back on.

White light illuminated something in the road. Aaron only caught a glimpse. It stood on four legs with metallic eyeshine the shade of gunmetal. In a horrifying instant, Aaron realized they were going to hit it. The full weight of Thor's hammer seemed to crash down on the hood. Everything rushed forward to the sounds of breaking glass, skidding tires, deploying airbags, and screaming. Ice from the cooler rose up, hung in the air, then showered down like Texas hail. Aaron tumbled over the backseat, unable to give any resistance as cold cans of soda and beer pummeled his back.

He careened into an un-seat-belted Max and they both slid to the floor in a tangle of limbs. Collin's rap music sadistically rose in volume like background music to a bad horror film as Aaron struggled to right himself in the dark. With arms and legs flailing all around him, he grasped something soft.

Realizing it was some part of Carole he quickly let go as the SUV slid sideways. He braced for another impact with either a huge hundred-year-old pine tree or one of the colossal boulders that dotted the roadside. But it didn't come.

The sound of sliding tires suddenly ceased as the vehicle jolted to a stop. One or more doors had buckled enough to turn the interior lights on and Aaron looked down and saw his feet floating in the air. His blood felt as if it were flowing in the wrong direction, then he realized he wasn't looking down. He was looking up.

"Carole," Max said. "You all right?"

"Yeah, I think."

"Aaron, you alive?" Max said.

Aaron thought about that for a second. The cold rubber of the floor mat pressing on his face seemed to indicate that he was. "Guess so."

"Then how about getting your ass-cheeks out of my face?" Max said.

Aaron felt Max's hands clasp his belt, lifting him like a crane. He flopped back into the rear compartment. He then tried to look outside but most of the view through the front windshield was blacked by deployed airbags. The view on either side of Max and Carole was also obstructed by airbags.

A head rose from the front seat, hair in disarray. Collin's girlfriend moaned, touching a finger to her bruised forehead.

"Debbie, are you okay?" Aaron said, bringing out a pocketknife.

She moaned again. "My name is Deedee, you total asswipe."

Aaron sighed. "She's fine." He flipped open the blade and handed the knife up to Max. "Hey, Collin?"

There was no movement from the driver's seat. Max

plunged the blade into the backseat airbag to his side; a soft whistling sound filled the car. He reached out and put a hand on Collin's shoulder. "Hey, man."

Collin made a grunting sound like a gorilla fighting to wake from a nap. His head flopped to one side. "Feels like there's something sitting on me," Collin said. "Can't feel my legs."

Everyone sat still for a few moments. Collin's heavy breathing was the only opposition to silence.

Aaron glanced over at Max who seemed to take a deep breath, then said, "Okay, let's stay calm. Carole, call nine-one-one."

"I'm on it." Carole began digging for her phone.

Max handed Aaron back his knife, then opened his door.

Aaron grabbed Max's shoulder. "Where're you going?"

"I'm gonna check out the car. You stay here with Deedee and see what you can do for Collin." Max stepped out.

Aaron lowered his voice. "Why me?"

Max stuck his head back in, extending a hand toward Carole. "Cuz, you're studying to be a doctor."

"I want to be a biologist."

Max cocked his head. "What's the difference?"

Carole slid across the backseat to follow. Before she stepped out she whispered to Aaron, "I know the difference."

Aaron took a moment to watch her leave, then hopped into the backseat to take a look at Collin, while his girlfriend pushed on the steering wheel.

"Donna, what're you doing?"

She stopped, glancing over at Aaron. "It's Dee—oh, never-the-fuck-mind. Just help me."

"Let's get this out of the way first," Aaron said, then stabbed the muffin-top-shaped airbag that had deployed from the steering wheel. As the bag deflated, Aaron leaned into the front seat, looking into Collin's lap. The entire steering column had been bent downward, pressing into Collin's stomach. "Aaron," Collin said. "Can you see my legs? I think I'm stuck" Aaron put a hand on Collin's shoulder, peering down.

"Everything's gonna be okay. Help is coming. Just hang—"

"I can't move, man?"

Below Collin's knees, Aaron couldn't see anything. The area around the pedals was completely caved in. Whatever they had struck must have been solid, and very heavy. "You're pinned in real good," Aaron said, trying to muster up some genuine concern for a guy he couldn't stand, the same guy whose dumbass antics had caused this mess. "I don't think you're getting out without help."

"Geez, my head hurts." Collin touched a golf ball-sized welt on his forehead.

Aaron eyed the lump. "Are you dizzy, tired, nauseous?"

"Yes, yes, and more yes," Collin said.

The door of the rear compartment swung open. Aaron snapped around, seeing Max riffling through the luggage. "What's going on?"

Max held up a finger. "Not now." He pulled out a flashlight and shut the door.

What the hell? What could be so damn important that Max didn't have time to answer? And why the hell am I in here taking care of his idiotic friend?

Collin's girlfriend raised a hand, pushing the front passenger-side airbag from off her face.

Aaron leaned forward with his pocketknife up. "Let me get that."

"No, I got it." She pulled a nail file out of her purse and stabbed the bag. It deflated in a few seconds.

Aaron looked at Collin, noticing his usually smug expression was slightly less smug. "Aaron," Max called from outside. "Get out here."

"You need to stay awake," Aaron said as Collin let his

head flop back onto the headrest. "How about just a little nap?" Collin mumbled.

Max's voice sounded again from right behind Aaron, "Aaron, I really need you to see this."

Aaron turned and looked at Max. "What?"

Max made an insistent gesture with the flashlight then stepped away.

Aaron turned and met Deedee's eyes. "Look, keep him awake and I'll be right . . ." his words faded as he glimpsed the windshield. A spider web of white cracks filled the glass, but not enough to obscure his vision. Something else, lying on the hood, was doing that.

Is that hair, Aaron wondered. And that looks like a—a saddle.

"I'm gonna step out for a minute," Aaron said. "I'll be back."

He hopped out, following the line of Max's flashlight illuminating Carole who stood a good distance down the road, her smartphone pressed to her ear.

"What's she doing way over there?" Aaron asked.

Max turned around, his face lit eerily by the vehicle's only working headlight. "That's as close as she wants to get to this thing." He waved at Carole and she returned with a nod, then Max aimed the flashlight at the hood.

Aaron's mouth dropped open and he instinctively stepped back. In a kind of perplexed daze, he joined Max standing just a few feet in front of the bumper.

"What the hell is that?" Aaron said.

"You tell me," Max said.

"Is . . ." Aaron stepped forward, fascination beginning to override his initial horror. "Is it a horse?"

Max moved the light down toward the bumper, illuminating the thing's feet. "Do horses have toes?"

"Not lately," Aaron said. "Shine the light up on its back."

The beam drifted up the creature's alien, dark exterior. Its underbelly was gaunt, leathery, and disturbingly unfamiliar.

And then Aaron saw something that was at least a little familiar. "That looks like a saddle."

Max's head tilted a bit. "Are you sure that's a saddle, city-boy?"

"According to all the John Wayne movies I've seen, that's a saddle." Aaron held out his hand. "Give me that."

Max handed him the flashlight and Aaron brought it up over his head, aiming the beam down, illuminating the creature's entire form. "Jesus," he breathed.

"What the hell is this?" Max asked.

Aaron shook his head, taking in the enigma sprawled out on the hood. Its form resembled a horse, but that is where the comparison ended. Instead of hooves, the thing had three-toed, muscular feet, each toe encased in a predator's claw, wide and jagged, stained in an array of colors from bone white to deep crimson. The equine frame was covered in short hair that glistened in the flashlight beam like rows of staples. A tail dangled off the hood by the front tire, comprised of hundreds of thick rust-colored, and somewhat familiar, strands. Aaron stepped closer, wanting to touch the tail and confirm the image his mind must have been imagining.

At the last moment, he thought better of it and settled for shining the light on it and gazing at the strands.

Is . . . is the tail made of barbed wire?

"Damn," Max said. "Shine the light over here. Look at these teeth."

Aaron redirected the beam to the creature's head which lay on the roof; its lips receded along the protracted snout in an unsettling death grin. The light bounced off and through the teeth giving Aaron the impression that the fangs were ice sickles, frozen to its black gums. But as he moved the light back and forth, he realized the long, spike-shaped teeth were transparent, as if made from glass or crystal.

"What the fu—" Max moved away from the beast's head. "This can't be real. Right?"

Aaron was about to answer but he'd moved the light down the thing's neck and his words caught in his throat. Growing from the spot where a normal horse would have a mane, protruded thick slimy follicles with ungodly ridges spiraling around each strand. They, too, had an unnerving ring of familiarity. The beast's 'mane' seemed made of a thousand oversized, dead earthworms.

"I don't know what is creeping me out more," Max said, "the fact that I'm really looking at this . . . or that someone actually rides this thing."

"Could be pre-historic," Aaron said, moving around to its head.

Carole's voice cut through the dark, "You mean like a dinosaur?"

Aaron aimed the light at Carole, now standing just behind Max. "Not exactly." He gestured to her phone. "What'd they say?"

She rolled her brown eyes. "No one can get here for at least a half-hour, maybe longer. And my battery just died."

"Geez," Aaron said.

Max pointed to the front seat. "How is Collin?"

"He has a slight concussion; I'm guessing not his first. He's dizzy and stuck under the steering column. This thing caved in the area around his legs. He's pinned tight, and he isn't getting free until they can get here and cut him out."

"But he'll be all right?" Max said.

"Yeah. I mean, he'll still be Collin, but aside from that, as long as What's-her-face keeps him awake, he'll be fine."

"Is there anything we could do to help him while we wait?" Carole said.

Aaron shrugged. "I guess we could get this thing off him. Max, get its tail."

"You nuts? I ain't touching this thing."

Aaron shined the light on his friend. "It's dead."

"How do you know?" Max said.

"We just hit it with a two-ton car." Aaron turned the beam on the creature's defined ribcage, visible under hair-covered flesh. "It isn't breathing."

Max walked toward the creature's tail. "We don't even know if it needs to breathe. It might be from outer space or another time. Or it could be a robot, even."

Aaron shined the light on Max's face. "Dude, no more Syfy channel for you."

Max gazed down, clearly fascinated. "Man, just look at this thing."

Aaron turned his attention to the creature's head. Its face seemed too long for a horse, almost a foot too long, and its snout seemed to be designed for tearing meat from bone rather than grass in a field. He found the thing's closed eyes and placed a thumb across one eyelid. Through the thin layer of skin, he could feel that the eye underneath was ridged, not spherical, or smooth. He pushed the lid up. There was a suction sound like someone pulling a shoe out of mud.

He aimed the flashlight at the thing's eyeball. It wasn't an eyeball at all, but a small human skull cast from gray metal like a pinky ring on the meaty finger of a Hell's Angel. "Ah, crap-weasel," Aaron said, letting the eyelid fall closed and stepping back.

"What is it?" Max asked, his voice noticeably elevated.

Aaron staggered further away, the flashlight still aimed at the thing's face. He took a breath. "Just reconsidering your alien-time-traveling-robot theory." He looked up at Max. "I don't think we should move it."

Collin's girlfriend stuck her head out the window, placing a hand on the creature's rump. "Hey, what is this?"

Max stepped forward and removed her hand. "Be careful. Maybe . . . don't touch it."

She recoiled. "Okay."

"How's Collin?" Max asked, standing just behind the thing's back legs.

She sighed. "He keeps trying to nod off."

"Well, help is on the way," Aaron said. "So, keep his eyes open."

She delivered a salute. "Yes, Sir, Captain Douchebag," then disappeared back into the car.

Aaron chuckled. "I might be starting to like her."

"There's no accounting for taste," Max said, then glanced down at the creature. He took a step closer holding his hands above the thing as if it were a warm fire. "Hey, Aaron."

"What?"

"Do you think it's worth something?"

Aaron furrowed his brow.

"I mean, it's gotta be one of a kind, right?" Max sounded excited. "A couple of months back, there was this three-headed dog that went for ten-thousand on eBay. Hell, this thing could beat that, easy."

Aaron rolled his eyes.

"I'm talking even split," Max said. "You, me, Carole, Collin, and even What's-her-name." Max grinned. "So?"

"So, what?" Aaron said.

"What do you think we could get for it?"

"I don't know, Max. My market knowledge of pre-historic-alien-time-traveling-robot horses is a bit limited. Besides, I think you're forgetting one minor detail."

"What's that?"

Carole pointed to the creature's back. "The saddle."

"Exactly," Aaron said. "Someone or something owns this .

. . whatever it is. And I'm not particularly interested in meet
—" Aaron's words stuck in his throat as his blood turned cold. His eyes went wide, so wide they felt as if they would pop from their sockets. "Max."

"What?"

"Get away from it."

"Why?"

"Now!" Aaron took a step back, his gaze locked on the creature's face. The eyeball-sized human skulls were wide open. Aaron heard several soft pings, like metal moving through air. He glanced down. Steak knife-sized claws extended from the creature's hind legs like rear hallux talons on a bird of prey.

"Max, get back," Aaron shouted. "It's not dead."

Max took a step, but it wasn't big enough. All four of the thing's legs kicked out as it tried to get up. The back leg talons slashed across Max's mid-section and he went down.

Aaron rushed around the car, meeting Carole at Max's side.

Max tried to sit up, his hands clasped around his abdomen.

Aaron aimed the flashlight at his midsection. Blood poured between Max's fingers.

Max glanced down, then back up at Aaron. "It really hurts."

Aaron handed Carole the flashlight and grabbed Max under the armpit.

"It's just a scratch," Carole said, taking Max's other side. "Stop acting like a girl."

Max smiled for a second, then pain seemed to erase the expression like chalk from a blackboard. They lifted Max to his feet, while he kept one hand fixed on his abdomen. He seemed to be pushing as if struggling to keep things inside.

They dragged him to the side of the road, Aaron fighting

the urge to look back even as he heard Collin and Deedee begin to scream. Max pushed Carole ahead toward the forest and said, "Run."

Carole hesitated, looking back at the boys, but then she glanced over their shoulders and clearly saw something—something horrible. Her mouth fell open, her eyes bulged and even in the thin moonlight, Aaron could see her tremble. "Just go," Max said. "Run!"

Carole spun on a heel and darted into the forest. The sound of bone and talons scraping on metal echoed behind them. Aaron and Max paused to look back.

The horse-creature had righted itself, now standing on the hood. The SUV's back wheels were several inches off the ground, teetering like a seesaw on the front axle. Collin's girl-friend screamed, looking up through the windshield, hands clamped tight on the dashboard. Her terrified shrills seemed to be aggravating the creature. The angular snout arched upward, and each hair in its mane moved under its momentum like the venomous strands on Medusa's head.

Aaron took a step toward the car but felt Max's hand around his shoulder holding him back.

Mouth open and transparent teeth glistening in the moonlight, the creature's head darted forward into the wind-shield like a predator bird diving into the water. Glass shat-tered and the whole car shook.

Deedee's screams stopped.

The creature pulled its head back out, something round and fleshy stuck in its teeth. Snapping its jaw shut the thing began to swallow. Aaron saw the outline of the girl's head moving down the long, gaunt throat.

"I told her I'd be right back," Aaron said.

"You lied, man," Max said. "Let's go."

Using the bouncing light from Carole's flashlight as a beacon, they pursued her into the forest. They hobbled in a clumsy entanglement of limbs, but even terribly wounded, Max seemed the more coordinated of the two.

Before they lost sight of the road, Aaron looked back to see if the horror was following. It wasn't. The beast stood on the hood, slowly sinking into the engine as unimaginable weight pulled it toward the ground.

Instead of getting down, the creature rose on its hind legs and reared its monstrous head back. The chest looked to be expanding as if taking in an enormous breath like a mythical dragon preparing to breathe.

Fire erupted from the beast's mouth as it thrust forward. The car's interior was engulfed in flame; smoke and ash exploded through the rear window.

"What was that?" Max asked.

Aaron jerked him forward. "Keep going!"

A tree limb smacked Aaron in the face as they crashed through the brush. Carole's bouncing light moved further away. Max moaned, and his head slumped forward. Aaron felt the pull of his friend's full weight and they both tumbled to the ground. Aaron landed on top of his friend, their lips close to touching.

Max pushed Aaron off. "Not even if you were pretty and made of money." He grimaced, shutting his eyes.

Aaron got to his knees. "Don't flatter yourself." He grabbed Max's arm. "Now walk it off, you big pie-hole."

Max pulled his arm away, falling flat on the ground. "I appreciate the words of encouragement, but I don't think . . ."

He pulled his hand away from his stomach briefly.

Aaron tried to mask his horror.

"I think I'm done."

Both of them sat still, breathing heavily. Aaron looked away.

Max lifted his head. "I'm slowing you down."

Before Aaron could respond, he felt something: a rhythmic vibration stemming from the ground, coursing through his body like precision lighting, striking his flesh first then going deeper to rattle his bones. A thunderous echo was just a step behind the vibrations, galloping through the trees. Getting closer. Coming fast.

"What is that?" Aaron said.

"You know what it is," Max said, softly. "Aaron, go. Catch Carole."

"Knock the hero shit off," Aaron said, pulling at Max's arm.

Max yanked his arm away, sitting up. "I'll slow it down best I can."

"Max."

"Just go," Max said, reaching for a broken tree limb.

Aaron stood up. "Max, I—"

"Please don't say anything weird, man. Just go." Max's eyes locked on Aaron's. "Keep her safe or so help me, I'll find a way back and kick your ass."

Aaron turned away from his friend and ran after Carole. The beam from the flashlight was at least a hundred yards deeper into the forest, blinking as it passed behind trees and bushes, fading from view. He was in danger of losing sight of her. He pushed himself harder. His chest pounded, sweat flowed, his lungs ached, and his legs screamed no more. He wished at some point in his life he'd taken up running, or jogging, or any kind of exercise whatsoever.

Tree branches slapped at Aaron's body as he ran faster than he knew how. The smell of pine filled his nose and he could feel his face beginning to rub raw from the scraping of needles. A pinecone hit him square in the forehead and he slowed to shake it off. He blinked his eyes a few times then the sound of a bonfire being ignited with far too much accelerant boomed behind him. He looked back just in time to see a fireball in the distance ascend into the underside of the forest canopy. Max screamed.

Aaron started running again. The bouncing light ahead was less than a hundred feet away, and he was closing the gap. When he could see her thin silhouette, he called out.

Carole stopped, aimed the beam back at him.

Aaron held up a hand to block the light. "Turned that off."

"Why?"

"You're like a freakin' lighthouse."

"Where's Max?"

"He . . . he went a different way."

"He did what?"

"He's trying to keep it off our tail." Aaron pushed her forward. "Go, go."

She turned toward him, defiant. "How is he going to keep it . . ."

Her words faded and sadness flickered in her eyes as understanding washed over her features.

Aaron shook his head. "There's no time for this." He grabbed her wrist and pulled as he started to move. She resisted for only a moment. Then they ran in the dark, stumbling every few yards. Aaron fell twice and Carole stopped each time, pulling him to his feet. After several more minutes, Carole smacked into a tree, tumbling backward. Aaron hit the same tree and fell across her legs.

Crap. Aaron rolled off her, feeling the damp needles covering the ground beneath him. "You okay?"

"Yeah. Need to rest."

"Just for a few . . ." Aaron breathed deeply lying flat on the ground. Fear-induced adrenaline flowed through him but he could do nothing with it. It was fuel for a machine that was grossly out of shape and all it did was cause his head to pound, his limbs to shake, and a wave of displaced nausea that moved into parts of his body he wasn't aware could even feel nausea. A part of him wanted this to be over. Just let it end. But another part, the part that was focusing on the distant vibrations in the earth bearing down on them like a heard of buffalo, had another idea: Embrace the adrenaline. Aaron sprang to his feet. "Break's over."

"Just a few more—" Carole began to say but stopped as a distant galloping began to resonate through the trees. "I'm ready." Carole jumped up and took off running leaving Aaron standing still.

Soon, Aaron was on her heels again, the galloping growing louder behind them. Aaron knew it was his imagination, but he swore he felt the thing breathing on his collar. He slapped at the rising hairs on the back of his neck, dirt and sweat running down his shirt.

The galloping was so close now; it couldn't be more than ten or twenty yards behind them—thunderous, pounding.

Carole turned hard to the right and ducked at the base of a wide tree. Aaron joined her, tucking in behind. They cowered at the tree's base, one of many that lined a small, oval-shaped clearing where only moss-covered boulders and dead pine needle littered the ground.

The galloping stopped. The forest went still for a moment; nothing moved, nothing breathed. Carole put her hand over her mouth, trembling.

Something moved by fast, forest debris caught in the enormous wake showered down in a rain of dirt, bark, and pine needles. As the debris settled, Carole and Aaron stood slowly, each having a tight grip on the other.

"Where'd it go?" Carole whispered.

High above, a tree branch snapped in the distance. Then another. Then a symphony of breaking limbs sounded. Aaron looked up, but couldn't accept what he saw. The creature was above them, moving within the forest canopy like a snake through grass, defying gravity, reason, and sanity. Branches and pinecones hit the forest floor with echoing thuds forcing Aaron to believe.

The trees went quiet, needles continuing to float down in the silence.

They looked at each other, Aaron's nose inches from Carole's. "I think it's gone," he said.

Carole breathed deep. "What the hell is that—"

The ground shook, sending a tremor through Aaron's body.

The four-legged beast straightened up ten feet in front of them. Enormous, leathery, black wings slowly folded to its side, tucking just beneath the saddle. The creature blinked and jostled its fire-breathing head. The hairs on the animated mane floated all around as if submerged underwater, giving life to each individual tendril. Teeth bared, the thing reared up on hind legs and the already-wide chest expanded to the sound of air inhaled down the gullet.

"What's it doing?" Carole said, her nails digging into Aaron's back.

Aaron put a hand on her chin pulling her face toward him. "Don't look, okay." He closed his eyes, resolute that after a few painful moments it would all be over. "Sorry, Max."

A wave of cold rushed by, icy, biting. Aaron opened his eyes.

A towering figure stood with its back to them, a dark cloak shrouding it from head to foot.

"Take it easy, my friend," the cloaked figure said in a deep and hollow voice.

In one hand, the figure held a macabre looking bridle. Aaron narrowed his eyes. There was something wrong with its hands. They were bony. No, not bony. They were bone.

"Please, excuse my pet," the newcomer said, sliding the bridle around the creature's snout. "He's naturally very curious about your world." The skeleton hand reached into its cloak and pulled out a pile of something worm-like, fleshy and placed it under the creature's mouth. "He wanders off whenever he gets the chance. Don't you boy?"

Aaron watched as the creature began to feed on the pile of nightcrawlers and maggots being offered. He loosened his grip on Carole. "That thing killed our friends."

"Yes, I suppose," replied the bony figure. "Would it help you to know that it was their time?"

"What?"

The cloaked form turned around to face them. Aaron and Carole recoiled, bumping into the tree behind them. There was no flesh on the man's face, only a skull, with dark eye sockets cast down. He pulled a long scythe out of the night air and pointed it at Aaron. "When it is your time," Death said, "the circumstances are irrelevant."

Aaron pushed away from the tree. "My friends aren't irrelevant."

Death shook his head. "You don't understand." He turned away and swiftly swung himself into the saddle. "But you will."

He gripped the reins and turned his mount. From under the saddle, the bat-like wings uncoiled and began to flap. Death and his mount rose off the ground, the forest floor swirling beneath them.

Aaron and Carole stood still in the center of the clearing and watched Death ascend, then disappear in an ocean of stars.

In the thin moonlight, Aaron and Carole stared at one another, neither of them sure exactly what had just happened. After a silent moment, Carole grabbed Aaron's hand and they started walking back to the road. They stumbled in the dark, unsure if they were heading in the right direction. Twinges, and debris they couldn't see snapped under their steps. Aaron searched for a tree that was smoldering, the tree Max had been sitting under, not because he wanted to gaze upon his friend's remains but because it would mean they were near the road. When he spotted it, he planned to veer away, go around. Carole didn't need to see that. He didn't need to see that. But he never got the chance. They came across a burning tree or the remains of a fire.

Like waking from a nightmare, they stepped from the woods onto the asphalt. The trees fell away and they were again under stars. Aaron took a deep breath smelling pine with a hint of ash as he peered up into the night sky.

"Look," Carole said, pointing to their right.

Less than a hundred yards down the road from where they had emerged, flashing blue and red lights lit up the scene. A dozen silhouettes moved about the emergency vehicles, and before too long, one noticed Aaron and Carole standing in the road.

A flashlight was aimed their way, then another. Aaron looked at Carole not knowing what to feel. Her exhausted and spent features seemed to express the same emotional uncertainty. They took deep breaths, turned toward the silhouettes, and stepped toward the light.

"I'm just trying to get this straight. In your nine-one-one call, you said that only one in your party was injured," the highway patrol officer recounted. "Can you tell me why three of your friends are now deceased and appeared to have expired on impact?"

Carole brought a hand to her brow. "I must have hit my head harder than I thought. I mean, I swear they were alive and talking after the crash. I guess that was just wishful thinking."

The officer flipped the page in his notebook. "Uh-huh."

Aaron could see disbelief in the officer's eyes. "Yeah, she

ran off into the woods, talking like someone was with her. I went after her and I guess we got a little . . . lost." Aaron swallowed hard. Lying was not really a part of his skill set.

The officer didn't write anything down, just stared back at them.

"Hey," someone yelled from behind. "Smoking gun."

Aaron and Carole turned around looking back at the SUV, no longer in the middle of the road but wrapped around an enormous pine tree. Aaron could just see Max's head slumped in the backseat, a torn airbag lying in his lap.

A fireman stood next to Collin's crushed body in the driver's seat, his girlfriend, head and all, next to him. The fireman held up an empty beer can. "There's more than one," he yelled.

"Yep, that's a shocker," said the officer taking Aaron and Carole's statement. He looked down at them, clearly not trying to hide his disdain. "You kids care to tell me how much the driver had to drink?"

Aaron met Carole's gaze. Her lips quivered but her eyes were dead still. He couldn't tell if she was putting it together or not, but Aaron could feel the cold touch of understanding slowly washing over him.

When it is your time, the circumstances are irrelevant, Death had said.

Aaron looked the officer dead in the eyes and said, "Yeah, he had a couple of drinks." He turned his gaze to Carole. "Isn't that right, Carole?"

Carole took a breath before she answered, "Yeah," she said. "More than a couple."

The officer closed his notebook. "You two are lucky to be alive."

Aaron smiled. He knew luck had nothing to do with it. The truth was much deeper than that. He met the officer's unsympathetic eyes and said, "It wasn't our time."

THE DRIFTER

JAMES FLYNN

They were basically a bunch of amateurs with some rented equipment, way out of their depth, and they knew it. Navigating their way across South Vietnam in the rumbling 4x4, cameras and emergency gear bundled all around them, they couldn't help feeling like a bunch of frauds.

There were three of them: Josh, Denis, and Lance. Josh was the unofficial leader, the one who'd put this insane plan together, the one who was crazy enough to have actually come up with the idea in the first place. They were making a low-budget documentary, travelling around Southeast Asia gathering footage, and, even after two months into the project, none of them could believe that they were actually doing it.

Laying down the money for the plane tickets, cameras, shipping fees, hotels, hired vehicles, and all of the other unexpected costs associated with the project had been brave—or stupid—enough, but the actual subject of the documentary itself was arguably even braver. Possible names upon release included: The Search for the Drifter, The Hunt for the Drifter, and The Man that Time Forgot.

If you were to mention the name Drifter to most members of the general public you'd most likely get a blank expression; either that, or people would perhaps think that you were talking about some kind of chocolate bar. Mention it in a pub and someone might think that you were referring to a new sports car. But if you were to mention the name whilst in the company of certain niche circles, however, people who were inclined to spend vast amounts of their time scouring the internet in a darkened bedroom binging on strange videos, it would trigger a look of knowing recognition as an icy chill ran up their spines.

The legend of the Drifter went back for generations. Hearsay and old wives tales of a wandering, timeless man had been in circulation around the globe for decades and beyond, but with the advent of cameras in the 19th century, followed by the ubiquitous rise of smart phones in the 21st, there was now a sizeable amount of photographic and digital evidence to back up these ancient tales. Nobody really knew anything about the Drifter, but that certainly didn't stop people from speculating.

Some people claimed that he was the ghost of an escapee from a lunatic asylum, others claimed he was a government spy. Certain researchers and investigators swore that he was the result of a botched laboratory experiment, whereas some believed he was a robot or a cyborg. And, if one cared to comb through special forums for long enough, they would find posts claiming that the Drifter was actually Elvis or D.B. Cooper.

The first photograph of the Drifter surfaced all the way back in 1892. To describe the picture as being grainy would be an understatement. Shot out on the Yorkshire Moors in the north of England by a dog walker, the black and white image showed a spindly figure strolling along in the middle distance, surrounded by grassy slopes. The thing that led many people to believe this hazy figure was the Drifter was the distinct shape of the hat he wore. Most of the tales and legends surrounding the Drifter included descriptions of a wide black hat, something like a fedora or a warped cowboy hat, along with the rest of his black attire.

Other photos popped up here and there during the first half of the 20th century, but the turning point for most people was a video clip that emerged in 1984. Shot on a family camcorder in a rural hillside area in Tenerife, the recording showed a tall, gaunt figure traipsing across a sandy, cactus-infested field adjacent to a disused industrial estate. Despite only being about twenty seconds long, the clip clearly displayed a figure which strongly resembled the standard description of the Drifter, reigniting the ancient legend for a new generation of curious, impressionable minds.

And since the famous Tenerife clip appeared there had been others uploaded onto the internet, originating from all four corners of the globe. Teenagers exploring a deserted airbase in Russia uploaded a brief clip in 2007 of a darkly dressed man loitering near a metal hangar, backpackers in Japan uploaded a video of a "wandering beast" walking through a forest in 2010, some shaky footage from Turkey in 2013 showed a hatted man walking along a rocky shoreline, and in 2018 a clip surfaced in Cambodia showing a disturbing figure shuffling through the remains of an old temple on the periphery of Phnom Penh.

For some, the most disturbing aspect of all of these photos and video clips was the way that the Drifter moved and carried himself. A common thread among all of the separate sightings was the lethargic, drained movements of his gangly limbs, like some kind of slo-mo button had been pressed. A certain graininess or haziness seemed to be present on every picture and video of the Drifter, but it couldn't always be explained by crude camera equipment or bad weather. Eyewitnesses sometimes described a difficulty focusing on the man, like an invisible film covered his ragged clothing and lofty physique.

The team's last port of call had been Phnom Penh, where they'd managed to gather some half-decent footage of the temple where the Drifter had been spotted, plus a few brief interview clips of local tuk-tuk drivers explaining how they'd seen a "strange foreigner" walking along the shore of the Mekong River for a few weeks before he suddenly vanished, never to be seen again.

The newest sighting of all, however, had occurred just three months ago, and it'd been in a semi-rural area in Vietnam, hence the reason Josh and his team were now driving through the outskirts of Sài Gòn in the sweaty, afternoon heat.

THE VIETNAMESE ROADS HAD BEEN CHAOTIC AND HECTIC since they'd left the car rental lot, packed with mopeds, motorbikes and speeding buses that stopped for no one. Families of three or four rushed past on all sides, all on one bike, along with delivery drivers carrying stacks of unsecured boxes behind them on the seat.

They were travelling along a road called Đường Mễ Cốc, a long pothole-ridden stretch that ran parallel to the Kênh Tàu Hủ River in District 8. The latest sighting had been witnessed and filmed by a local man to the area known as Chú Đức, and after some correspondence online with his English-speaking daughter, the man and his family had agreed to show them the original footage as well as answer any questions they had.

'This is it,' said Josh, sat in the passenger seat looking down at the map app on his phone. 'Take this turn here.'

Denis, who was sat behind the steering wheel covered in sweat and dust, nervously steered the vehicle across the never-ending tide of mopeds and motorbikes, taking a small slip road that ran beside a concrete bridge. Lance, the youngest of the three of them, was in the back of the vehicle, trying unsuccessfully to insert a new battery into one of the cameras.

After a couple of sharp turns they found themselves driving down a narrow alleyway with rows of colourful houses on either side, and low-hanging electrical wires dangling from wooden posts that threatened to snag the roof of the car. For a moment they all thought that they'd taken a wrong turn, but up ahead a small cluster of locals came into view, waving them over to a sliding metal gate on the right-hand-side.

'Hello,' said a young woman, as they climbed out of the car.

She was about mid-twenties, long black hair flowing down either side of her smooth face, with a floral dress covering her slim body. Her English was broken, but intelligible.

'Hello,' said Josh. 'Nice to meet you. You must be Ngân.'

'Yes, yes,' she smiled. 'And this is my father, Đức.'

Đức was a friendly-looking man of roughly middle-age. A large grin seemed to be constantly present on his weathered features, and a semi-casual collared shirt hung from his thin shoulders.

'Please come inside,' said Ngân, waving a hand towards a blue house with a corrugated roof forming part of a mini neighbourhood.

They all went inside the house, watched closely by an assortment of neighbours who sat on their doorsteps or lay in hammocks. Once inside the main living room they sat themselves down on the tiled floor, and were brought a tray of fresh spring rolls and iced tea from a woman who Josh guessed was Đức's wife.

'Cảm ơn,' said Josh, to the woman, reeling off one of the survival phrases he'd memorised during the plane journey over.

'My father, he fish by the river,' said Ngân, sitting opposite them all. 'He saw strange man by the old hospital, and he film.'

Most of the details were already known to Josh, and he'd even seen a small section of the video already, but he nodded and listened politely as the girl spoke.

'The man, he walk around one of the old buildings, but my father filmed him for a while.'

'How did you know who he was?'

'I show video to one of my friends, and she tell me that he's the ghost. After that, I put video online.'

'But how did your father know? Why did he film him in the first place?'

'The ghost is famous here,' said Ngân, running a hand through her glossy black hair. 'After people see it in Cambodia, it famous here.'

Ghost, thought Josh. He'd been wondering how the Drifter would be perceived in Vietnam, and now he knew. 'Can we see the video?' he said, at last.

'Yes, you can see,' said Ngân, turning her amiable gaze towards her father, who then rose to his feet and retrieved his mobile phone from the armrest of a lacquered, wooden sofa.

The grin on her father's face widened and morphed into a smile of genuine excitement as his fingers swiped at the device's screen, eagerly searching for the infamous video that'd gone viral on certain websites. The phone was then passed over to Josh, and his two companions leaned closer to him, itching to see the full footage in its entirety.

The first thing they saw on the small screen was a shaky

view of the Kênh Tàu Hủ River. After a few seconds the shakiness levelled out, and a crumbling building came into view on the opposite bank. For a while, nothing happened and no one was seen. An excited mumbling could be heard from behind the camera, presumably from Đức, but the dusty landscape was empty apart from a couple of stray dogs hobbling about.

But then, like a wiry apparition entering the frame from another dimension, the unmistakable outline of the Drifter came into view. His slow, fuzzy form undulated across the dirt and gravel like a dark snake standing upright, the blacked-out windows of the old hospital serving as a macabre backdrop to his unsettling gait.

'That's him all right,' Josh muttered, squinting down at the section of unseen footage with keen, borderline-obsessive, focus.

In line with the several other videos of the Drifter, the black-clad figure appeared to be completely oblivious or indifferent to the fact that he was being filmed, heading towards some unknown destination off screen with his long steps. He eventually disappeared around the back of one of the dilapidated hospital buildings, his mirage-like outline merging into the simmering heat waves of the sun-beaten vista.

Josh handed the phone back to Đức and thanked him. Then, he turned to the young woman. 'We'd like to interview your father on film as part of our documentary. Would you be able to act as an interpreter? Your voice will go over the top of his when it's broadcast.'

'Yes, I help you,' she said, her deep brown eyes lighting up with curiosity. 'That's fine.'

Looking over at both of his comrades, Josh said, 'Let's do this.'

If the neighbours within the small congregation of houses had been secretly curious about Josh and his team when they first arrived, they were now not even bothering to hide it. A wall of onlookers huddled around the open doorway of the house as Josh interviewed Đức in front of a chunky, tripod-mounted video camera, the lighting made dramatic with the help of a couple of strategically-placed lamps and mirrors. The interview lasted for around ten minutes, and they all knew that the intense scene would add a considerable amount of value to the documentary once it was released. Đức was very open to all of the questions that were put forward to him about his encounter with the Drifter, and his daughter Ngân translated his answers very well.

Once it was all over, Josh had just one more question for the man.

'Can you take us there?' he asked, in his friendliest tone.

Ngân leaned over to her father and whispered a few words into his ear. When he nodded in response, the whole team felt butterflies in their stomachs—the most important stage of the documentary was about to be put into motion.

⁂

THEY WERE BACK IN THE 4X4, RUMBLING ALONG THE riverside highway, this time accompanied by Đức and Ngân. Denis was driving, following translated directions from Ngân as she leant over the back of his seat. There was a tense, nervous atmosphere in the car as they made their way through the quiet town, as though they were driving into the arms of a beast that lurked just out of sight.

It didn't take too long to find the old hospital, around twenty minutes or so passing tiny food outlets and empty coffee shops, but when they arrived they were far from relieved. Worried, disappointed looks were present on all of their faces as they parked the car and took in the sight before them, their hopes emptying away. It wasn't the unsettling eeriness of the old medical facility that drained their spirits, nor was it the unbearable heat that showed no sign of easing off—it was the ten-foot-high barbed wire fence that menacingly loomed before them.

'What the hell is this?' grumbled Josh, squinting up at the long steel fence with despair seeping into him.

Ngân came up beside him, sensing his confusion and worry. 'Maybe it's police fence,' she said. And, after an awkward silence, she added, 'I don't know when they did it.'

Things had been going relatively well so far. They had some pretty good footage and interviews to use, all filmed on location, but the success of the project ultimately rested on Josh getting some close up shots of the hospital. Even if he didn't manage to get an exclusive clip of the Drifter himself the show could still do well, but at the very least he had to get into the derelict hospital and film some of the interior. This latest video clip of the Drifter in Vietnam was rapidly becoming the most famous one of all, and exploring the building for the documentary was of paramount importance. This realisation, along with the searing afternoon heat, was grating away at Josh.

'Well that's just great, isn't it?' he fumed, finally giving in to his irritation. 'How are we supposed to get in there now?'

Denis and Lance were short of ideas, the vast array of anti-trespassing signs and tall steel posts stunning them into silence. They were both avoiding Josh's gaze, but after a few moments Denis cleared his throat and came up with a suggestion:

'We'll have to just get some shots of the exterior, and then maybe add some commentary over the top of it.'

'Shots of the exterior?' sighed Josh. 'You think I've come all the way out here just to get some shots of the exterior? You can't even see the bloody exterior, anyway! It's fifty metres away and obscured by that poxy fence!'

'Well, I'm sorry Josh! What am I supposed to say? I was just—'

'Okay, okay. I'm sorry,' said Josh, taking a few deep breaths. 'I'm just getting stressed right now.' He wiped some sweat from his brow, and then turned towards Ngân and her father who were standing by the car. 'Ngân, what'll happen if we go in there?'

'You mean, go through the fence?'

'Yes.'

Sweeping a strand of charcoal-black hair from her forehead, she looked towards the metal barrier with unease. 'I don't think it's good idea. The police, they arrest you.'

Josh paced around for a while, kicking the stones and gravel as he pondered the predicament. He wasn't prepared for this, and yet he should've been. He should've seen something like this coming; it was just the kind of unexpected hurdle that arose whilst embarking on a crazy adventure of this kind. There was really only one option available to him if he wanted to make the documentary a success. Denis and Lance must've known this, too, because they were still avoiding his gaze, fiddling with some tripods and lenses in an effort to make themselves invisible.

'There's only one thing for it,' said Josh, coming to a halt before his two cameramen. 'We need to get ourselves in there, get the golden footage we need, and then leave.'

'What about the police?' said Lance. 'You heard the girl.'

'If the police come, we'll just act dumb.'

'Act dumb?' snapped Denis, throwing his tripod down on the ground. 'You're talking about trespassing onto Vietnamese property! They'll—'

'Calm down, Denis! It's an old hospital, for crying out loud! You make it sound like we're about to rob a bank or something. The council probably put this fence up for health and safety reasons; to stop kids from running around in there, that's all.'

'I'm not doing it, Josh. And even if the police don't come, what about the person, or thing, we might find in there? Have you thought about that?'

'Have I thought about that?' screamed Josh. 'Of course I've thought about that! That's why we're here! That's the sole reason we've been travelling across South East Asia for the last two months! Or did you not know that?'

'Fuck you, Josh!' shouted Denis. 'There's only so much I can take.'

'Suit yourself,' said Josh, shaking his sweaty head. 'Lance? What about you? Are you with me?'

Lance, the youngest of the three of them, looked down towards his feet. 'I'm sorry, Josh. I'm committed to this project, but I'm not willing to get arrested in a foreign country. I'm just not.' The words fell from the young man's mouth in a weak spill, like the utterance of a schoolboy shamefully turning down a dare.

'I see,' spat Josh, derisively. 'Well, I suppose I'll have to go in there by myself. You two can wait out here and look pretty.' Walking over to the boot of the car to grab a camera bag, he added, 'Make sure you don't break a nail or anything.'

'Come on, Josh!' cried Denis. 'You're being unreasonable! You're obsessed over this thing!'

Denis never got a reply. Josh ignored his outburst and stormed off towards the fence with a camera bag slung over his shoulder, leaving all of them to watch on in disbelief. Nobody tried to stop him as he angrily tore up a corner of one of the fence posts, yanking it back and forth until a sizeable gap had been created. Nor did anyone try to stop him as he painfully dragged himself through the gap on his hands and knees, ripping his shirt and trousers in the process.

Moments later, once he was on the other side of the

fence, he followed the exact path that the Drifter wandered along on the video, disappearing around the back of the same crumbling structure, its cracked brickwork rising up from the dirt like a rotten, decaying tooth.

OBSESSED? YEAH, TOO RIGHT I'M OBSESSED, THOUGHT JOSH, as he walked gingerly around the deserted medical facility. He'd been obsessed about this thing before it'd even begun, obsessed after first hearing about the legend of the Drifter as a child in his primary school playground. Solving the mystery had turned into his main purpose in life, his ultimate ambition, and he certainly wasn't going to let a barbed-wire fence stop him from doing it.

It was getting later into the afternoon now, but the relentless tropical sun was still smothering the land like a humid blanket, scorching the cracked concrete edges of the various buildings. The atmosphere was eerie, mysterious, borderline miasmic, and Josh's senses were on overdrive as he nervously looked around. But apart from a few rats scurrying around, and a steady trickle of cockroaches crawling over the empty beer cans and plastic bottles lining the curbs, there was no sign of life.

Things changed when he turned a corner, however, creeping silently around the edge of a crumbling plastic security hut. There was a sudden shift in the air, a feeling that he was no longer alone, and the dry landscape heaved with tension. The main hospital building towered over him like an overgrown tombstone, and the setting sun shone through its empty window frames creating bizarre, surreal shadows over the stony floor. These shadows stretched out before Josh like long grey monoliths, the windows giving them a grid-like effect.

It was on one of these shadows that Josh saw the first sign of movement. A shape passed across one of the square window frames on the ground, a silhouette crossing from one edge to the next, and the sight of it took his breath away. By counting the windows cast across the shadow, Josh calculated that whoever was in the hospital was up on the fourth floor.

Did I just see the Drifter?

An overwhelming wave of panic and fear took hold of Josh as he contemplated this question, as well as an impulse to leave. But leaving was absolutely out of the question, and he knew it. Not only was he in serious debt due to the expenses of the expedition, not only had he committed a ridiculous amount of time and effort travelling and preparing, but now he'd also pissed his two cameramen off in a big way. Redemption was the only way out of this mess, and an award-winning documentary was the thing he needed to pull it off. A prize-winning cult hit would pay off the debts, make all of the stress and hassle worthwhile, and win back the respect of his fellow crew members. Was he scared? Yes. He was terrified, even. But so what? This was it. This was his moment, this was his dream, and he was doing it.

Moving stealthily like a cat, he prepared to enter the hospital.

THE INTERIOR OF THE HOSPITAL WAS LIKE A SETTING FOR A demented dream. Old-fashioned relics and artifacts of a time gone by sat in every crevice of every room and hallway, all covered in dead flies and dust. Metal trolleys with torn tablet boxes in their compartments sat beside stairwells, bed frames with mouldy mattresses occupied empty wards, and small storage cupboards here and there were filled with broken mops and half-disintegrated rubber gloves.

Josh recorded all of this through the lens of his camera, working his way up the many floors with the device held up against his chest. Terror and trepidation rattled his bones and ignited his nerves, but he refused to give in to it. He was going to confront whoever—or whatever—lurked upstairs above him, no matter what the outcome may be.

It was on the third floor that he began to hear noises.

Light footsteps and shuffling started to echo down the concrete stairwell, a peculiar sound that permeated straight through to Josh's core. A voice seemed to accompany the sound, but the exact words were too distant and low to make out. This unsettling murmuring and shuffling continued as he climbed the filthy, littered staircase, and he followed it carefully.

His earlier calculation had been right: the sound was emanating from the fourth floor of the building. It eventually led him to the open doorway of a dormitory, where he lingered for a moment whilst peering in. The long room was filled with intense rays of orange light as the sunset penetrated through the remaining glass panels and empty frames, highlighting the spirals of dust and dirt that hung over the empty beds like miniature sandstorms. At the far end of this rectangular room, behind what might've been an old doctor's desk, a hatted silhouette pranced up and down like a shadow puppet.

Josh edged further into the room, his presence seemingly undetected or ignored, holding the camera at chest height. After a lifetime of searching and studying he was now actually in the same room as the Drifter, and he had no idea what to say or think.

The Drifter, on the other hand, showed no sign of discomfort. His incessant pacing and shuffling did not falter for one second with Josh now in the close vicinity, he simply continued to twist and gyrate in his elastic way, letting a string of words flow from the neat crease of his mouth:

> Has it really come to this
> Despite the planet's size?
> No nook or cave to sit and rest
> To hide from prying eyes?

The voice. The voice. It was like a needle that pricked the centre of Josh's heart, the tainted echo of a damaged instrument. The camera had slipped from Josh's hands upon hearing it, but he hardly even noticed. For several minutes he could do nothing but stare across at the partially-obscured features hidden under the rim of the big hat, trying to decipher the meaning of the rhyme he'd just heard.

'Wha...What? What do you mean?' he eventually said.

Without breaking his graceful stride, the Drifter sang again:

> This globe of many wondrous things
> I've sat and watched it grow
> It started off so desolate
> But now it's quite a show

Taking another few steps into the room, passing along the rows of rusty bed frames either side of him, Josh formulated his next response.

'Who are you?'

> A splendid thing you ask of me
> For sometimes I forget
> It's been so long since I've been home
> I sometimes have to guess

The combination of the loose pacing, the rhyming dialogue, and the piercing voice was making Josh's head spin. It was like being in the presence of a tormented circus animal that'd been locked away in a cramped cage for too long, or a trapped insect buzzing away under an upturned glass. It took a large amount of discipline and self-control for Josh to hold himself together and think clearly amongst this onslaught of insanity, but he persevered.

It's been so long since I've been home? he thought. What could that mean? Calling out again to the moving figure up in front of him, Josh said:

'Where do you come from?'

And then, another tainted melody rang out across the room:

> My city is a distant speck
> So far away from here
> They banished me with no remorse
> And did not shed a tear

The rays of sunlight cascading into the room made it hard to focus on the Drifter, but there was something else too. His nimble, arachnid limbs were clouded by a mirage-like haze, making the edges of his form flickered and blurred. Even his words seemed to lack solidity, undulating through the air before seeping into the listener's skin.

'So how long have you been here?' asked Josh, straining his eyes through the dusty haze.

The Drifter's rhythmic pacing altered at this question, and he began to gravitate towards the old wooden desk. Then, in one fluid motion, he scooped up a small item from its surface and tossed it over to Josh.

> There was a dirty, nasty war

It really was no fun
The soldiers sleeping in the dirt
They call it World War One

An antique whisky flask sat in Josh's outstretched palm, and he looked down at it in bemusement. Its metallic surface was scuffed and dented, worn with age, but before he could comment on it another item was thrown over to him.

I once bore witness to a time
Caligula was king
The fights, the battles, and the deaths
A sight it did so bring

Now he was gazing down at a small Roman coin that he'd caught, the inscriptions barely visible. The implications of it were crazy, but things were about to get even crazier.

You want to go back further still?
For that, I can oblige
A token from an ancient past
All witnessed with these eyes

With a graceful twist of the torso, the Drifter hurled another small object over in Josh's direction, which he barely managed to catch. This one was a reptilian tooth, large and sharp at its tip.

This beast I fought with my bare hands
In the Mesozoic
I roamed the plains with ancient forms
Mighty and heroic

'Is this a dinosaur tooth?' asked Josh, his face now solemn and deadly serious.

There was no reply to this, though. The Drifter was off again on his maniacal pacing, his dizzy wandering of the room, his...drifting. Josh was close to him now, only a few metres away, but he still couldn't make out any crystal clear details. It was like trying to focus on something through a rain-spattered window, or trying to read a page of a book just seconds after waking from a long, deep sleep. This continuous confusion and failure to understand what was going on made Josh snap. 'Look!' he said. 'How are you even here? How are you still alive?'

Like a gangly spider stumbling about in its web, the Drifter paced and sang his reply:

> I broke the law, on my own land
> And paid a hefty price
> They dropped me down on this wet rock
> Then rolled the dice of life

'Dropped you down on this wet rock?' Josh cried. 'You're from another planet?'

> They wanted me to suffer hard
> Throughout millennia
> To live among the vicious forms
> From their panspermia

This last word hovered around Josh's head, circling his brain. He'd heard it somewhere before, probably on the internet. Panspermia? he thought. Isn't that the theory that life on Earth came from another planet? He was pretty sure that it was, but he wasn't certain. Fortunately, the Drifter had more to say:

Before they brought me to this place
In a shiny vessel
They strapped me down on to a bed
Injecting me with metal

Inside my body sits a sphere
No bigger than a dime
Its function is a simple one
To bend, and distort time!

Josh carefully placed the tooth and the rest of the items down on a bed beside him, and tried very hard to get his head around what he was hearing. If all of this was to be believed, he was in the presence of someone who'd lived through millions, if not billions, of years, witnessing the evolution of Planet Earth first hand. A time dilation device sat inside his slim body somewhere, keeping him young as he traipsed across the eternal landscapes. And as for the panspermia comment: was he trying to tell Josh that his race planted the seed of life on Earth 4.6 billion years ago?

'Tell me more,' cried Josh, determined to solve this torturous riddle. 'Tell me what you've experienced.'

The Drifter's haunting face stared out across the room from behind a thick sunbeam infused with dust, his pointy features lost in the glowing swirl. Then came a melody, a string of sounds that caused the hairs on Josh's neck and arms to turn end-wise.

For hundreds of eternities
I've walked the Earth alone
I've scavenged things and pillaged things
And carved out many homes

The languages and dialects

I've seen and spoke them all
My eyes have seen ten million suns
They rise and then they fall

The population of this place
Is on a rapid rise
But I will always walk alone
And no one hears my cries

For perhaps the first time ever, Josh was seeing the Drifter not as a monster but as a victim. It was clear now that time had rendered him insane, the decades, centuries, and millennia melting his brain into a tortured mush. Always an outsider, he wandered along the periphery of the societies and cultures that he saw come and go, trapped in his own bubble of existence. Regressed into his own head, he lived out his lonely days within the walls of his cranium, his thoughts and musings heard only by him, the outside world nothing but a transient, ever-changing backdrop that had no place for him.

Maybe his rhyming talk was simply a way for him to occupy his mind, Josh thought, a distraction from the terrifying predicament that he found himself in. In the same way that an incarcerated man may develop eccentric, psychotic habits and rituals to pass the long hours in solitary confinement, the Drifter may have developed his own bizarre habits to pass the long millennia that he was trapped inside.

But what about this talk of panspermia? Josh had to know more.

'What did you mean by panspermia? Did life on Earth come from another part of the universe?'

This life that's all around you now
The life on planet Earth

It's all a big experiment
Concocted and researched

My race came here with cells and genes
To see if they would grow
But they could not just stick around
To sit and watch the show

The evolution takes so long
For things to take a hold
So I was left here on my own
To watch the thing unfold

'But what was your crime?' asked Josh. 'Why did your people leave you here like this?'

The crime that I was guilty of
That got me many years
Was my affront to their big plan
Of planting life down here

So there it was. The mystery that'd sat in the background of Josh's life, as well as countless others, was now solved. The Drifter was a convict of his planet, sentenced to become an observer of an extraordinary biological project. The punishment for his crime of being opposed to the terraforming of Earth was to be left here alone to watch the evolutionary show unfold. But was his punishment eternal? Or would his race one day return to collect him and take him back to his distant city, wherever that was? Josh had neither the energy nor the willpower to find that one out. The atmosphere in the old hospital wing had become suffocating, the Drifter's strong presence adding a sickly weight to the air. His agony and torment radiated outwards from his restless body, his loneliness and isolation surrounding him like a magnetic field.

It was time to leave. Without saying another word, Josh began to tiptoe back through the rows of empty beds, retreating to the doorway. The Drifter made no attempt to follow him. In fact, he didn't even notice him leaving. Josh was merely another shape in the transient landscape, another meaningless object that came and went, another blurred movement in his peripheral vision.

There was one last shock for Josh before he left the room. Just a few feet away from the door, he lost his footing and almost dropped to the ground. He'd forgotten all about his camera, and he nearly stepped right on it. Once he'd steadied himself he picked it up and cradled it in his arms like a comfort blanket, then got himself out to the stairwell as quickly as he could.

To his emotionally-distressed eyes, the building appeared to warp and distort around him as he hurled himself down the chipped stairs, the architecture bending and breathing like the arteries of a concrete heart. He could still hear the Drifter's shuffling and murmuring as he reached the ground floor exit, the faint rhymes orbiting the edges of his consciousness like the echoes or residue of an hallucinatory dream.

IT TOOK A WHILE FOR JOSH TO NAVIGATE HIS WAY BACK OUT of the disused site. Stumbling around in a stupor, his bearings were all over the place. After stuffing the camera into his bag he searched for the hole in the fence that he'd made earlier, but it was easier said than done. And, once he'd gotten himself through the fence and away from the buildings, he was faced with a fresh problem—everyone was gone.

The area was deserted. As he stood there in a daze, head turning left and right for signs of life, all he could see was an empty patch of gravel where the 4x4 was previously parked. Denis and Lance were nowhere to be seen, neither were Ngân and Đức.

Paranoid thoughts instantly began to surface in his mind: had the police turned up? Had there been some kind of accident? Were they all so pissed off at my decision to enter the hospital they simply left me to my own devices?

Things didn't improve when he took his phone out of his pocket to make a call, either. There was no signal, no data, nothing. He'd purchased a new SIM card upon his arrival into the country; had it run out of credit already?

Effectively stranded in a small corner of Sài Gòn, all he could really think of doing was to walk back the way he'd come, following the roads that Denis had driven down on the way out there. If he could get himself out to the main road again, he could try to hail a cab and get back to Đức's house. With any luck, they might all be there waiting for him.

The sky had grown very dark, the palm trees and empty shops lining the river discernible only as faint outlines, but he made it back out to the main road easily enough. There was a strange disorientation gripping him now, however, and everything around him seemed altered and unfamiliar. Houses passed by that he didn't remember seeing on the way out, and even some of the bikes and cars on the road were peculiar-looking and sounded too quiet.

One of these slick, silent cars pulled over for him when he stuck out his hand, though, and it came as quite a relief. The offside door slid open on its own, and the driver—a middle-aged cabbie—waved him in. Flopping down in the passenger seat, a dazzling array of miniature screens and luminous buttons screamed out at him from the dashboard, and the driver had to call out to him twice to get his attention.

'Err, sorry,' Josh mumbled, fumbling around in confusion. 'Can you take me to...'

It soon became apparent that communication was going to be quite hard, so he just pointed a finger in the direction he remembered the house being in, and attempted to direct the driver en route. And, surprisingly enough, it worked. About twenty minutes later the small alley that the house was on came into view, and things were looking promising.

But then it went strange again.

The driver didn't seem to like Josh's money, despite it all being in Vietnamese dong. The colourful bank notes first made the cabbie smile and chuckle to himself, but then, when Josh persisted and made it clear that this was how he was seriously intending to pay for the ride, the man's smile transmogrified into an angry scowl. Tapping his finger impatiently against a card reader on the elaborate dashboard, he demanded some kind of digital currency. There was a flurry of shouted obscenities from the driver, and Josh was eventually pushed out of the car. A few seconds later, the cabbie sped off down the small road in a huff.

It wasn't an ideal turnout by any means, but at least he was back at the house now. Walking over to the sliding metal gate, he peered in at the cluster of houses, then entered the small estate. To his horror and dismay, he noticed that even Đức's house looked different than it did earlier, the paintwork and corrugated roof constituting a different design. How could this be?

He tapped on the front door a couple of times and waited. A few seconds later a young man answered who looked completely unfamiliar, as well as hostile.

'Bây giờ, mày muốn cái gì?' he said.

Peering over the man's shoulder into the house, the entire layout of the living room looked different, the furniture of a completely different design.

What the hell's going on? I don't like this!

Josh had no idea what the man said, but he was pretty sure it wasn't good. He'd never seen him before, and even the neighbours in the surrounding houses looked unfamiliar too. Sensing trouble on the horizon, he made a swift exit from the small estate and walked back out towards the main road.

A concrete bridge sat next to the main road and he stopped by it, taking a few minutes to gather himself and decide what he was going to do. He was alone in a foreign country, he had no vehicle, his money appeared to be useless, and, on top of that, he appeared to be losing his mind. Was this really happening? Was he dreaming? The encounter with the Drifter in the derelict hospital already seemed like a sketchy dream rather than reality, so he couldn't rule it out.

Remembering that the camera was in his bag, he took it out to see what'd been recorded. The device came alive easily enough, despite having been dropped, and within seconds the rectangular screen lit up to reveal its usual symbols and functions.

He pressed play.

Shaky images of the crumbling stairwell began to play out, confirming that the experience had been real, and then things were reinforced even further when the Drifter's dark silhouette came into view. The entire sequence of events played out as they should have, the scene crashing and shaking as the camera was dropped to the floor, but there was a huge anomaly that caused Josh's eyes to widen as he watched the screen—the date and time.

Was he seeing this correctly? Or had he damaged the camera when he dropped it? Something was wrong, because the displayed date and time read: 20:42pm 7.2.82. Pulling his phone out again, he checked the time on there.

His heart did a cartwheel inside his chest, then a somersault for good measure.

The same thing was showing on his mobile phone: 20:42pm 7.2.82. There were two possible explanations that Josh could see. Either both of his devices were faulty, displaying the same incorrect date and time for some unknown technical reason, or sixty-odd years had passed by while he was in the hospital. The former was more likely, of course, and more desirable, but bearing in mind the altered state of his surroundings, coupled with his awkward experiences with the cab driver and the man at the house, the latter was looking much more like the truth.

Had the Drifter's time bubble distorted his own time line? Had he strayed too close to the spherical device mentioned in one of his rhymes? He couldn't believe it, he didn't want to believe it, but yet...he had to.

So what was he to do now? Hitch a ride to the airport? Try and catch a flight home? After a quick calculation in his head he worked out that both of his parents were probably long dead by now, along with most other distant relatives. And as for Denis and Lance? Even if they were still alive they'd both be octogenarians, old and frail and tucked away in some cosy nursing home somewhere. Maybe they'd remember him, maybe they wouldn't.

Dark thoughts. Dark thoughts, indeed. A strong impulse to move suddenly washed over him, a desire to just walk into the night in an effort to distract himself from the terrible predicament he found himself in. He was now a lost soul wandering along the periphery of society, a forgotten face from another era.

The legend of the Drifter had been Josh's main obsession for as long as he could remember, and solving the mystery had become his main purpose in life. Now, not only had he solved the mystery, he'd also become a Drifter himself, an outsider destined to roam, traipse, and drift through a lonely existence.

THE BLOCKED CELLAR

MIHALIS GEORGOSTATHIS

The street used to be a nice, upscale neighbourhood of artists, merchants, and affluent individuals. Now, it was a dilapidated ruin of abandoned squats for homeless and drug addicts.

I wish I hadn't listened to Lena. But she was very clear, I should either come to help her with the video or never bother to call her again. Girlfriend problems, right?

"The old Alkminis Manor used to be famous in old Athens," she told me as I was making another round on the block, trying to find a parking spot. I had yet to see a parking spot that would guarantee nobody would break into my car.

"You told me before," I told her.

"Stop nagging!" She sighed. "I have to do a recap. I have to narrate as we move into the building."

"I thought you would be doing a voiceover."

"Don't be dumb! I'll do both. Some narration as we navigate the building and then will do voice overs over the B-roll."

"All right," I said, as I found a good spot to park. It was a good three minutes away from the manor. If I were lucky, we would find some of the car afterwards . . .

"Don't forget the lighting!" Lena told me.

"I won't." I sighed, trying to balance the camera, the tripod, and the microphone.

"Come on, move it!" she said and left for the house.

"Hey, wait! Don't go there on your own."

"Are you afraid?" she chided me.

"Come on! It's just – did we have to come here after dark?"

"Are you afraid of ghosts?"

I worried about whoever might be inside the house. Lena was not aware of the dangers in these parts of the city. But she was in a hurry, so she rushed inside the dark alley that led to the old mansion.

The street was narrow and paved with broken tiles. A large dumpster blocked access to all cars. Lena breezed past it, while I was running after her, expecting a dark shape to jump from behind the metal cannister.

Nothing happened.

"Come on, you slowpoke!" she said and ran further into the street.

I tried following her, but I was too burdened with our equipment. Breaking any of this stuff would mean we would have to return here another night, and it was the last thing I wanted.

I just wanted us to leave this damned place.

The manor had seen better days. But I seriously doubted it had seen worse . . . The building must have been, once upon a time, an architectural marvel. Lena had gone over the details of who designed it and how it was built over and over again. Now, it barely stood; its windows were broken, the front door was only held by one of its hinges, and either the roof had darker patches or the tiles had fallen in places.

There were also dark patches against the front wall as if somebody had set the place on fire.

"Can you turn the light to me?" Lena scolded me.

I did, turning the camera light at her, then I adjusted the lens. She was standing in front of the manor, fixing her hair and straightening her clothes.

"Do I look good?" she asked me.

"Hey, I am dating you, remember?" I told her, trying to frame her in a way that also showed the mansion. It was difficult, the street was very narrow and the lighting was non-existent.

"This is no big reassurance," she said and stuck out her tongue.

"We better move towards the end of the alley," I told her.

"Afraid?"

"No. There is no way I can fit the entire manor from over here."

Our first take was a tracking shot. Lena stood behind the garbage bin and walked towards the building.

"Ionas Dekris inherited this house from his maternal grandfather. So, he gave it her mother's name, Alkmini. He was a medical doctor of great repute and soon recovered most of his family's lost fortune."

She was walking towards the house with unparalleled grace as if she was performing a dance of subtle motions. She was truly alive in front of the camera and I was very perplexed why she had to pursue these macabre themed videos for her followers, instead of just being herself and talking makeup and all the stuff the other girls did. Must have been all those Tim Burton movies she grew up with.

"In this house," she went on, when we stopped in front of the door, "he treated the rich and famous of Athens. The years after World War One were not easy, but his medical skills and the charity work he did for refugees elevated him back into high society."

"Do I look good?" she asked me. "Should we do another take?"

"You were perfect, baby," I told her, too eager to finish this thing as soon as possible.

"You think?" she said, flattered.

We only did four more takes and no bums, hobos, or junkies tried to kill, rape, and mug us, so I was getting calmer.

"Time to go inside," Lena decided and posed before getting to the door. "Can you get me some Insta shots?" she asked me.

I obliged. I knew the more I tried to dissuade her, the more time we would remain in that accursed place.

Then, once she was satisfied, she ordered me to turn on the camera and she opened the door. The rotten, wooden door cringed as it opened, like a dark, yawning mouth in the manor's face.

Lena took one step into the house, and then, suddenly, she let out a piercing shriek.

I froze, then left the camera to hang from its straps as I run to her rescue.

Meanwhile, she stepped back, flailed her arms around then burst out laughing.

"Oh my god," she said, puffing, "a bat got in my hair! Yikes!" Then, calmer, she added, "Tell me you got this on camera."

"Some of it . . ." I muttered.

She then filmed a short segment, explaining to her viewers that a bat got into her hair and she was scared and her brave cameraman – she never called me her boyfriend in her videos – rushed to the rescue.

She talked for about five minutes then she went into the house. This time, it was uneventful.

I followed her in and I took a lot of shots around as soon as I entered the building.

Forget my irrational fear of hobos and junkies. Forget my worry that the bat might have given Lena rabies. This time, I was genuinely terrified the house would fall on us.

The hallway we entered must have been splendid back in the twenties. Now, marble that once adorned the floor was littered with rubble from the ceiling. Cobwebs were hanging over us like expensive chandeliers, and the frame of a wooden stairwell to the upper floor was barely standing, most of the steps broken or missing.

"Bummer!" Lena said. "We can't go upstairs. I read that Dekris' bedroom was a den of filth back then."

"Got any plans to restore it to its glory days?" I teased her.

"No, you dummy. But sex sells, you know that."

If it didn't, I thought, I wouldn't be here with you, risking life and limb.

"Take a good shot of the stairwell, and try to also film the upper floor, if you can. I need a lot of material for the B-roll. I have a lot to narrate". I did, too, trying to get as much footage as I could. The camera light was not as strong as I wanted, so I knew that, despite the lens, much of the footage would be grainy.

"Did we have to come at night?" I complained. "The light is atrocious."

"Don't be stupid," Lena said, "the area is full of drug addicts during the day. Plus, it is more atmospheric this way."

"There could be junkies after dark," I said.

"There are not," Lena said, "they're too afraid to stay nearby. The house has an ugly reputation . . ."

"Are you serious?"

"Do you see any needles around?"

She was right. I didn't.

Hell, if heroin addicts knew better and never entered the house, why did we?

"However," Lena narrated as we traversed the ground floor, "not everything about the good doctor was good. The rumors started early on, that not all of his upstanding clientele was visiting him for . . . proper treatments.

"This dining room", she said, as she waved around the spacious, dilapidated room that was missing a big part of its ceiling, "often entertained Athens' high society.

"However," she added, heading to a door against its north wall, "inside his office other dealings took place. Sinister dealings.

"It was a common secret that the doctor often helped maidens from proper families end their premarital pregnancies and did the same for gentlemen who were not willing to support their lovers and the children they were bearing.

"Sometimes, without their will."

"What?" I exclaimed. "You were telling me about a house of a century-old sex scandal, not this freaky stuff."

"I know you're a coward, that's why. I didn't want you to chicken out."

"Unborn babies died in here, Lena!"

"Are you suddenly a pro-lifer?" she asked then pointed the hole in the ceiling. "See if you can take any shots of the upper floor through this hole."

"Are you not worried the ceiling will fall on us?"

"A little. So, stop yammering and get the footage. Chop-chop!"

I did as she asked, while she was giving me directions, where to shoot, where to move, and all that stuff. I was seriously considering the future of our relationship. I mean, she was cute and we had fun most of the time, but was it worth occasionally putting our lives in danger?

Imagining the rest of the ceiling falling and crushing me under tons of rumble, I went on until I was eventually done.

"Perfect," Lena said. "Now to the office."

The office was half as large as the dining room and bare of furniture or rubble. That was quite a surprise. Dense cobwebs covered all four walls and they shimmered as the light hit them.

"This was Ionas Dekris' office. Where he admitted his patients." Then she ducked out of the room. "Fuck it, this is full of webs. Get as much footage as you can, I have five pages of script to narrate over this room".

"How the hell do you know so much?" I asked her.

"I did a lot of file diving," she said, "found a deep-buried police report about the case. Most of the details were never released to the press."

"I see." It made sense. She was constantly digging in libraries for spooky crime cases and urban legends.

Then I saw it.

"Honey," I whispered, pointing at it.

"Dammit!" Lena whispered. "That was not supposed to be here. Make sure you get a clear shot of it."

I did as I was told, focusing the camera on the used needle. I could feel Lena tense behind me. If one drug addict entered that building, he might still be here.

As I went closer, I also noticed tiny tracks, as if an animal was walking in the building. The tracks looked fresh in the dust. I didn't recognize them. They were too large for a mouse and didn't look like a cat.

"Let's go to the kitchen," Lena ordered me.

"All right," I said, taking some extra shots of the office.

As we walked back into the dining room, I thought I heard a faint sound from behind me. I instantly turned around but saw nothing.

I heard it again, this time from the hallway. It was barely

audible, yet in the still of the night, it sounded clear. It resembled something between a crawl and a traipsing. I looked around, alarmed, but I saw nothing.

"Is something wrong?" Lena asked me.

"No, Nothing," I said. It was probably my imagination.

I walked to the hallway, making sure I got more footage of the walk there. I turned the camera around, taking more shots of the ruined room, then I turned it down and noticed something weird.

I knelt and got a better look. "Dammit!" I whispered. It was those tracks I saw in the office. And I couldn't remember if I'd seen them before. But then again, I wouldn't have noticed them amid the rubble that littered the floor.

Upon entering the kitchen, Lena posed and took the mic. "The police finally came into this room." She moved deeper into the room. This one still had some of its furniture, splinters still strewn on the floor.

I followed Lena in. This room was narrow. The sound quality would be awful with reverb, but Lena seemed eager to narrate here. And I had no clue how police got involved.

She finally got to the other end of the room and knelt. Then she banged her foot against the floor, kicked the worn-out wall and glared at me.

"What's wrong?" I asked.

She sighed, then had me do the same route again. Until we got to the end of the room and, as she told me, I pointed the camera at the floor. There I saw a big slab of concrete, with a cross carved on its surface.

"This is the notorious cellar of doctor Dekris," Lena said as she knelt over it. "After his conviction and mysterious death, his surviving relatives donated the building to the church, as a way to redeem themselves of the shame. This is why it remains empty to this day.

"However, it seems that somebody took the effort to

block the cellar door. Maybe this is for the best. I don't know if I could visit the basement and the horrors that took place in there".

I was confused, but Lena had me take more footage of the kitchen and told me it was time to go. She was agitated, her mood ruined. We always had sex after each of our filmings, but seeing her like that, I knew I would be lucky if she kissed me goodnight once we were back at her place.

I filmed more of the kitchen while she was in the hallway. I spotted another set of the mysterious tracks as I left the kitchen. But I was too relieved we were leaving this place to examine them.

"The scandal was kept under wraps and most details were never published to the press. Since ministers and people of influence associated with the doctor, he was summarily convicted along with select members of his cult. But the rumors were there. Soon, the residents of this once beautiful street left their houses, looking for greener, more reputable pastures. This has led to the abandonment of the Alkminis' Manor and its surrounding buildings.

"Thank you for watching this expose. Like, subscribe, hit that bell. And stay spooky."

I put the camera away, put the tripod back in its case, and followed Lena, who was already trotting to the car. I heard her feet stomping against the tiles as she muttered under her breath.

"What is the deal?" I asked her as soon as I reached her.

She kicked the garbage bin. "Damn it! I had a video that could go viral! But those stupid priests closed the entrance to the basement!"

I almost screamed, "Amen!" I hated the idea we would enter the basement to this building.

"Let's get in the car," I told her.

"All right," she said, admitting defeat.

I put our equipment in the trunk, securing their cases, then went to the driver's seat. For a second, I thought I heard the mysterious sound from the house, but I ignored it.

"What was the whole deal with the police?" I asked Lena, as I turned on the engine.

"Do you remember Sakis? Tina's ex?"

"Vaguely," I said. "He was kind of a creep".

"He used to hang around here," she told me, "shooting up."

"No way!" I said.

"He's clean now. He was telling me stories about this place. About the spooky stuff some people have witnessed inside the house. He's a fan of the channel and suggested it would be a brilliant dark story."

"That's how you dug up the police report?"

"Yes." She beamed with pride, forgetting her disappointment.

If I let her talk, pep her up a little, I might get lucky tonight. These were my thoughts at that time.

"What was that cult thing?" I asked her.

"This is the amazing part", Lena told me. "While Dekris was studying in London, he got involved with the occult. Freaky stuff. He believed the Devil restored his fortune. When he returned to Athens, he recruited some socialites, businessmen in a bad spot, as well as some attractive women who wanted to escape menial labour and organized some sort of a satanic sex cult. As long as he pulled the strings of his clientele and connected his cult members to help each other – or just bang hot chicks."

"Makes sense," I said.

"Now, this is the sickest part," she said as I shifted into first gear and got out of my parking spot. "Dude was sacrificing the unborn to Satan. Or something like that. Therefore, he did the abortions. And he did them in his basement, in a secret room next to his cellar."

"Oh, really," I remarked.

"This is why I wanted us to go to the cellar, that would be awesome!"

"Yeah . . ." I barely noticed what she was saying. I was too busy looking at the rear mirror.

I stepped on the brake.

"The Hell!" Lena hollered, annoyed. "What happened?"

"Nothing," I said, too scared to tell her.

"You are such a scaredy-cat! I tell you about the ravings of junkies and old stories about a doctor and his strange devil worship and you freak out. Damn it!"

"Sorry, darling . . ."

"Next thing you will tell me is that you saw some sort of ghost foetus roaming inside the house. Like some junkies imagined while they were high."

I laughed. "Of course not," I told her.

Then I took another glance at the rear-view mirror.

No. There was no malformed baby crawling by my rear window.

THE NIGHT WATCHMAN

MARIE MCWILLIAMS

I t was just after eight PM when the last staff member left for the day. Tonight, was Mark's first duty as the night watchman at the Titanic Museum, a role created solely for the newest exhibition. The museum was playing host to several items recovered from the actual wreckage. "History incarnate," that's what the museum's manager had called it during Mark's interview. Mark considered it to be more along the lines of grave robbing, but then, what museum in the world didn't contain something pilfered from some tomb or gravesite. Mark thought it was more respectful to let these things lie, to respect the wishes of those long since passed. He found the whole concept a little creepy. Then again, he wasn't about to voice that opinion to the manager, not with a well-paid job at stake in this current climate. He had simply smiled, ensuring he oohed and aahed at the appropriate moments. It had worked. Two weeks later, he was handed a uniform, torch, and a large set of keys which weighed down the right side of his belt and jingled slightly as he walked his rounds.

The museum had never had a night guard before, believing the replica items and white-star line pieces were secure enough under lock and key, but with the new items, treasures recovered from onboard the ship itself, used and touched and held by the actual passengers of that tragic voyage, these items would require a little extra for the insurance company to remain happy. So, here Mark was, wandering around the large, empty halls, moving from room to room to check the place was indeed empty. His boots echoed on the hardwood floors and his torch being the only source of light other than the low green glow of the emergency exit signs, created a myriad of shadows that danced and flitted alongside him.

With less than half the building checked, Mark began to feel unease settle in; images from a dozen horror movies and ghost stories told around campfires as a child spinning inside his head. He picked up his pace, hoping to get this first sweep over with so he could return to the safety of the security room. It was small and cramped, but it had a kettle and a radio, so it was more than enough to deter his overactive imagination.

The museum was set up with large circular floors, allowing you to look down the middle at the bottom floor. The view gave Mark vertigo at the best of times, so he stuck to the walls as he wound his way upward. The new exhibit was on the very top floor alongside the replica staircase made famous by the James Cameron movie, a film which Mark had seen only once when he took Margaret Smith, his first teenage crush and first taste of heartbreak. They had spent most of the movie snogging on the back row, so he hadn't taken a lot of it in, but what he had seen hadn't been for him —soppy romances were not his cup of tea.

He gave each exhibit he passed a cursory glance, having

already visited the museum when it first opened, but when he reached the very top floor he found himself mesmerised by the artefacts encased in large glass boxes. This room had large windows giving a panoramic view of Belfast and what would have once been a busy shipyard filled with the cacophony of noises made as giant metal behemoths like the Titanic were built. It was a clear night and moonlight spilled into the room, giving each of the cases an eerie glow.

The first cabinet contained items from the dining area. Plates with the white star-line logo sat alongside silverware and a crystal glass, whole and completely undamaged. Mark marveled at how something so delicate could have survived a ship being torn open and split in two before sinking into the black depths of the cold North Atlantic ocean. He imagined the gloved hand of a first-class passenger as it rose the glass in a toast to a successful voyage, a journey on the "unsinkable ship." Mark scoffed. He didn't believe in things like luck or fate but he still considered it a bad idea to declare your ship to be unsinkable before sailing into the vast and perilous ocean. The word ironic didn't do it justice.

The next cabinet contained personal belongings from some of the passengers. There was a necklace, a simple silver locket, its pattern almost worn completely away by the ebb and flow of the water. Beside it sat a silver baby rattle, a little bell on an ivory handle.

Mark moved away from it quickly, a wave of sadness washing over him. The thought of someone so young, so innocent losing their life in such an awful way was too much. He silently prayed that the owner had made it off alive but something in his gut told him they hadn't.

The last item in this cabinet was a simple leather boot. Judging from its size and style it had belonged to a woman. The plaque next to it described how the crew recovering the items had discovered the shoe lying as it now was, fully laced and buttoned, indicating the shoe's owner had been wearing it when the boat sank. Their body likely became food for the local sea life, decaying and rotting to nothing. A small leather gravestone, the only thing left to represent an entire life ended too soon.

Mark had enough for one night. Some might find the items interesting but he found the whole thing morbid. He quickened his pace, determined to finish the sweep and get back to the security room. A large cup of coffee and some Jaffa Cakes and he would feel himself again.

As he neared the exit at the far end of the room, something caught his eye. A blur of movement in his peripheral vision that vanished as soon as he turned to face its source. He moved his torch slowly around the room holding his breath, hoping it had merely been a trick of the light; a mirage created by the combination of the exhibit's morbidity and his own overactive imagination.

The light glinted off each of the glass cabinets as it passed until it reached the second. It fell upon the edge of a face peering back at Mark. Mark gasped, dropping the torch, sending it spinning several feet away before stumbling backward into brass stanchions roping off a staff-only area. They clattered to the ground alongside him, the noise of metal against concrete echoing around the large, quiet room.

He had landed badly, his left hip aching, a sharp pain shooting through his left wrist. The torch continued to spin for a few seconds before stilling, pointing in the direction of whoever, or whatever he had just seen. The beam diminished in brightness closer to the case before fading into shadow.

He was about to laugh at himself, chalk it up to first-night jitters when he saw a black silhouette flit across the torch's beam before disappearing into the darkness.

Mark, his heart thumping, scrambled to his feet, grabbing the torch and frantically throwing light all around him, searching for something he hoped he wouldn't find. There was nothing, only the glass coffins containing their ghoulish trinkets and the quiet hum of the nearby exit sign.

Mark took a deep breath trying to calm his nerves. He wanted to laugh it off; turn this into the funny story he would tell his colleagues in the morning. "You'll never guess what I did last night." But first, he had to make sure he was alone; he had to suck it up and do his job because having someone steal or destroy priceless artefacts on his first night on the job was something he could never recover from and the ever-growing pile of unpaid bills and late fees which littered his kitchen counter were a daily reminder of how much he needed this job.

Slowly, he moved toward the cabinet from where he had seen the face, constantly swinging his torch around him, looking for some indication he may not be alone. It was the case containing the shoe, serving only to increase his sense of unease. He checked the case and those surrounding it for fingerprints, scratches, cracks, anything which would indicate tampering but found nothing save his own reflection cast dully in the glass.

He sighed with relief, embarrassed by his foolishness when his foot slid from beneath him. He managed to right himself before taking another tumble, using the case to steady his stance. It felt surprisingly cold beneath his hand, so much so that he immediately withdrew it. A shudder snaked its way up his spine.

That's when he noticed the water.

There was a pool of it in front of the case with a trail leading in the direction he had seen the shadow move. Had that been there before? He leaned down and touched it finding it to be as ice-cold as the glass. It almost looked as if it had come from the case itself, oozing from the bottom edge of the glass. For a moment he contemplated whether the cases were refrigerated, that perhaps, because the items had spent so long in the freezing cold waters of the North Atlantic, they needed to remain at a similar temperature in order stay preserved and this unit was merely leaking. That would explain the coldness of the glass and the fluid.

But the cases did not make the familiar hum of an electric appliance. There were no cables or plugs around them. No thermometers or temperature gauges within. More than that, this hypothesis did not explain why the water led away across a level floor, or why it smelled faintly of the ocean.

Mark followed the water. Each puddle growing smaller and more defined until they became footprints, clear and distinct on the concrete floor. His torchlight caught the watery outline of a small shoe with a delicate heel.

Multiple scenarios flitted through his mind: perhaps someone had broken in or stayed behind after closing, remaining hidden in one of the many nooks and crannies such a large building inevitably possessed; perhaps it was one of his new colleagues playing a prank, hazing the new guy; maybe the water had been there all along, unnoticed, a spillage left behind by one of the museum's cleaners. But every instinct he had cried out that these explanations weren't the case, that something was happening that had no rational or sane explanation.

He followed the wet footprints out of the room onto the corridor outside, his own steps echoed around the large, central chamber. He was nearing the escalators which sat still and unused when the footprints suddenly stopped.

He moved the torch around him, searching for the rest of the trail but found none. They simply stopped dead in the centre of the walkway. There was nowhere they could have gone, no raised area or bench they could have stepped upon to explain their sudden cessation. They just ended. His heart thumped inside his ribcage when he heard something barely audible above the sound of his ragged breathing.

At first, he couldn't work out what it was or where it was coming from. It sounded distant and muffled, like hearing sound underwater. Straining, turning his head this way then the other trying to make it out, he slowly realised it was a melody of some sort; a haunting tune being hummed or sung so quietly he could not make out the words. The voice was female, he knew that much and whoever she was, she was sad. Even with the voice being as quiet and distant as it was, he could hear the sorrow in it.

"Hello?" As soon as he spoke, the sound stopped, returning him to eerie silence.

He longed to return to the security room, to get as much distance between himself and this floor, these ghoulish arte-facts, but he still had the bathrooms to check before his sweep would be complete. He contemplated skipping them, lying on his timesheet but was painfully aware of the many cameras dotted about the building and the idea that his new boss might check up on him, that he might lose this vital source of income as soon as he'd gotten it, sent more fear through his body than any ghostly image his mind could create. So, he took a deep breath and hurried on.

The women's bathroom was first. Slowly, he pushed each stall door to reveal nothing within; no ghosts or ghouls; no thieves or bad guys. With each empty stall, he felt himself relax. Next, he checked the men's room, again finding the few stalls inside empty, the room quiet and untouched. He sighed with relief as he exited, half laughing at himself for being such a wimp when he heard water running inside both sets of toilets.

He peered inside to find every single tap running at full

capacity in every one of the sinks. It was the same in the women's bathroom, too. Every one appeared to have been turned on simultaneously. The taps were not the type that could be turned off, so all Mark could do was stand perplexed and wait for the water to stop. But they didn't.

The water kept gushing from each of the taps and, despite the absence of any plugs, the water soon reached the top of each sink and began to flow over onto the floor, snaking its way toward Mark.

He backed away, watching dumbstruck as the water poured from beneath both of the now-closed bathroom doors. He knew he should call someone, a plumber or the head of maintenance whose number was already saved inside his mobile phone, but he couldn't think straight. He knew this shouldn't be happening, it didn't make sense. He just kept backing away, afraid of what might happen if the water touched him as if it were acid or some terrible poison.

The voice returned, nearer now, clearer.

He froze, listening to the words, no longer thinking of the water which now reached his feet. He didn't recognise the song but it sounded like a nursery rhyme of some kind, like something sung to small children to lull them to sleep.

He turned to find its source and saw her. A young girl, perhaps fifteen or sixteen. Her clothing was old fashioned, like the pictures of the many passengers displayed around the museum. She didn't seem to notice him, instead, staring blankly, singing her sad, lonely tune.

He realised with horror that his torchlight seemed to pass right through her. She cast no shadow. Her hair moved unnaturally as if it ebbed and flowed to an invisible sea. She appeared and disappeared in a juddering motion, like an old movie reel caught inside the machine; an image fading in and out of view.

He noticed her dress and hair, dripping wet. Her shoes, the same small, brown boots he had seen inside the cabinet.

Mark wanted to run, to yell, to do something, anything. Instead, he stood transfixed, rooted to the spot. He felt fear gripping him, surging through his frozen body but also something else—an icy cold had descended upon the building. His body erupted into convulsive shivers and he could see the plumes of his breath. He had never experienced a cold like it. It moved from his core, snaking through his veins to every inch of his goose-bumped flesh. He tried desperately to move, but the cold was so overpowering, lulling him into a sleep from which he knew he would never wake. He summoned every ounce of strength he had and forced one of his feet, now soaked through, to move. Through gritted teeth, he let out a guttural yell.

Suddenly, the girl's face turned to his, their eyes meeting for the briefest of moments before her mouth opened wider than any mouth should as if her jaw were unhinged, detached from her body. A screech emanated from her, so loud that it caused Mark to wince in pain. She shot forward, impossibly fast.

Instinctively, Mark threw himself back, away from the danger but immediately lost his footing. His black shoes, polished especially for his first night's work, slipped on the large pool of water which now surrounded him. He slid backward, hitting the rail with enough force to throw him completely off balance, sending him toppling over the edge.

Everything seemed to slow down, his movements now in slow motion as he fell the one-hundred and seventy-five feet toward the solid concrete floor below. It felt like he was falling through water, being dragged down; pulled by a current so strong nothing could break him free. He felt the coldness worsen, this time reaching his lungs, stinging him with every breath.

He saw the girl walk away from the edge, out of view, as he continued his descent. His only thought was why? Why?

It only took a matter of seconds for him to drop, but it had felt like minutes, torturous and terrifying, before he felt the sudden, painful impact. Then, black.

ALONE AMONG THE GUM TREES

CAM WOLFE

Gum trees surrounded Alex on every side. They towered high above, into a canopy of pale, skeletal branches, and impenetrable black night. The campfire stood at least three-feet-tall, but the warm orange glow did little to pierce the darkness between the thin tree trunks. It gave rise to a prickling in Alex's chest, an uneasy anxiety that stiffened her joints. During the daylight, the trees had felt almost comforting. This part of the Australian bush was unlike the forests she knew back home; the trees here were narrow and easy to step through, you could see your friends for ten or twenty yards before they disappeared from sight. Now that night had come, the trees felt much closer. It was as if they were creeping in and reaching over, shielding the night sky from view so not even a single prick of starlight could shine through. Now, the dark here was just like the dark back home.

'Alex, you okay?'

Alex snapped out of her trance and looked from the shadowed forest scrub to her sister. 'Huh? Sorry, I was—I was just thinking.'

'Yeah, okay.' Nora didn't try to hide her concern. One eyebrow was raised and she had shuffled her chair closer to Alex's. 'It's your—'

'It's your turn,' said the young man on the other side of the fire. He was looking over at the sisters with a wicked grin. 'If you can guess one thing about me I haven't told you, I drink. If you're wrong, you drink.'

Alex looked down at the beer in her hand. There wasn't much left, but it was also only her second can. She was sure the rest of the group knew this too. It was embarrassing, she didn't like being the boring one, especially not around her little sister.

'Take your time, Alex,' said Nora, shooting the man a sarcastic glare. 'Sid hasn't shut up the whole month we've known him, it wouldn't surprise me if there's nothing left that we don't know.'

Sid laughed and drunkenly waved his middle finger towards Nora, nearly falling from his chair in the process.

'Um.' Alex looked up at Sid through the dancing blue and yellow flames. 'I think maybe you didn't do too well in school?'

Nora shrieked a single, 'HA' before breaking into a hysterical cackle. Krish – who was seated next to Sid—spat the drink from his mouth, some of it leaking from his nose. Alex's comment even managed to bring a small smile to Luis' mouth. That made her breath freeze for a moment. Sid didn't seem bothered by the comment at all, he shrugged and threw back his can, sculling at least four mouthfuls of the foamy alcohol.

'Well played,' he said through a tremendous burp. 'Next!'

Nora leaned forward in her chair, eyeing Sid through narrowed lids.

'I think,' she said, clicking her tongue, 'you were the one

who asked Quinn out, and I think you had to ask more than once.'

Everyone around the fire laughed again and Sid gave a theatrical gasp of fake indignation.

'I'll have you know, she never said no.' Sid took another long drink from his can before crushing it in his grip and throwing it into the fire. 'But she did just walk away the first few times I asked.'

'I can't imagine why,' said Luis, giving Sid a half-smile. His voice was deep with bass and curled with a French accent.

'Yeah, yeah, whatever. I'm done with this game.' Sid got to his feet, staggering a little and holding out his arms for balance. 'Where is Quinn anyway?'

'She said she had to use the bathroom,' Krish said quietly.

He didn't look up from the can in his hands, the label peeling under his thumb. Alex knew she was shy, but this boy was something else entirely. When they'd first met in the tour group, he would not even say a word. They caught him looking up at Nora every now and then —when he thought they wouldn't notice – so it was she who decided to get him talking. After just a few weeks they were friends, so inviting him on their road trip of Western Australia seemed natural.

'Bathroom?' Sid laughed, waving an arm around at the wall of pale trees and dark night.

'She has been gone a while,' said Alex, unable to mask the worry in her voice.

'She's probably taking a dump,' said Nora casually, taking a swig from her beer. Everyone looked over at her.

'What?' Nora rolled her eyes. 'You do know girls take shits too, yeah?'

'She's probably gotten herself lost,' said Sid. He burped again and stumbled towards the tree line. 'I'll be back in a bit.'

'Hey,' said Luis, grabbing at Sid's arm.

'What?'

'Take a light, fool.'

He held out a bright yellow flashlight, the fabric of his shirt stretching against bulges of muscle. Alex adjusted her stare as he turned back, but saw that Nora was now smirking in her direction. She could feel her cheeks filling with warmth and quickly buried them in her hands. She leaned forward with her elbows on her knees, pretending to be extremely interested in the depths of the crackling fire.

'If you hear any weird moaning, I wouldn't come looking,' Sid said as he vanished into the black. His drunken chuckling could only be heard for a few seconds before both he and the dancing torchlight vanished.

'Should someone have gone with him? He's pretty wasted.' Krish was looking at the spot where Sid had left, concern carved into every inch of his face.

'You can if you want,' replied Nora, chugging more of her alcohol.

Krish looked over at her, his eyes flicking over her exposed thighs and up to her wet lips.

'H–he'll be okay.'

'If he's not back soon, I'll go take a look,' Luis said calmly. He gave Alex a comforting smile and she felt an involuntary grin spread across her face.

'You probably camped out in heaps of places like this in the army, right?' Nora said.

It was too obvious what Nora was doing—it was obvious to Alex at least. It was even more clear when Nora gave her a sly wink as Luis set down his drink.

'Absolutely. I've spent many nights in forests and jungles, without tents or fire.' Luis waved an arm towards their camping gear as he spoke. 'Places like this are a dream, it is the wet places that are the worst.'

'Oh, you don't like it when it's wet?'

Alex would have kicked Nora if she weren't out of reach.

'Not at all. It is cold, your gear becomes so much heavier. The worst part is that you can not hear when the enemy is approaching.'

Alex looked away from Luis' tanned, chiseled face to survey the dark spaces between the trees again. A gust of wind rolled through, creaking the branches and hissing against the leaves. The breeze didn't reach through to where they sat; the air was still and jarringly quiet between each word they spoke, each pop from the fire.

'I'm not much of a fan, but Alex loves camping and traveling and all that,' said Nora, giving her sister a suggestive look: Talk to him, you idiot.

'Is this true? You like adventure, Alex?'

Alex loved the way her name sounded out of his mouth. For weeks she had found her mind wandering to fantasies of running her fingers through his dark hair, of holding his jaw as they kissed.

'Yeah, I guess,' were the only words she found.

Nora sighed, loudly.

'One second guys, I need to talk to my sister for a moment.'

Alex felt her stomach drop, she knew what was coming. Luis nodded nonchalantly and turned to talk to Krish about his time in the young man's home city, Kolkata. Nora dragged her fold-out chair next to Alex's and slumped forward, giving her big sister a stern look.

'Alex.'

'Don't Nora, please.'

'Alex, you have to lighten up.'

'I am.'

'You're not. I mean, you do when it's just us, but as soon as the other guys are here you go all quiet again. This isn't like you. Since when do you let me do all the talking?'

'I just have a lot on my mind, okay?'

'You should talk to Luis, instead of just staring at him all the time. It's getting kinda creepy, sis.'

'I don't stare.'

Nora gave Alex an exhausted look, raising her eyebrow. They both knew this was a lie, they both knew Alex knew it was a lie.

'I—I just don't think it's a good idea right now.'

'Alex,' Nora's voice softened, and she put a hand on Alex's knee, 'he can't do anything anymore.'

There was a moment of tense silence before Alex replied.

'I know.'

'No, Alex, listen to me. He can't do anything to you anymore. He's back in Boston and we're in Western Australia, we're on the other side of the world, sis.'

Alex fought the urge to cry but her stomach tightened, and her vision fogged. Nora grabbed her other knee and moved to block her sister from view of the other two men.

'He can't follow you this time. Even if he could leave the U.S., which he can't, Australia's a big place. You're free, sis, and by the time we get home he'll either be in jail or on the other side of a restraining order.'

'The lawyer said it'll be hard to get him jail time because he didn't actually hurt me.'

'Bullshit. Stalking like that, the threats he made, it's enough. Even if it doesn't happen, he won't be stupid enough to violate the restraining order. Trust me.'

'Okay,' whispered Alex, quickly dabbing at her tears and blinking away the moisture. 'Thanks for coming on this trip with me; I don't think I could have done it alone.'

Nora smiled at Alex and leaned forward for a hug.

'It's okay, I would have preferred Bali, but a holiday is a holiday.'

'Hey,' Krish's raised voice broke the quiet moment and the

girls turned to see the men looking out into the dark of the bush. 'Sid has been gone a while, hasn't he?'

'Okay,' said Luis before sculling the last of his beer. 'I will go fetch the clumsy couple.'

'Actually,' interjected Nora, 'why don't I go?'

'On your own?' Krish said.

'Why not?'

'What if there's something out there? Maybe that's why they haven't come back yet.'

'Something like what?' Alex said, feeling her heartbeat rise.

'I don't know, like a snake or a tiger?'

Luis chuckled. 'We're in Australia, friend, not Siberia. There are no tigers here.'

'What about the snakes?'

'Well yes, the snakes could get you.'

'Okay whatever, I'm going.' Nora crossed her arms and tapped her foot impatiently. Krish's eyes flicked from the bulk of mass named Luis to the curve of Nora's backside and he closed his eyes as if plunging into icy waters. 'I will come too.'

'Cool, I feel much safer.' Nora rolled her eyes and leaned down to give Alex another hug.

'Talk to him,' she whispered.

'Maybe you should tell Krish he's not your type, so he stops getting his hopes up,' Alex replied just as quick.

'Cool. I'll break the news that I fuck women to my friend of one month, in the middle of the night, in god knows where bushland.'

Alex watched anxiously as both her sister and the thin, mop-haired boy disappeared into the tree line.

'I don't like this,' she said out loud.

Luis cracked the seal on a fresh drink and moved his chair closer to Alex. 'It'll be okay,' he said.

The flash of white teeth and his large, brown eyes had her convinced almost instantly. 'You think so?'

'Oh, yes.' He looked over his shoulder into the darkness. 'There aren't any hills or valleys around here and the roads are not too far on either side. It would be hard to get lost.'

'What about what Krish said, about the animals?'

Luis smiled and guzzled some more of his beer. 'Most animals are more scared of you than you are of them. I'm sure they're okay.'

The branches rustled with a rolling sweep of wind again and Alex felt her fear fading.

'You don't speak much, may I ask you why?'

Alex flushed with embarrassment.

'You don't either, y'know.'

Luis laughed, holding Alex's stare with his. 'I like talking to you, you're funny.'

'My sister would probably disagree with you there.'

'Your sister is funny too, but not quite as gorgeous.'

Heat in her face, excitement in her chest and crotch. She could swear he was leaning closer, she could feel his breath now; it stunk of beer but bristled her with anticipation all the same.

They heard a scream.

'Nora?'

Alex and Luis both shot up from their chairs. They stood frozen, the air around them felt dead and suffocating. It was so quiet that they both wondered if they had really heard what they thought they did. Then they heard it again. It was a shrill, sobbing shriek.

'That's Nora,' Alex said breathlessly.

Luis took off towards the trees, and still dizzy with confusion, Alex found she was following close behind. They ran, weaving between pale, thin trees that glared out from the dark. Each step pounced quickly after the last, bringing them closer towards the desperate, shattering cries. In a matter of seconds, they were sliding to a step behind two figures, standing almost invisible in the dark. Alex knew the bright, blue tank top to be her sister and she pulled her into a tight embrace. Nora was rigid, sobbing, and gasping for breath. Krish was also standing solid, his flashlight fixed onto a spot on the forest floor. Luis stepped past the young man and brought his hands to his head.

'What the fuck?'

Alex was gripping her sister's hair and trying to calm her hysterical wheezing. 'What is it?' she said, half-dazed with wild confusion. 'What is it, Luis?'

The man didn't answer, he too was frozen now. His hands were shaking and glued to the back of his head. Alex looked over Nora's shoulder and down into the beam of light. It took a few moments before she understood what she was looking at.

At first, it looked like some poor animal had become food for something bigger; pieces of bleeding red meat glistened in the luminance, and shards of what appeared to be skeleton were scattered around the gore. The splintered bones were glazed with red and chunks of flesh and viscera were sprayed onto the pale bark of the tree behind the mess. Then Alex saw the belt. The ribbons of red fabric and what was undeniably a human hand. She looked over the decimated body with her stomach spinning in sickening spirals and she saw a face, caved in and pierced with cracked skull fragments.

'Is that–'

'That's Sid,' Luis said. He gagged and fell sideways into a tree. 'That's fucking Sid.'

Suddenly a sound stabbed through their collective gasping and sobs; it was a loud thump, like someone dropping a body.

'Run,' said Luis stiffly.

Nobody moved, everyone was glued to the bush floor.

Something moved in the dark, snapping twigs and moving leaves.

'Run!'

In a chaotic instant of frantic motion, they were all sprinting. Leaping through the forest. Luis grabbed Krish by the arm, dragging him. The boy's feet nearly left the ground from the speed. Nora was screaming. Alex couldn't breathe. She could hear movement behind them, she didn't know if it was Luis and Krish or something else.

They all burst into the clearing, charging through one of the tents in an explosion of canvas and rope. The fire was low now, the light cast from the licking flames was a weak, yellow glow. Alex panted, collapsing forward onto her hands and knees, fighting to keep her dinner from resurfacing. All she could see was Sid's face – what was left of Sid's face. Nora dropped too, she curled into a ball and hyperventilated into her arms. Krish stood frozen, his eyes wide and glassy.

'We need to get the hell out of here. Now.' Luis was marching around the clearing, stuffing things into his bag. 'Get what you need, quickly.'

Alex was the only one who moved, she crawled for her sister. 'Nora,' she said weakly.

Nora was shaking violently, still refusing to look up.

'Nora we have to go, come on.'

'Krish,' Luis was shaking the young boy by the shoulders. 'I need you to focus.' The large man slapped him. Hard.

Krish looked up at Luis wildly, as if he had just woken from a deep sleep.

'We need to go,' Luis said again.

This time, Krish nodded with trembling lips.

Alex got to her feet and dragged Nora with her. She took her sister's face in her hands and forced her to meet her eyes. 'Nora, it's going to be okay, but you need to hear me. We need to run, okay? Don't let go of my hand.'

Nora was still crying, but she nodded.

'Okay,' said Luis. He stood in front of the three and withdrew a long, thin pouch from his bag. 'We need to go this way. It's not too far to the road, we'll be okay.'

He slid a glinting machete blade from the dark green fabric and a look of firm determination washed over him. The gears in Luis' mind had revolved into place with mechanical precision and his military training had been triggered.

'Stay behind me, and stay close.'

The giant, muscular man shouldered his bag and gave the group a small, stiff nod. Before anyone could take another step, something dropped from above and landed directly on Luis' back with a nauseating crunch. Alex squealed and they all watched helplessly as an enormous, dark-furred creature ripped into Luis' neck with its teeth, silencing his scream instantly. A mist of blood sprayed all three of them as the beast buried its claws and mouth into the man's head, swallowing chunk after chunk and chewing the bone with moist crunches. The creature's fur was matted and twisted into filthy knots and its limbs were long and thin. They stretched out, wrapping Luis' body into its grip like a spider would its prey. Large, circular ears trembled on the monster's head, twitching this way and that with every strangled sob from the others.

'D—drop bear,' Krish gasped, so quietly that it could barely be heard. 'I thought th—they weren't real.'

Alex heard the young man take off, sprinting into the woods, but she could not look away from the carnage at her feet. The creature had turned Luis' head into a stump of spine and goo and was now working on his torso. It dug through the ribs and cartilage like a dog digging a hole. Alex may have stood there until she too was dragged to the floor and eaten, but a hand gripped her wrist and pulled her away, back into the black of night. She ran, bashing into trees and stumbling. Her knees were weak, her vision was swimming.

What's going on?

She heard Nora speak through panting wheezes just a few feet in front, and realized the fingers curled around her arm were her sister's. 'Run Alex. Don't look back, just run.'

She heard branches snapping behind her, she knew the creature—the Drop Bear—was coming. They ran until their sides burned in protest, ducking between trees and kicking through shrubbery. Then Alex heard another loud thump and she felt her sister's hand jerk away from hers. Nora screamed with inhuman terror and disappeared between two towering tree trunks.

'Nora!' Alex tried to run after her, listening as hard as she could over her own panting. 'Nora! No, Nora!'

Alex fell, her legs finally giving way and she landed in a thick tussle of shrubbery.

'Nora,' she whimpered, clawing pathetically into the dark and willing for her little sister to emerge.

She lay there in the dry, prickly bush scrub for what may have been a minute or an hour. She gasped and clawed at old scars buried beneath her hair, scars from other times she had hidden in the night. The white-hot prickling of panic and terror was familiar, but the shame of not protecting her sister was new. She saw Luis' body as clearly as she had in the fire-light, it was twisted and mangled, no more than a pile of blood, bone, and gore. She saw the creature, wrapping her sister in its long arms and burying that blood-slicked mouth into her neck.

Suddenly she heard movement.

It was rapid and advancing towards her with dreadful speed. Alex recoiled further back into the shrubbery and peeked out, holding her mouth to stifle a scream. She saw a thin frame dash past, a mop of wet, black hair reflected the tiny amount of moonlight that found its way to the bush floor. It was Krish, clearly lost and desperate for escape. Alex leaped to her knees, clawing at a tree to pull herself to her feet. She turned to yell for the boy and stopped when she saw a dark shape jumping from tree branch to tree branch above. The long-limbed silhouette of the creature chased Krish from above, with inhuman speed. He never stood a chance.

Alex collapsed back into the bush and shielded a hoarse scream with her elbow, trying to drown out the sound of Krish's body being torn piece from bloody piece. She was so dizzy that all she could do was lay still, the white of the tree towering over her faded to black as the shock took over.

It was still dark when Alex opened her eyes, she blinked against the gloom for a few seconds before the memory of where she was stabbed through her chest like a hot blade. There was nothing she could do to stop the scream that escaped her lips. It was a bloodcurdling, heartbroken, ear-splitting wail of grief. She was screaming because her friends were dead. She was screaming because her sister was dead. She was screaming because she was lost and alone in the dark, and because clinging to a branch above her and looking down, was the creature.

It opened its mouth, revealing a row of sharp, bloody teeth, and it screamed back. If H.P. Lovecraft imagined the marriage of a spider and a koala bear, this monster would be the beast it birthed. The creature dropped from the branch with a hiss of nails on wood and landed heavily onto Alex's frozen body. She felt her ribs shatter immediately. It burned through her body in paralyzing waves, forced the air from her lungs. She could feel its claws pressing into her flesh as easily as a knife through water. Alex did not want to die, but all that was left was to hope it would eat her head first and end this quickly. The creature seemed to agree.

It lunged forward, sinking its teeth into the side of her

face. She didn't feel much as it pulled away, strings of elastic gore hanging from its mouth. Perhaps it was the adrenaline or the shock—it was welcome all the same.

'Fucking die!'

A figure charged from the dark and swung something long and narrow into the creature's skull. They pulled it back and brought it thundering down again, cracking bone and spraying Alex with waves of hot blood. She could taste it in her mouth, acidic and bitter. With two more hacking chops, the beast's head came off entirely, falling with a wet thud to the dry dirt. The body rolled away, still twitching and spewing liquid.

'Alex!'

The figure crouched down and pulled Alex onto her backside, leaning her against the tree. In the weak glow of moonlight, Alex saw Nora. Her little sister's face had a deep slash below the eye but was otherwise in one piece.

'Nora?'

Nora's bottom lip quivered and she stroked the good side of her big sister's face.

'I'm here, sis. I'm here, don't worry.'

'I thought–' Alex felt her vision fading out again and she had to claw for every word. 'I thought you were dead.'

'No, no, no, I got away. I was looking for you and I ended up back at the camp,' Nora said with a trembling voice. She dropped the machete onto the ground and put her hands under Alex's arms. 'Come on, let's get out of here. You need a hospital.'

New pain ripped through Alex's body and she screamed, 'No! I can't–I can't move. I can't.'

'You have to, we have to get help.'

'You have to,' Alex gasped, feeling her face grow heavy with cold sweat. 'Go get help, please.'

'I can't leave you, sis.'

'Please.'

'No.'

'I can't move, and if I don't get help, I will bleed out, Nora. Please go.'

Tears streamed down Nora's face and she put her face against her sister's shoulder. 'I'm coming back,' she whispered. 'Don't you dare die before I do.'

'I promise,' Alex replied. She attempted to give her little sister a comforting smile but wasn't sure she could move her face anymore.

Nora gave Alex one last, remorseful look before blinking away the tears and getting to her feet. She turned and ran, vanishing into the void between the trees.

Alex knew she wouldn't see her sister again. They were far from any hospital and the pool of blood moistening her arse was quickly deepening. At least Nora wouldn't have to see her die. That and one other thought gave her comfort as she felt the dark and the numbness set in:

He can't own me anymore. He can't own me ever again.

A rolling gust of wind shook the branches and Alex breathed deep. She leaned her head back and watched the pale limbs dance against the black night sky. Just before her eyes fell closed for a final time, she saw something strange. Shapes – long-limbed and big-eared. At least thirty of them racing through the dark in the direction Nora had run. They creaked the branches and rustled the leaves in a familiar, rolling motion. As the breath left her body, Alex finally understood why the wind wouldn't reach below the trees.

HIGHWAY TO HELL

NICHOLAS GRAY

So, there we were, playing Highway to Hell for what seemed to be the ten-thousandth time. The song was playing on repeat, with the occasional "Hells Bells," and "Hell Ain't a Bad Place to Be," all performed by AC/DC —my favorite band. This playlist was on for a special occasion though, for we were literally going to Hell.

Hell is a small town in the Great Lake state of Michigan. My brother, Wesley, and I were on our way to Hell, so we could say we've been to Hell and back! We were also heading over there to get a t-shirt for Wesley, which was a major reason why we were making this trip in the first place.

Oh, I forgot to introduce myself. My name is Sydney, and I had just gotten out of my last year of high school and was working at a local pizzeria for extra money. That all was displayed on my shirt that read, in bold, "Give me a pizza that pie," with the name Joe's Pizza arching over the saying. I didn't like my job, but I figured nobody does and muscled through my days of rolling dough and baking pizzas. Besides, it was better than being at home, I figured.

I became sick of pizza, just the smell of it made me ill, but occasionally I would bake a free pizza, which Joe allowed. My family wasn't great on money at the moment, so any time I could bring home free food, well it made a great day.

One Friday, while I was getting off my shift to enjoy the weekend, I fixed myself a pizza for the road. I drove home in my old silver minivan with a Joe's pizza box sitting in the passenger seat. Rock tunes booming out of the car's speakers, I pulled into my family's driveway, slammed the car door behind me, and approached the entrance with slight unease.

I could hear my parents arguing inside. It was never fun to be stuck in the middle of my parents' fights. I felt like a referee in a cage match at times, sometimes being a part of the fights when my parents would look to me for confirmation to their argument like I would agree with them. Their fights were always petty too. You were supposed to take out the trash, she'd say. It was your turn to pick Wesley up from school, he'd say. They'd argue, throwing insults at each other, then mom would slam the door to their bedroom, while dad would head to the old, familiar confines of the couch.

Who knew why they were fighting this time. I intended to race past that mess and go to my brother's room, who was probably looking forward to my return.

I opened the door and ran up the stairs, slipping past the argument ensuing in the kitchen. Walking past my bedroom, I was now facing my brother's door, which was covered in horror movie monster stickers. I knocked on the door gently and slowly opened the door, emerging into Wesley's bedroom.

Wesley was my small chubby brother, who at that moment was playing video games, but I could see he wasn't fully into the game.

"Hey buddy, how's it going?" I said with a caring face, our parents still could be heard yelling at one another downstairs. He paused his video game and turned to me, but just looked down to the ground. I shut the door behind me, muffling our parents fight downstairs with the shutting door.

"I . . . I started this one," Wesley said, referring to the fight happening downstairs.

"No, you didn't buddy. Mom and Dad are just . . . going through some things. It'll get bet—"

"No, no, I started it this time!"

"Why do you think that?"

"Because I asked dad if he'd take me somewhere and he said no, which got mom to yelling at him and he started yelling back and, and . . ." he trailed off, wiping his eyes with his sleeve to clear them from the tears falling down his cheeks.

"Where'd you want to go?"

He sniffed a few times, then began to talk, "Well, you know the small town called Hell. I thought it would be cool if we all went to Hell, like that one time we did when we were younger."

He was remembering a happier time. A time when they took a family trip to Hell, Michigan to say our family could survive a trip to Hell and back. But it didn't go well. Wesley begged mom for a shirt and she said no. Ever since then he's wanted to go back and get a shirt; specifically, the one that says 'See you in Hell' in bold, with Michigan in small text just under the word Hell.

I frowned. I understood where my younger brother was coming from.

"You know what, we'll go to Hell! Just you and me. It'll be fun! And we'll get you that shirt you've always wanted!"

He got his chubby body off the ground and slammed into me, clasping his arms around me for an embracive-bear hug. I set the pizza box on the bed and held him tightly.

"Thank you, Sydney," he said, his voice muffled by my shirt, which was covered in flour.

So, we packed our things, got in the car, and hit the road.

We drove for quite a while. Eventually, we turned onto M53 while jamming out to Hells Bells. It was known as the highway to Hell, for it was the last road you hop onto till you reach Hell, Michigan. I was banging my curly fro side to side, while my little brother head-banged offbeat in the passenger seat. He wasn't much of a rocker like me, but my music was perfect for this occasion. I was paying little attention to the road in front of me, but then something caught my eye. Something weird up ahead.

"What is that?" I said, staring at what seemed to be a red fog in the distance.

"I don't know. Maybe it's a flare," my little brother said while paying no mind to what I was seeing, switching the song over to Highway to Hell.

"It could be a flare . . . but what if it's a fire?"

I kept driving, and when we got closer it wasn't any easier to figure out where the fog was coming from.

"I don't know about this. Maybe we should turn around."

"No! We're almost there, Sydney. Just drive through it," Wesley said, looking up at me with a face you just couldn't say no to.

"Okay, but if I sense any danger, I'm turning this car around."

He nodded, and we pursued toward the fog.

When we reached the red fog, it was dense. It was hard to see through, but I could just make out the road in front of us. My biggest fear was that I was driving on the wrong side of the road and that an oncoming car might hit me if I was not careful. I started to drive under the speed limit, going about ten miles an hour, just to make sure I didn't get hit by any cars that could possibly be coming from up ahead that couldn't see us. I also turned on my fog lights, since visibility was low, but it didn't seem to make much of a difference.

Then something changed. I didn't notice it at first, but it became noticeable the deeper we went into the fog. The road was unusually bumpy like we were driving on a brick road or something. As I squinted at the little bit of road, I could see in front of me and I realized that the road did indeed change; we were now driving on a path that was cracked with a bright red light piercing through the ground.

"I really don't like this," I said nervously.

As Wesley was turning the volume up, the music suddenly stopped in the middle of the song, looping the word Hell repeatedly, like a broken record. Wesley struggled to turn off the radio as it pierced our ears. I winced at the increased volume and yelled for him to turn it off. He hit random buttons and twisted dials till it finally stopped. Relief hit us both as the volume ceased. I looked over at the station playing now: 66.6 FM.

Weird, I thought, didn't know such a station existed. A slight shiver went down my back at the thought of the sign of the devil: three sixes. Even though I wasn't a firm believer in the afterlife, it still made me a little uncomfortable to be on this station.

"Hey, are there any other stations, like, anything besides this one?" I asked.

He hit the seek arrow and it flipped through a bunch of numbers until it landed back on the same station.

"Nope," Wesley said nervously, looking over at me with a concerned look.

"Is the volume down?" I asked, wondering if the station was naturally silent or the volume was just low.

"I tried turning the volume down before," he said, testing the dial to see if it was turned all the way down, "and it looks like it's on mute."

"Turn it up."

He slowly turned up the volume and I instantly regretted

asking him to do so. Screams screeched through the car's speakers and nearly deafened my brother and me. I almost let go of the wheel to shield my ears from the violence being put upon them.

"Turn it off, Wes!" I yelled.

Wesley reached for the dial and spun it in the direction to mute the screams, but to no avail. The screams sounded horrific and blood-curdling.

"I can't turn it off!" Wesley yelled, as he stopped attempting to silence the screams and instead covered his ears, the only defense he had against the banshee noise.

The red fog lifted, and what we saw was, well, hellish.

The sky was dark red. Before, it was a little gloomy outside, but you could just make out the sun in the sky above. Now, there was no sun in sight, just an all-red sky, with a few black clouds. The road up ahead turned into a red-bricked path, the car bobbed up and down as it lumbered across the cracked road.

That was only the tip of the iceberg in changes we perceived as we continued to look around.

Large spikes speared into the red sky, and as my eyes followed one spike to its peak, I noticed something on the tip. A naked man! A naked man impaled on the giant spike! And it wasn't just one man—there were people impaled on spikes as far as the eye could see!

Wesley whimpered in the passenger seat.

"I don't like this, Sydney!" Wesley said, sinking into his seat.

"Close your eyes, Wesley!" I demanded.

He quickly followed the command, covering his eyes with his palms.

I checked the rearview mirror, but all I saw was the red-bricked road; no red fog. I looked forward, making sure I wasn't going to hit anything, then peered back into the rearview mirror. That's when I noticed something was starting to emerge a good distance behind us. It peaked over the horizon. Whatever it was, it was getting closer, and fast!

I kept my eyes on the road but constantly looked out the rearview mirror, trying to ignore the scenery around me. My ears adjusted to the screams through the radio. It was just background noise. As we kept driving forward, hoping to reach our destination, if that was even feasible at this point, the thing behind us came into view.

"What is that?" I said in an alarmed tone.

The thing behind us appeared to be a skeleton. A Skeleton with black wings. In its hands was a scythe. Its wings flapped vigorously as it approached, closer and closer.

Wesley was now turned around in his seat, peering out the back of the van to see what I was captivated by.

Fuck speed limits, I thought. I knew it was time to floor it.

I slammed my foot to the pedal and the car shook as it switched gears. The van wasn't used to going over seventy-miles-per-hour.

"Hurry, Sydney! It's gaining on us!" Wesley yelled.

"I'm trying, I'm trying!"

The thing was just behind us now, no more than twenty-feet away.

"Fuck, fuck, fuck, fuck, fuck!" I finally said, releasing the panic I was holding within.

The thing was now fifteen feet away. Ten feet away. Five feet.

Crack!

The car halted. I turned to the rearview mirror and looked as the skeleton was holding its ground behind us; its scythe piercing the top of the trunk, getting stuck there. I'd have to find a way to explain that to mom if we made it out of here alive. If this thing didn't kill us, she would kill me.

Sparks flew up from the back of the car as the bumper made contact with the brick road. I had to think fast, or we were doomed. I hit the brakes, causing the van to lurch forward before I threw it into reverse.

I contorted my body, so I could properly see out the back window and slammed on the gas. The skeleton behind us got into the pushing motion. We were in a tug-of-war; we were going in reverse and he was pushing us forward. The car's tires released smoke as the wheels turned in place, but we were slowly backing up. The skeleton switched positions, shouldering the weight of the van. Then he collapsed underneath the vehicle as the van overcame the skeleton's strength and reversed two tons of minivan on top of him.

I hit the brakes. Wesley and I were breathing heavily as the lights of the minivan shone onto the skeleton.

"Is he . . . dead?" Wesley asked.

The skeleton twitched, got to its knees, then it began to prop itself back up.

"Run him over! Run him over!" Wesley yelled.

I hesitated at first, then threw the van into drive and slammed on the gas again. The skeleton pushed against the hood of the car, pushing us backward a bit. I could tell it was using all of its strength to stop us from moving forward.

"Run him over!" Wesley yelled again.

"I'm trying!" I yelled back

Smoke appeared from the van's tires once again as the skeleton pushed against it. This time the skeleton was winning. I cursed, then began to think on my toes. I threw the car into reverse. The skeleton fell forward onto its knees, then stood up, preparing for the next move I had planned. It probably thought I was going to ram him again. Fuck that.

I slammed on the gas, making my way toward the skeleton. Then, right before making contact with it, I veered, like I would for a deer. I floored it and we made our way past the skeleton, or at least I thought we did. I took in a deep breath as we drove forward onto the brick path. I could hear my heartbeat in my ears, that's how much adrenaline was flowing through me at that moment.

Then I heard footsteps coming from the roof. It was on top of the van! The skeleton was on top of the van!

I hesitated again as my brain lagged. I whipped the wheel back and forth, hoping to get the thing to tumble of the side of the van. It was fruitless.

I then heard the scythe being expunged out of the top of the trunk. Shit, I thought. I looked over at Wesley, who was in tears.

"It's going to be all right, Wes. We got this." I gave him an unconvincing smile as thuds on the roof could be heard. I veered the car again and again, but it remained on top of the car. There was only one thing left to try . . .

Suddenly, the windshield was impaled by the scythe, which missed my face by mere centimeters. The scythe retracted, and I could feel another swing coming. I had to make my move. I slammed on the brakes, causing the car to skid and rumble to a halt. The skeleton went flying forward and tumbled to the ground. I hit the gas and ran over it. This time, I looked into the rearview mirror to make sure he was left in the dust. The skeleton stood and stared at us, wings starting to flutter.

The car started to sputter, then it stopped.

"NO! No, no, no, no, no!" I yelled.

"What's happening? Why aren't we going?" Wesley asked.

"I can't believe it! We're out of freaking gas!"

A loud thud landed on top of the roof. The skeleton was back.

He walked onto the hood of the van, turned, and knelt, peering into the van's windshield. He looked at both of us, then a deep, disembodied voice burst through the car's speakers.

"You don't belong here," the voice said, as the skeleton pointed a boney finger at me.

"No, we don't!" I screamed.

The skeleton looked back and forth between us. Then it turned and hopped off the hood. It walked a couple of steps forward, then lifted a hand in the air. A red fog began to appear, covering the area around us with its eeriness.

"Go," the disembodied voice said.

We sat silently, not knowing whether to trust the skeleton or not. We really couldn't move anyway, since the car had no gas left in it.

"LEAVE!" It yelled, and I quickly hit the gas pedal, which moved the van forward into the fog. I looked over at the gas gauge, which still read empty.

We journeyed into the fog for a few minutes; the fog turned into a pinkish color, then turned white, until it finally lifted, and a normal paved road came into view. Just ahead of us was a sign that read "Welcome to Hell." Our van sputtered then came to another halt as smoke began to emerge from the hood.

"What was that?" Wesley said, breaking the silence between us.

"I think Hell is precisely what it was."

We let out a nervous laugh, hopped out of the car, grabbed a gas can from the trunk, and walked into Hell, where a restaurant and souvenir shop were calling our names.

THE ROOM WITHIN

D.L. TILLERY

I finally found the house. It needs a lot of work, but soon I will make it home. I buy old run down homes and restore them, then sell them off for a profit, well that's in most cases. Today, the home I have purchased at a bargain price will be my new home. I saw it in the paper a few weeks ago and I just had to have it...there was something about it that called to me.

Upon contacting the owner who, on the phone, seemed odd, agreed to meet on location. Seeing it up close sealed the deal, I made the purchase and at a bargain price. I know that wasn't the brightest move I've ever made, but the outside of the house is the design I want, and the pictures I saw online are enough for me. With over six thousand square feet of living space, high bay windows and pillars decorating the front of the home... I'm in love. The owner seemed a bit shocked that I wanted to purchase it without even looking inside. In fact, he asked that I explore it before deciding. I told him I was in a hurry, that the pictures were enough, and that I would take it as is. To be honest; I knew what I was getting. I didn't want anything I might see inside to change my mind.

THIRTY DAYS LATER

Driving up to the house on my first day of officially owning it is surreal. In anticipation of the cold, I'm wearing a heavy coat and dark blue jeans to fight the bite of the last days of winter that always seemed to linger near the end of March.

I can hear the wind blowing hard as I stare at the front of the house. I pull my hood up before stepping out of the warmth of my Honda Civic, drawing the strings to make sure it stays in place. I should have grabbed my gloves. Man it's cold today. I lick my lips and blow on my freezing hands.

As I approach the large double burgundy front doors, I reach to retrieve the house key from my pocket only to find it's not there. I search all of my pockets and come up with nothing. What the hell! I know I had that key when I left this morning! Before I can turn and head for my car, the door creaks open.

"Hello?"

I guess the previous owner must have forgotten to lock the door. I enter even though a chill runs down my spine while crossing the sill.

Wow! I can't help but gasp at the site. Solid oak floors are what I find under my booted feet. The pictures I'd viewed before had shown marble tiles throughout. I guess the owner replaced them. Dust covers everything, yet shockingly not much, considering it's been empty for years.

"Beautiful. I can't believe he let this go for only ninety grand."

As I walk into the foyer, two carved pillars framing the archway into the next area of the house grace my sight. How romantic.

The curtain-less windows give me a little light to see, but not enough, I grab my flashlight from my left coat pocket. Damn it's dark. I should have had the power turned on before this little visit. Walking under the archway the flashlight helps me see better, so I continue on.

Ahead I see a large spiral staircase that goes up three flights with a landing on the second floor. Shining my light upward, I make the first step when a second chill runs down my spine.

"Welcome."

I quickly look towards the sound of the voice. I know I heard...

"Hello?!" I yell. Waiting, I receive no answer. It was a soft feminine voice. I'm sure of it. I shine my light every which way yet I find no one. Must be my mind playing tricks on me.

Making my way up the long, spiral stairs, flashing my light all around, I find even in the dark, this house is breathtaking. Amazing designs of angelic carvings and antique paintings hang from every wall on my way up. Soon I find myself on the first landing; the long hall that's lined with floor-to-ceiling windows feels both ominous and inviting.

On this level, I find silk, cream-colored drapes that hang to the floor. I could tell they have been hanging for many years as they are dusty and yellowing. I continue down the long hall until I come to a green door. Turning the knob, I enter. I'm immediately met by a hail of dust. Coughing and waving my hand helps to avoid inhaling the rest.

"Thank God there's a window here." I try to open it but it won't budge. "Damn."

Giving up, I walk towards the old hearth and a single chair sitting near it. I guess I know why the door was green. Taking note that the entire room is the same color. The daylight streaming in from the window illuminates the room, but the rest is dark. Aiming my light around the walls, I spot another door on the other side of the hearth. I approach and attempt to turn the knob.

"Welcome. Who might you be?" Says the same soft, feminine voice I heard earlier. Jumping away in surprise, I drop my flashlight, which I quickly retrieve. The voice must have come from the other side of the door. I wait...and wait, but I hear nothing. I press my ear to the door. Still, I hear nothing. Stepping back, I chuckle.

"Did I say something funny?" she asks in shock.

"Who are you?" I ask the disembodied voice. Turning in a complete circle I face the door again.

"I asked you first, if you recall," she replies in an annoyed tone.

"I'm Daniel Elliot and I own this house. Excuse me, why are you here? Who are you and where are you?"

"Ah, yes, a very likable name...Daniel. I'm locked in and can't leave."

The door-knob jingles. Eyeing it, I step back. "I'm sorry but this is nuts, and I'm nuts for talking to myself. I need to get out of here—like now."

"Please, don't leave me. I have to get out before he comes back! I'm being held!"

"How's it I can hear you as if you're inside my head?" I ask, stepping closer to the door again.

"I'm speaking to your mind...it's odd, I know, but it's something I could always do." she says, calmer.

"Odd? Yeah, cause that's the word I'd use. Listen, I'm not doing anything until you tell me who you are? And who is 'He'?"

"My name's Dalidah," she replies.

"Okay, and how did you get here, telepathic Dalidah?"

"He put me here against my will... only you can free me Daniel," she says.

I feel hazy and out of sorts. Something's wrong; I want to

open the door, to free her with no more questions asked. My hand moves of its own accord, turning the knob. "What the Hell!" Pulling away, I land flat on my backside.

I feel overheated, my mind still hazy, I pull off my coat, and sweater. Only my long-sleeved black shirt remains but I feel a relief by lightening my burden.

"What did you do to me?!" I yell at the door.

"I don't know what you mean. I have done nothing. How could I? I'm trapped,"she says, emotions choking her.

Shaking off the odd feeling, I come to my feet. "How would I get you out even if I wanted to? There's no keyhole... not that I have a key. And what of the past owner? Is it the 'He' who put you here?"

I know I should run... everything in me says to run... but what kind of person would I be?

"Please, Daniel!"

Grabbing the knob, I turn and pull. Nothing happens. Not that I'm shocked. I try again and again.

"I can't get it open!"

"It's held by a force stronger than either of us. Believe me, you will never get me out by physical means."

"What does that mean?" I ask in frustration.

"That, you must find another way to release me."

"Let me think a minute." I sit in the only chair available. I try to think of what to do. So many thoughts run through my mind. Why would the previous owner sell it to me, but leave her here like this? Maybe I'm imagining it all. It's all so bizarre...Dalidah, this house, the old owner. I really want to save her, if I had my cell, I could call for help. The only other option is to leave and come back with help.

As I am about to do just that, everything is darker. I can no longer see anything. Then, as if they have always been there, I'm surrounded by lit candles; the room all ablaze in fire light.

Jumping out of the chair, I look around. The room looks the same except for all the candles. No, no, no. The window's gone. I run over to feel the cold wall where it once was. My mind screams to find a way out. The door! It's also gone!

"What the hell is happening?!" I scream, banging both fists where the door should be. Heart racing, I turn all about the room—and there I see a woman's figure standing in the far corner. The only part of the room shrouded in shadow.

I walk toward her. "Dalidah?"

Her head is down, but as I get closer, I can see she is watching me. From beneath her waist length, cold black hair that looks like silky ink, a small pale hand reaches out to me. I don't take her hand. Something feels wrong, I step back instead.

Her head comes straight up and she steps into the fire-light. I can see her eyes now, they are as black as her hair and as cold. Her cream-colored dress hugging her frame, yellow-ing... much like the curtains from the hall.

"Where are we?" I ask, stepping further away. "This isn't the same room. it can't be." I look around for a moment , my eyes coming to land back on her face.

She smiles, yet it's sinister, and I know I've made a grave mistake in not running fast and far.

"He makes me feed," she says, stepping closer still.

"No! Stay back!" I yell, yet she continues her advance.

"Though I love the taste of your fear..." Her tongue darts out, licking her lips slowly as if she can taste my fear on them.

"My father... you met him. He sold you this house or at least that's what he made you see. He's much like me you know... making people see things... so I can... eat."

She's so close now and I can no longer move. I can see the hunger in her eyes.

I attempt to run but can't move. My feet feel encased in

stone. She lays both hands on either side of my face looking into my eyes. I can't look away no matter how hard I try.

"Please. I was trying to help you."

She laughs. "You are helping..." Leaning in, until I can no longer see her face.

I feel something hot, like iron cutting through my left shoulder. I grab for her hair, to stop what she's doing, but to no avail. She grabs my wrist, fire, and pain follow. I can hear the sickening sound of my severed hand hitting the floor. Ripping, tearing, now my screams only bounce off the walls. The realization that I am dying hits me as she slides me to the floor.

Above I see my blood dripping from what looks like fangs protruding from her mouth. She slides down my body, continuing the feast. The pain is too much to bear, yet I find the strength to scream one last time. I only wanted a place to call home to build a family. Now I will never have it.

FADING APPLAUSE IN QUINTLAND

LYDIA PEEVER

Weeds grew among a couple of old, tilted sheds. They dotted an overgrown field in grey countryside between old farmhouses. The shadow of a nearby stone mansion loomed over the quiet copse to one side, and vacant land across the road reached forever toward it; barren. Only people with a knowing eye saw the remains of a war-time attraction called Quintland, and the ghosts that lived there thrived forever on memory alone.

"So, you bought the entire area?" Kate asked, making her way through the tall grass behind the old farmer, Jeff Hughes. He led them, Kate and Sarah, through the field. The clearing was a rough circle, ringed by shrubs and the dilapidated sheds. She looked back at Sarah who kept up while taking photos of the journey.

"Yup, I bought what I could from the gal that used to run the gift store. So many people forgot exactly why she carried on with all the mem'bilia with her other store in town. They'd forgotten she owned all this land at one time. She was the last person from Quintland who really hung on." He stopped and seemed to consider for a beat, then gestured to the farther, and much larger stone house. "Well, her and the big house still stand, but it's a retirement home, now. Just as well."

Both girls looked over to the mansion, the house the quintuplet sisters once lived in as medical wards of the province, then fled and avoided until the Crown sold it off. They knew the story well. "You don't count yourself among them? The ones that hung on?" Kate asked.

"No, no, not at all. I'm not looking to make a buck. I'm not even looking to raze the past. I just take care of the land here; someone has to. They could plow it over." He stopped again. "You don't plow over a graveyard. In some sense, that's what this is."

The area they stood in had once housed a playground. Like most parks, it had teeter-totters, bouncing animals, swings, and a merry-go-round for the five little girls. Unlike all the others, there was an observation hall built around it. A circular hall of wood and mesh screens. Wire screens meant to hide the ring of crowding people somewhat, but the girls later said it did little. They could see the thousands of visitors filing through the corridor to watch them play. They could hear the legion of feet shuffling past. The cooing, catcalls, morbid comments, and adoration all the same.

At the time, the little girls, toddlers then, barely understood the concept of Quintland. To all others, it meant hope, tourist dollars, cheap entertainment, and enterprise; five little national treasures paraded around with viewing twice daily for a dollar.

Sarah had been quiet until this point and she finally spoke up from behind her camera lens, "That's why a seance might be a good idea. You're right, Mister Hughes. We can't thank you enough for showing us this and letting us on your land and all." It was Kate's experiment, but the filming had been her idea, too. In her mind, Kate had the face for what could be part of a larger film.

"Well, it's the least I could do. You know there are people who still find a lot of fascination with what those girls went through and who am I to deny it just because I've set up camp here." His house was to the right of the field, far from the old mansion on the opposite hill.

"You sure you don't mind?" asked Kate. "I mean, we won't be here long, and it's not like we will actually do anything. We're going to just sit here and, you know, see what we see. I just want to be sure—"

Hughes laughed. "You ain't the first, you know! If there's anything this land has seen, it's a bunch of people coming to looky-loo. I mean, that's what it was all about, right? Quintland, the girls, all that; it was about people come to satisfy their curiosity, and a mite better than a Freak Show, I'd say," he paused, maybe to stop from saying more. The girls knew local sentiment about the place ran hot and cold. "But, well, some sort of show, anyways."

"I don't know about that," Kate's tone became heavy, "I think that was straight-up abuse, really. If you ask me, putting the girls on display like that." She shuddered visibly. "They were just twins, you know. Two-and-a-half twins, I guess, but just twins. That's not so special. They didn't deserve that treatment and they had no say in it. Had to run away the moment they could. Child abuse really . . . I can see them being restless spirits here if anywhere."

Hughes smiled gently despite Kate's simmering. "Well, I guess only they know and we don't. I have to say, there was some small piece of happiness found here for them. And people watchin' too. Really. I believe that. They were taken care of, they had nice clothes, food, and shelter. Friends. Even put in a schoolhouse down the way. I don't know if anyone down there is still living but there were people who went to school with them."

Kate suppressed a snort of disbelief. "Handpicked by the

damn government, that's what, and they weren't allowed friends . . ."

"Well, it was kind of arranged, yeah," Hughes countered softly, and added after a moment of thought, "Not like they didn't spend time together though. It's not like they didn't become friends and even the family would invite people over, like my brother sometimes. Play basketball with the boys, even sometimes hang out with the girls for a soda. Supervised and all, but he counted them girls as friends never'less."

Sarah had heard these debates run circles before and did what she did best to get the show back on the road. "Either way you slice it, it's passed. One very tangled web we still follow the threads of. The worst came after they had grown, but they were happy here. They all agreed on that. Before we start, can I get a picture of the two of you?" Her soft smile calmed them both, and she gestured with her camera lens as a gentle reminder of what they were there for.

Hughes smiled right back. "I'll break your camera if we don't warm it up some. I'll take one of you gals first, standing with the old school in the background."

He took the camera and, having held at least a manual one in his time, grabbed an easy digital snap of the two girls—waves of grain behind them, high grasses to their knees, buttercups framed them to either side. A ray of light among the decay and sorrow that was once a bustling, awkward carnival.

Sarah caught photos of Hughes with his house in the background, looking over the site with tired eyes. Eyes that glinted despite his years. Shone bright with memories of this ghost land. He hulked in the foreground, every inch the weathered farmer with the ruins of Quintland on the horizon in shadow. Hughes walking toward the mansion, dwarfed, his hand grazing gently over weeds in the fallow field.

"Well, I guess that's it." Sarah looped her camera off her

neck and placed it into the bag at her hip. "We won't be here long. Should we come to the house and let you know when we're done?"

With a wave of his hand and grin, he bid them well. "No need girls. People come and go often enough, me and the missus are used to it. You don't need an audience. We'll be at the house, so if we see other cars or any trouble, one of us'll head down here. Holler, and we'll hear you, but, otherwise, well met."

Kate spread a blanket on the ground. It was the perfect time to start as the sun sank minute by minute into darkness. The camera blinked away on its tripod, zoomed in on them from several feet away.

Facing one another, with their knees touching, Kate pulled a small cloth bundle from her pocket. Pink linen, white lace; the small dress could be a doll's but they knew where it had come from.

"How much did you pay for this again?"

With a sly grin, Kate held the dress up. "Less than you think, but more than I have, that's for sure. And it really is one of theirs, before you ask."

"How do you know? What if it doesn't work?"

"They have the same dresses on display in the museum."

Sarah looked relieved if not more uncomfortable all at once.

"Four of them. No pink. That's when I knew that this was worth every penny."

"And you think it will really help conjure them?" Kate looked up from the dress with a barely suppressed glower as Sarah stammered. "I don't doubt this, I don't doubt you. Believe me when I say I believe you, I've just never seen anything like this."

Kate softened somewhat. "Even if we make contact you

realize I don't know what to expect beyond that? It's not like a Ouija board."

"I get that, I do. I just want some impression that they weren't full of pain like I worry they were."

"Will you just take this seriously, please?"

"Of course I'll take this seriously! You went through a lot of trouble and I'm not about to piss on your parade."

Kate sighed, realizing she was lashing out and wasting energy. She was nervous, that was all. "It just means so much to me. Thank you for coming along."

"I may not be psychic but if there's anything that I know about conjuring the dead, it's that I can't sit here and not trust you. You have my faith and that's all I've got. Well, that and my camera." She glanced over to be sure it was still flashing away, trained on them.

"Okay, let's get started." Kate held the garment out. "Take hold of the dress"

Sarah grasped the edge with both hands. They held the pink fabric taught. The neckline to Sarah's right and the hem of the dress fluttered a little in the breeze.

"Now, I'm going to say their names, then a few lines I wrote while at the museum so they're imbued with the power of their home and imbued with the power of my ancestors. If I make some sort of connection—" Kate faltered, unsure of what that would even look like. "Just don't let go of the dress and don't say anything I haven't said. I think that'll be enough to maintain the spell."

Sarah nodded, not one question stirring behind her gaze.

With a soft voice, Kate spoke one of the quintuplet's names. With as much tenderness as she could, Sarah repeated it. With growing gravity and volume, they repeated each name in the same soft tone. The third and fourth names were louder, and the last, a little louder still.

Wind lazily stirred around the two girls. Fluttering fabric

broke the silence as the dress came alive, caught in a torrent of wind they could not perceive.

"We come to you in peace, and we hope to find you peaceful," Sarah said, as if to Kate.

Kate spoke it back as the girls locked eyes.

The phantom wind grew around them. While the field stood still, their own clothing ruffled, their hair swam in the air.

"Please, let us know if your soul is grounded here on this earth that knew your footsteps well." Sarah extended one hand to the ground and pressed her fingers into the dirt among roots and matted grass.

Kate repeated the gesture while the sound of gusting wind finally broke through. Carried on the wind was the rustling sound of footsteps. At once, far away and near, the sounds of a thousand onlookers crowded and encircled the girls.

"We come to you in love," echoed by Sarah.

"We wish to leave you peaceful," louder, once again.

"Please, let us know if you are here with us now."

To punctuate the final word, a whirlwind erupted around the girls. One wall of dust and debris whipped up, sending tall grass streaming, whipping their cheeks. The centre was calmed as the dress they clutched between them stayed still. Then, bit by bit, it began to fill with a shape. Slowly, the dress grew heavier in their hands. The small frilled-shoulders stood round, ready for tiny arms. The hem of the dress floated in the air, bowed in the centre as if around two small legs.

Dorothy Hughes looked out her kitchen window while drying the few mugs from tea. In an instant, she saw the wind whipping in a circle around the two girls, and had to catch a mug before it dropped from her hands. "Jeff! Did you leave them two girls out there doing an exorcism?" Her rage mixed with disappointment as she barked, not even sure if he was in the room.

"Not an exorcism, a conjuring," he replied plainly, looking up from his newspaper as his wife turned and glared.

"Bloody hell, have you not learned a thing? Hungry ghosts are out there and they'll come to anyone who calls. You know that!"

Jeff remained pinned to his chair, paper in hand.

Dorthy stood her ground, her silence damning.

"Come now, Dotty, how else do you expect to scare people away?"

Dorothy, not soothed by her pet name, exploded, "Well hell, not telling them the field is haunted! No! You go out there and you chase them off by telling them . . . I don't know what to tell them—tell them your wife wants them off the damned land! I don't care, but you don't just let them conjure the God-damned ghosts, Jeff!"

"All right there, I'll head out and send them on their way. I always figured it's best to let them scare themselves off . . ."

"Oh hell, the best part of me thinks you just plain find more fun in scaring the brains out of them than just telling them to go away as a nice man would."

Jeff smiled, looking forward to a little fresh air at least. "You know me best, Dorothy. You do know me best."

THE RING OF WIND SPUN FASTER AROUND THE GIRLS. Oddly, Jeff had never seen anything quite like it before. He'd seen quite a lot on this little haunted stretch of fallow field, too. Crop circles; that was what he thought it was starting to look like. If those were real, that's what was happening here.

The girls sat in the centre of the storm. With eyes rolled

back in their heads, hair all over the place, they stared straight up at the sky. Totally out to lunch, but the wind, God, he'd rarely seen wind like this.

Sure, there was something to that field being haunted, but maybe there was something to these girls, too.

The wind was racing as teeming figments beat a track around them. He was about ten feet away from the cyclone before he realized not one hair on his head stirred. One step closer, and he could just feel it on his face. Another step and it took his breath away with force.

He inhaled, and along with cold night air, the familiar spirit of the doctor settled into his chest. The sensation of slipping into coveralls was about all he could equate it to. The onetime caretaker of the quintuplets and erstwhile ring-leader's smile broadened. He'd taken on this host before, on a night a lot like this. He looked around, seeing the ghosts of the little girls he'd once known hovering just inside the wind cylinder. Two of them hung over top of the girls looking down into their eyes. The teen girls sat looking up, enraptured, locked into a ghostly gaze. Had someone taken a photo with the right kind of lens, it would capture gossamer floss in the shape of two girls, screaming waterfalls into the gaping mouths of young women.

"That's enough. Playtime is over." That is all it ever took to end the show. Hughes never questioned why it worked so well because the doctor knew.

Dejected, a breeze of protest wound around the grain, but the doctor held his ground. Wails of protest drowned out the whipping winds, which died down. Raising one hand into the air, the doctor used the farmer's body to wave goodbye. He turned to his side and continued to wave. As the ghostly girls dissipated one by one, shadows in the field rustled with coos of delight. Applause sounded softly, distantly. The shuffling sound of feet along gravel, long taken over by the field, rustled in the night.

Hughes shook off the ghost of the doctor as if it were a coat he wore, which on some days, it was. The doctor came about when there was a crowd; those hungry ghosts. In turn, the little girls came when the doctor was about. This circle turned as often as it had to. The audience was demanding, even in death. Hughes, when he was between thoughts like this, was never sure exactly who the ringleader really was.

For a moment, he could picture the five perfect little girls clearly. They skipped, single file, into the small hospital in the care of nurses after the crowds had come and gone. He could still hear their laughter, their cries, the crowds. Then, the visions were gone.

Kate and Sarah rose, suddenly exhausted and confused about what had just happened. Hughes mumbled something about the weather, and they said it was okay, and thank you, things like that. He may hear from them tomorrow as they pieced the night together, but then, he may not.

One almost forgot their camera. Their car was started and backing up before the second door slammed and they hit the road, shaken.

Hughes looked out over the field as the final wisp of the doctor's ghost left his mind. There was a piece of pink fabric caught in some bramble before the wind whipped up and blew it away. He thought it was still part of the show. He'd look for it tomorrow, same time, same place. Rain or shine. Hughes and the doctor would walk the grounds like he always did, and always had.

A FULL MOON OVER BLACK STAR CANYON

MATT WALL

There were four of us. We were sixteen and hanging out in my garage. Chris, the intellectual. Dave, the drunk. Scott, the chick-magnet, and me. I didn't have a cool thing about me; I was just me. We noticed it was a full moon out. I started telling stories of the local place everyone was afraid of: Black Star Canyon.

We had been drinking and all of us started telling stories and, for some stupid reason, we all decided that since none of us had ever been there, we should go out, and see if all the legends were true.

We got into Dave's truck and drove the long way over. Dave and Chris were in the front and Scott and I were in the back, covered by the shell. Dave opened the window so we could talk on the way and all of us were pouring machismo through every pore of our body. Once we hit the canyon though, a lot of our verbal swagger seemed missing. We took a few windy roads and then a dirt road, deep into the canyon. We came to a metal gate. The gate said this:

ALL LAWS OF STATE AND COUNTRY DO NOT EXIST PAST THIS POINT. ENTER IF YOU DARE.

That was enough for me. "Okay, looks like a dud. Let's go back."

"Fuck that," said Chris. "I came out here to prove to you idiots there is nothing to be afraid of. We are going past the gate!"

There was a short silence in the truck.

Chris got out and tried to open the gate but it was locked. He walked back to the driver's side and said through the window, "It looks like we're going on foot."

"Fuck that," I said. "This is how every stupid horror movie starts. No fucking way in Hell am I going through that gate."

"Come on, you pussy," Dave said, then everyone but me laughed.

The engine turned off. Doors opened. People exited. I was the last one out. Even though there was a full moon, it seemed dark. The trees overhead blocked out most of the light. It was colder there than it was back in my garage and I didn't like it.

Chris walked to the gate and was able to get over it with little trouble. Dave followed. I stood my ground. "I think I'll keep an eye on the truck," I said, and was surprised to hear Scott say, "Yeah, me too."

"Suit yourself, ladies," Chris said as he and Dave walked into the darkness and disappeared.

Scott and I stood and listened to crickets, frogs, owls, and all sorts of night creatures while we swallowed hard and sweated in the cold.

"This isn't that bad," Scott said.

"Yeah," I said. "It's actually pretty nice out. Nice night."

"Yeah."

Then we heard some small rocks slide down the slope to our left, we jumped to the tailgate of the truck.

"What the fuck was that?" I asked.

"I have no idea and don't want to find out," Scott said.

We peered into the darkness and I said, "Do you see that?"

"What?"

"That, right there in front of us. Maybe ten feet down." I pointed.

"I don't see—" he stopped talking.

It was like the wind was being pulled out of our lungs. There, not too far away were a pair of red eyes staring at us.

"Shit," I whispered.

"There are more," Scott said.

I looked to where he was looking and sure enough, there were more. Then more, then more. There looked to be five or six different pairs of red eyes staring us down.

"It's kinda cold," I said, "let's get in the truck."

"That's a good idea," Scott said.

We quickly got in and pulled the tailgate shut and brought down the hatch of the shell. I wasn't surprised when Scott also locked the hatch.

"It's pretty nice and warm in here," Scott said.

"Yeah," I agreed. "Beats being out there in the cold. What a couple of idiots Chris and Dave are."

"No shit," Scott said.

We both laughed faintly then sat in the quiet, both scanning our surroundings in fear.

"I've never heard of red eyes out here," I said.

"Yeah, that's the first I've heard of it," Scott said. "The best one that I've heard, was the skater."

"What skater?"

"I heard that some kids were out here skating and one of them was doing a big ollie and then the board came down, but no kid."

"Bullshit!"

"True story," Scott said. "No one ever saw him again."

"That's a load of crap. Now that we are out here, on a dirt road, I can't see any kid skating here at all."

Scott thought about it. "Maybe it was a bike. I can't remember."

"I like the story about the lady walking her dog."

"Which one is that?"

"The one where the lady is walking her dog and then the leash feels funny and she looks and there is just a collar she's dragging. No more dog."

"It probably just got off the collar and chased a rabbit or something," Scott said. "There isn't anything weird about that."

"I guess so." I nodded.

"What about the virgin sacrifice?" Scott said enthusiastically.

"What?"

"These guys were out here paintballing, and they came upon a group of monks in brown hooded cloaks in front of a fire with a naked chick tied down. One of them had a knife over his head and he was gonna kill her as a sacrifice to some god or something."

"Bullshit," I said. Then thought about it. "What happened next?"

"Well, it turns out the guys held them up and were like, don't move or we'll shoot, and the monks got scared and they tied the monks up with zip ties and called the cops."

"Bullshit! And what about the girl?"

"It turns out the girl was pissed at the guys because she wanted to be sacrificed, can you believe that shit?"

"No, cuz it ain't true, man."

"It is!" Scott demanded.

"No, man. Too many problems with that story. First off, how did they not know they were being held up by paintball markers by guys who probably had paint splotches all over them? Second, why would the paintball guys have zip ties? That's a little too convenient."

Scott rubbed his chin and said, "Yeah, I guess you're right."

"The story I heard about the monk is that this couple was out here boning in the back of a VW and the monk came up with an ax and beat the shit out of the car. They wouldn't get out of the car for obvious reasons and the monk kept fucking the car up until morning then vanished. The car wouldn't start and the couple had to walk back to town."

"That sounds made up," Scott said.

"No, man. It happened to this guy I know, well, his roommate's cousin."

"That is complete shit, man and you know it." Scott chuckled.

After the chuckling stopped, our eyes grew large. We both knew that the other heard what we were hearing. There were footsteps walking around the truck. Without moving, we looked out the windows but no one was there. The steps continued. I noticed we were both holding our breath. It seemed like it was going on forever. I thought I would faint from not breathing. Then . . . it stopped.

We both laughed.

Scott wiped his forehead and said, "What about the school bus full of kids that fell down the canyon, killing all of them?"

"What about them?"

"Well, I heard they come out at night looking for their parents."

"So," I said. "What's so scary about that?"

"Little ghost kids?" He looked at me like I was nuts. "That's scary shit, man."

"No way. Little ghost kids aren't shit. They're looking for

their parents and I ain't them, so that's no skin off my back." I sat up a little straighter, suddenly finding balls.

"Well," Scott said, "that would scare the shit out of me."

"Cuz you're a big, hairy puss. Where the fuck are Chris and Dave?" I said, looking out the back window.

"It's been almost an hour," Scott said. "I wish they'd hurry —not because I'm scared, but it's cramped in here and I'm cold."

"It is a little cramped in here. You're right."

Off in the distance, not too far away, were headlights. Pair after pair of headlights, coming our way. It sucked the air right out of the truck.

"What the fuck do you think that is?" I asked.

"I don't know," Scott said. "Do you think there's some church up there?"

"I sure fucking hope not." I looked at my watch again and saw it was almost two in the morning. "What the fuck kind of church meets in the middle of the night?"

"On a full moon? I'll tell you: devil worshippers! It's the monks!"

"Jesus fucking Christ!" I shouted. I tried to get through the little window into the cab of the truck but was too fat. "Jesus fucking Christ!" I shouted again. "Get out! Get out! We got to get the fuck out of here before those fucking monks show up and chop us up!"

Scott opened the back and we jumped out. I ran to the driver's side door and opened it. "Shit! It's a stick! Do you know how to drive a stick?" I asked.

"I don't even have my learners permit yet!"

"What the fuck good are you?" I jumped in the driver's seat and Scott ran around to the passenger seat. I reached for the ignition and there weren't any keys. "Shit! Dave has fucked us, man! We are gonna die! Chris and Dave will come back and find us all hacked up! They'll have to deal with all this shit!"

"Fuck, fuck, fuck!" Scott shouted. "The headlights are getting closer!"

"Jesus, please save us! I promise to be good!" I cried.

Then, there was pounding on the windows. Scott and I screamed. Then stopped.

It was Chris and Dave.

"What the fuck are you doing?" Dave said.

"Oh," I thought fast. "I was just gonna turn the radio on. It's boring as fuck out here."

"Yeah," Scott said. "You find anything cool?"

"No, this place is shit," Chris said.

"Yeah, it's a total sham," Dave said.

"Well, look at that," I said, and pointed up ahead to where the headlights were, but they were gone.

"Look at what?" Dave asked.

"Uh . . . your mom," I said. "I saw her over there dry-humping a tree stump."

"Yeah!" Scott added. "She looked like she was really digging it."

"Get the fuck in the back of the truck, you assholes."

We did.

The whole way home Chris and Dave talked about what a bust Black Star Canyon was. Scott and I never said a word, then, or since.

LONG BURIED

E. D. LEWIS

he house stood lonesome upon the flattened lawn. Out in the distance, wind turbines loomed as giants waiting to swat at the local inhabitants. A few birds glided overhead but diverted once they had come within the vicinity of the farm. Minimal trees stood close to the house to distance themselves from the little building with the peeling paint and the fragmented roof. Stepping out of the car, I caught the wild scent from the nearby woods and the grainy dirt road. The cloud of dust that had come in with me had already long dissipated and settled back into place. I stared, taking it all in, contrasting the changes to what was once the setting of my childhood.

My feet had to drag me over the dry gravel that crunched like withered bones. The house was a mighty beast waiting for me, filled with cobwebs of memory. The cracks in the steps were wider than I remembered. The porch boards had started to rot. Terracotta pots sat almost empty except for barren unfertile soil still resting within them. Old rusted paint cans adorned the porch's corners, and a couple of wind chimes dangled in empty space. The window blinds were drawn, closing out as much light as possible. I glanced around the corner of the structure, taking view of the old car nearby; if it weren't for the vehicle, I'd have thought the place deserted.

Moving closer to the entry, I stopped, staring at the door. It dared me to proceed. My courage was getting the better of me. Shaking my head, I raised a hand and gave the door a firm thump, thump, thump.

The creaks and groans of the old floor warned me of approach. My heart was uneasy in my chest. The lock clicked back, the wood of the door popped as the knob turned and light slipped into the house through the growing opening. Staring back at me was a causally dressed woman of medium height, pale eyes, long wavy hair, and a wrinkled face sporting jowls. Though it had been so long, I would always know her. Age had taken its toll, and her skin was no longer fair, but sallow.

We stared at each other, me growing a little sick and help-less at the sight of her after so long. Feelings tried to squirm to the surface, but I wouldn't let them get free. I wasn't sure if she'd cry or let her anger out on me; either way, I was ready. But she just stared at me as if trying to determine if I were real or some apparition, a ghost from these old grounds.

"Well," she said, hushed, yet above a whisper, "you better come in."

I couldn't tell much from her tone. Neither pleasant nor upset, it was almost neutral. This will be fun, I thought and stepped over the threshold of the old house. Faint wisps of anxieties and unease pricked at the muscles beneath my skin. Did they know? I shook my head, stopping myself before I started. They didn't exist.

The house looked as it usually did, except for the stacks of cardboard boxes sitting here and there. I will admit that it was odd seeing that place in such a state as if a death had occurred. It had that same strange heavy, yet empty presence. I wondered about the furniture and the cabinet. Would they stay, would they go with her, or would she sell them? Other than the bizarre funeral-like atmosphere, the house looked much as I remembered it.

I looked upstairs, where I would sleep once again, and placed a hand upon the railing. Some of the varnish still clung to the wood. Above where pictures once hung, the great archway divided the living and dining rooms still housing the same wooden table and chairs, a little more worst-for-wear, and the antique china cabinet. The kitchen was just beyond.

She stood watching me as I looked around. Turning my gaze to her, I figured I'd break the awkwardness. "Hasn't changed much."

"No reason to, not..."

I knew what she was going to say. She didn't finish. I took a drawn-out breath and nodded. She blinked, eyes full of empty feeling and some sort of uncertainty. I had to look away. Just seeing it made me...uncomfortable.

"Your room is still the same," she said. Was there some sort of a catch in her throat?

I nodded some more and looked up to where the stairs disappeared into the upper floor.

"I stored some things away, in the barn, and kept a little in there, but it's as you..."

God, it was coming, starting already. I wasn't ready for it, not yet.

"Cool." I looked at her from the corner of my eye. She was looking down at the floor.

"Are you hungry?" I heard her utter.

Good, a distraction. "I could eat."

I looked her way. She was staring at me, that same look plastered on her face. I wondered if it was a front or genuine. She gave me a nod and started to shuffle her feet over the worn-out carpet before picking them up as if she had to force herself to get going. I inhaled and held it for a bit before following her into the kitchen.

The room was still and calm. There had been no packing in there. Everything was as it should be for everyday use. Her steps were thunder on the linoleum tiles, which had started to break apart and crumble in places. My sight drifted to the door off to the side, a tense tingling came over my skin, and I looked away, reminding myself that it was just a damn basement. Focusing on her, I watched as she made her way around me and over to the counter. She grazed a callused hand over the smooth green metal of the lifeless cabinet next to the stove. Her eyes scanned the cluttered room before going about her task. She moved around to the icebox and took out the evening's supper. I observed as her body moved back and forth, readying her spices and seasonings and her pans and cutlery. At one point, I caught a lingering glance at the stunning slick carcass of the bird upon the white marble cutting board, a naked corpse resting on a cold stone slab. A dry swallow caught in my throat. I expelled a cough. She looked up from preheating the oven with surprise on her face as though she had forgotten I was there. Her eyes showed a soft yet weak sympathy.

"Are you coming down with something?" she asked.

I shook my head. Her gaze lingered on me a bit, and then she turned away. She picked up a knife and began to slide the blade into the moist flesh, through meat and vein and fat, slipping the edge into the joints and popping bones from their sockets. The oven came alive with a ghostly red glow within its window. Something about it was haunting to me, but I didn't know why. The spell was broken the moment she started to crack the bones. My guts shifted and begged me to get out of there; I accidentally caught sight of the basement door again, and my skin prickled.

"I'll go out to the barn for a bit."

She looked over her shoulder. "What for?"

"Look at some stuff, and... you know."

"Food will be ready in an hour or so."

More like two hours. I scrambled out of there as fast as my legs could take me, the cabinet in the dining room rattling as I passed. The last I thing heard before disappearing outside was the old, "No running through the house!"

THE GROUND POPPED AND CRUNCHED AS I MADE MY WAY across the lawn. I bounded the twenty-yards or so to the neighboring building. The empty chicken coop, just outside, stood barren and half-eaten away by erosion, reminding me of some ghost town. I shivered as I came near it. The barn didn't give much relief with its paint-stripped edges, graying wood that looked dry as discarded bones, and violent jagged splits upon its surface. It had an almost sickening impact on me. The woods peeked around the barn at me. I chose to ignore them, nothing I needed to distract me from the task at hand, but I felt I wasn't alone, as if someone was standing just within the trees. Figuring it had to be a neighbor out for a hike and gazing at the farm's eyesore, I proceeded.

The barn was filled with the typical junk that any family would store: chairs, desks, stacks of filled cardboard boxes creating a maze of mountains. Included were a couple of large wooden crates, some tables, rows of dust-encrusted wooden planks, metal pails of filthy nails infected with rust, an old piano she used to pound her fingers on during her weekend lessons. I wondered if she had plans for it or if she was going to leave it.

The loft overhead was a craterous mass of odds and ends, most of it draped in old tarps.

I stared up at it and rolled my eyes.

"Leave that shit," I said to myself and went to work on what was loaded on the ground floor. Much of what I found, or rediscovered, was useless to me—old sheets, schoolbooks, toys, knickknacks; nothing I wanted or needed. I did find a few minor pieces of interest, but the rest could go to wherever. Maybe there'd be some stuff I wanted in my old room, I thought.

WHEN I RETURNED TO THE HOUSE, THE SUN WAS ALREADY starting to set, bringing with it the coolness of enveloping darkness, and I found myself starting to run on the way back. It seemed that some reactions never die, even those we think we have long shed and left behind. Before heading through the door, I threw a glance over my shoulder, almost certain I could feel eyes on me, stronger than I did earlier before I set foot in the barn. I rolled my shoulders and shook it off. Inside I could already smell the savory aromas of home cooking, attempting to pull me back to my childhood, like so much that was around me. But I refused to go, no matter if it took me back to good times or bad. I hollered that I was back and went up to my old room, my bag in hand; I'd retrieved it from the car when I dropped off the stuff I salvaged.

My room was as I had left it except for minor changes. My bed remained in place, but my collection of bubblegum dispensers were gone from the shelf above; I found them in the barn. Some of my clothes remained, the old gaming system that I owned as a teenager and odds and ends, but the TV was gone. None of it was weird, except that I didn't find any dust and barely a musty smell, which made me realize that she kept the room up, as though she expected me to return one day. I sat down on the bed. I swear I could see her coming into the room and sitting, waiting, remembering, maybe even crying a little.

After my sit-down, I tuned my senses to the food smells. It was time to head down.

She was still in the kitchen, completing the meal. I breathed in the aroma of baked chicken and potatoes. Everything was set up buffet style on the counter, which was the usual, not that there was much of a buffet. I grabbed a plate and flatware.

While I piled my plate, she went to the dining room, switching on the light, then she returned and fixed her plate as I went to seat myself. She joined me, sitting a short distance away. A silent prayer formed on her lips, and we ate. It was good, as usual; she was never a bad cook. It was just that sometimes she ran out of ideas, or they didn't quite pan out. I tried to focus on my plate, but I found myself glancing at her as she stared at an empty spot on the table. I wasn't sure what to say, if anything. Or if I should wait for her to start.

At one point, she caught me staring at her. "How is it?"

"Good." I nodded.

"Was it a long trip?"

"Yeah."

Her turn to nod. Was this what it was going to be, a bland going-through-the-motions conversation? It was painful enough to sit in awkward silence, but this was killer, and I figured it'd be worse if we went back to silence. I decided just to dive in.

"You didn't exactly explain to me one thing on the phone."

Her eyes were blank. "What?"

"This whole thing."

She gave me a quizzical look.

"The move, the purchase."

She shrugged and nibbled on some potato.

"Why would anyone want this place anyway?"

She looked at me for a while then dropped her gaze. "I don't know. There's always someone wanting something."

I realized that I had insulted her. This was where she had brought me home from the hospital, raised me, the place I had both laughed and cried, learned to walk and talk, had my first birthday and first Christmas, pretty much the majority of my firsts, as well as where her parents had lived for the latter half of their lives. This place held many good memories for her and some not so good; it was much the same for me, but those were all marred by anger and resentments, and other things that I must have imagined. I went back to my food and decided to focus on that again.

"A good home to live in and full of memories. Once happy..."

A piece of food caught in my throat, and I erupted into a coughing fit. While I recovered, she reached out a hand, and I pulled away just out of reach. She sighed in an irritable huff. The tension made everything thick around us. I needed only to shrug it off and let it go, but something nagged at me.

"What?"

The look in her eyes, anger mixed with hurt. "Nothing."

I let my fork drop upon the plate with a clang. "No, what?"

"You."

"What about me?"

"Your attitude."

I stared at her hard. Throwing up a hand and asking, "What attitude?"

"The way you flinched just now and the way you look at this place."

"I just flinched." I knew that wasn't true. "And what way? I just look around, I haven't been here in years."

"That's your fault."

"Don't!" I demanded.

"It is. You walked, leaving everything behind, leaving me to—"

"I don't want to do this."

"It's kind of late."

I didn't want to rehash what had happened that last day, but she wouldn't back down, no matter what I said. "You know why I left. I needed to, to have a life."

"You had one."

"No, I didn't. And I needed to go to college. You wanted me to, remember?"

"You could have gone here, to the community one."

"You know they didn't have the program I wanted."

"That's just an excuse."

"Bullshit!" I screamed.

"Garrison Allan Lowes!"

I hated it when she used my full name. It always made me cringe and back down, but not then. She opened the door, dug up what should have remained buried.

"You know I wouldn't have had opportunities here." I stood up, the chair nearly toppling behind me, my legs bumping the table and giving it a faint rustle. She flinched, eyes growing wide.

"Besides, I didn't have much of a life. Isolation, imposed by you, is not a life!" I shouted.

"I didn't isolate you!" she shouted back, matching me.

I let out a laugh. "Oh, yes, you did."

"How?"

"Let me see, you didn't like me hanging out with class-mates, or anyone for that matter, you didn't like people coming over, not that that mattered after how everyone talked about the 'alleged' shit that went on around here."

"I didn't want anyone picking on or taking advantage of you."

"You did it before the bullying. And you were always afraid I'd be kidnapped, or molested, or something!"

"You were a cute little boy!"

"You still felt that way when I was a teen! You always treated me like a child!"

It was becoming as it had been all those years ago, on that last night. I was finished with supper, so I stomped into the kitchen and deposited the plate into the sink. I didn't even have to avoid that door.

I went back through the dining room, not even looking at her, and announced I was going to bed. My feet thundering upon the stairs emphasized my anger and radiated it outward into the decrepit structure, culminating in me slamming my bedroom door.

I didn't want to do it, not during the visit. I was hoping things would be peaceful, that at worst, the few days would be simply awkward.

I lay on the bed and let my brain swim. My thoughts drifted between the present and that last night, which pretty much went down the same way, except the things we said then came to light for the first time. It was in the past, yet it still held power over both of us. A ghost that wouldn't remain at rest.

Through the door, I could hear her moving about in the hall like she was attempting to tiptoe. Once her bedroom door closed, I stripped down to my shorts, switched off the light, and crawled into bed. The air seemed to vibrate all around, as though electricity was surging in and out of the walls. I was already hating being back.

I tossed and turned, pulling the sheets over me and throwing them off again. My mind raced. It got to the point that I was growing paranoid, convinced that I saw a figure standing against the door, staring at me from the shadows, waiting for me to fall asleep or lower my defenses—a familiar nightmare, one that had kept me up for months. The figure seemed to be there, solid as the bed I slept in, and at times it seemed to be gone as if it were never there. It was like I was regressing to my early years. At one point, I imagined that she might come into the room and watch me sleep, attempting to grasp at fond memories that I probably ruined. She never came, and I finally slipped into a stifling form of sleep.

I AWOKE EARLY AND WENT DOWN TO THE KITCHEN. Luckily she was still in bed. I remembered her mentioning, during our brief phone call, that she was taking the week off from work to focus on the move. I was glad she was still asleep, so I wouldn't have to relive the incident from my first night back.

For breakfast, I fixed myself toast and a cup of coffee, which had been preset the night before, as always. I was so tired that I remained in the kitchen to eat, leaning against the counter. All that kept me company was the dreaded basement door. I hated looking at it and tried to focus on other things. It stood there, daring me to come closer, but I refused.

I still remember how, when I was little, the basement freaked me out so much I had to run into the kitchen for anything I wanted and run back as if the devil were hot on my tail. It wasn't anything that happened at that point to terrify me. It was just creepy. I'd never go down there, not even to help with laundry unless she went with me. I never outgrew it, and finally, there came an incident that didn't help.

One afternoon I was on the couch watching TV. I was thirsty and figured that if I hurried, I'd be able to get something before the commercials were over. I made my way to the kitchen. Nothing was out of the ordinary except that the basement door was open. Now earlier in the day, she had been doing laundry, and I figured she left the door open by mistake. Knowing that nothing could get me during the day, I promptly closed and locked it, then got my soda and returned to my show.

When the program was over, I finished the drink and disposed of it, but something startled me: the basement door was open again. How? I was alone in the house. I remember staring at the door until finally I re-closed and re-locked it. I tested it afterward, making sure the lock wasn't broken. It was weird, but not as weird as what followed. Ever since then, until the day I left, I felt like I was being watched. It wasn't all the time, but often enough to be disturbing—in the house, outside, near the barn, even when I walked through the woods.

I finished my breakfast and hurried out of the kitchen, returning upstairs to dress. I was out of the house while she was in the bathroom. I wanted to clear my head and let off what remained of the steam from the night before.

THE CAR NEEDED A GOOD WASH AFTER THE JOURNEY AND the drives along the country roads. Town hadn't changed too much. A few new businesses had cropped up, a few had closed, no doubt due to the pandemic, and at least one new street had been built, which to me was the most surprising. I chose an automated car wash instead of a do-it-yourself one. My car deserved the treat after lugging me all those miles to a place I thought I'd never see again.

After a good wash, I decided to vacuum her. I went into the office to get some change, and after I came out, I was accosted by a man with a crooked face, which was a mass of wrinkles and darkened age spots. His skin sagged just a little and held a grayish hue. Dark circles rested just below his empty eyes. I cringed when I saw him and looked down, trying to avoid him. A low wheeze escaped from his mouth as I passed. My feet tried to keep a distance from him; I knew things had gotten back to normal, and the pandemic had been over for a while, but there was still that hint of fear that persisted.

"You gotta smoke?" he asked, his voice dry and patchy. The sound made me wince.

I looked at him in disgust. "No," I said, certain that the annoyance was clear—what a revolting habit.

I walked back to my car and turned my attention to my task. I tried to keep my focus directed, but my eyes couldn't help but stray.

The man stared at me with those lost eyes while I worked. I felt as though they might rip out my soul and absorb it into his tired body. Damn, my imagination was working overtime. I finished with the vacuum, shutting my car's back door with a firm click. I was readying myself to complete my errands when I felt the overwhelming sensation that eyes were on me again. I tried shaking it off, thinking it was that old man. I looked in his direction. He had gotten up and was starting to wander off, but that didn't satisfy me at all. My back flexed, and the tension tiptoed up my vertebrae, sending pain and chills through my body.

"Stop it, Garr," I demanded.

My body stiffened, and I felt the urge to bang my head against the car's side. It wouldn't solve anything, just cost me a few bills and pain, but it was tempting. I got into the car, ready to go about my business. Before I had left the car wash,

I passed that old man. He gave me a bizarre grin as if he knew something I didn't.

When I returned to the house, she confronted me. She had been packing up the kitchen and swore she heard me earlier. She couldn't have. I was in town for a few hours. Her face was startled at first, fearful, but her expression softened, and she brushed it off. Oh God, it was all happening again. I refused to believe it. It had to be childhood trauma, resurfacing. I had to keep telling myself that all of it wasn't real.

IT CAME IN LOW DRAWN-OUT DRAFTS, FOLLOWED BY A stuffy wheeze. At first, I thought I was dreaming because I saw Virginia Shulman beckoning me to a steamy hot tub, in her sexiest bikini. I struggled to get at her, tossing off my shirt and trying to wiggle off my shorts, before plunging into the foamy froth. But once I lunged forward to take her in my arms, my breathing ripped me out of the moment. The scene from my subconscious and the cold dark of the old room were at odds, the room and that breathing were clawing me back to harsh reality and tearing my sensual fantasy world to shreds.

Perspiration clung to my chest, my lungs tight, a thick chill holding me to the mattress beneath its weight. All was quiet. It was all a nightmare created by the unhappiness that still lingered in the house. An urge to look under the bed came over me and I found myself starting to roll over. I stopped myself before dropping my head over the side, fearful of what I might find.

My eyelids fell back into place, then wrenched open again seconds later. The violent rasping dug into my ears.

It was hard to convince myself that it was only childish fears. Just being in that house, in that room, made me rethink the defenses I had built over the years. I was beginning to come to grips with what was going on, what was happening. As much as I wanted to deny it, to write it all off with some rationale, it was becoming impossible. When I left all those years ago, it wasn't only to get away from her, but the weird things too.

The next day was to be our last in the house. I got up and was surprised to find her in the kitchen preparing herself a cup of coffee and a simple bowl of cereal. I decided to do the same, and we ate together. It was still awkward for us, but less so than the previous night. She was chatty that morning, talking about her plans for her apartment and such. It was as if nothing had happened. After breakfast, she continued to pack up the kitchen, and I called to make sure the truck she requested would be available for the move. I went upstairs to see that the things I wanted from my room were packed and ready.

I had time to do a little digging into what I should do about *them*. I found dozens of websites dedicated to ghosts and the paranormal, many making suggestions for doing house blessings and cleanses. I didn't want to contact anyone. We were to be out of the house within the next few days, and I wanted it to be kept secret from her. My search was cut short by her calling me downstairs. She was afraid they might give her rental away if we didn't get things moving.

I PARKED THE TRUCK NEXT TO THE PORCH, TO MAKE THE haul easy; she parked in her usual spot, making it appear that she had never left. I moved the books I'd found at the local bookstore beside me into the glove compartment. I'd pick them up after supper and read up all I could for a few hours. I made it a point to drop into the store while we were out, looking for anything I could that would help. A few of the books suggested a séance. I grabbed a couple and purchased them in a hurry.

When I hopped out of the truck she came around to meet me, looking about and sighing. I think it was hitting her. This would be her last night in the house, the last time she'd sleep there, the last time she'd move about through its sad, gloomy enclosures. It was sad to think about it, and it made me feel what she probably wanted me to feel. I could have made it better for her, perhaps reinvented some of the happy times and moments that we had once shared, be the son she wanted me to keep being. But I was kidding myself. It wouldn't have happened that way.

"We'll get something to eat after we've finished for the night," she said.

I agreed.

I opened the back of the trailer, while she got the door, and we returned to the house and went about our duties. She took on the position of director of operations, and I was her laborer. I was right. It was a workout. I was sweating so much I could have flooded the damn place. We got most of everything from the living room and the kitchen. The rest would be saved for the morning. Anything else that she wanted would be picked up later on.

We went out for Italian food at a local family-owned place. I'd showered before we left the house, making sure I looked presentable for the restaurant. Not that it was any high-end place, but it was decorated nicely, and I felt that going in all sweaty would be offensive to the servers and other patrons. It was a nice change from what we'd been eating at the house. But my mind was distracted, which took away from the experience.

THE BOOK SOURCES DESCRIBED WHAT A SÉANCE WAS. IT differed from what I'd seen in movies. There were warnings, too, which I doubted I needed to take into consideration much, especially the one referring to calling up specific individuals since I didn't know the identity of those haunting the farm. It was all pretty simple, and I figured I didn't have much to lose on that last night.

I waited until it was around eleven, sure she would be asleep before I crept downstairs and out to the truck to locate the candles and anything I could use for an atmospheric tablecloth—I happened upon a black one. Once back inside, I readied the dining room table, setting it up as if I was about to partake in some performance. I threw the cloth over the table and placed the candles in an arrangement that seemed appropriate. But at a second glance, it looked like just a clump of glossy white and cream-colored wax.

I made sure all the electronics were off and then placed my hands upon the porous cloth, pausing, debating with myself. Should I be doing this? I shook my head. I had to get a grip. I followed what the sources said to do and attempted to focus. If there was any hint of doubt or skepticism, it wouldn't work. I took a deep breath, eased my shoulders, straightened my back against the chair, and relaxed every muscle in my body. Staring forward, I focused my mind, opening up to whatever was present. At first, nothing happened. I felt myself relax in the dark with only the candles' glow, shifting to the rhythm of my breath, making shadows appear and vanish from sight. I continued to sit there and concentrate, forming a question in my mind. Was anyone there? Would anyone want to communicate with me?

The boards under the carpet moaned as if some great weight were being pressed upon them. Eyes were on me from every direction, but no one was present, no one human that is. The air was heavy and damp, filled with something that made my stomach turn. My eyes skimmed the blackness, half hoping there would be what the sources called a "materialization" or some apparition.

"Is anything there?" I asked aloud, hoping that whatever it was would be willing to respond. The candles flickered. The room cooled, and my shoulders began to shiver, but not because of the cold.

"Can you speak?"

I smelled something foul, not rot or decay, but something dry and acrid like stale soil. Air caught in my lungs, and I couldn't expel it. God, what was happening now? I thought. A cold pricking nipped the back of my neck like icy fingers. What or whoever they were seemed angry. Why else would they attack me? Then, the breathing came from beneath the table. That horror from under my bed decided to join in and terrorize me as well. I prayed to God that it would stop, that whatever I had gotten myself into would go away. It was a mistake, a huge one, and the blame was on me.

Nothing was happening. Was I free? Had it, or they, gone? There was still a faint chill in the air, which I considered part of the after-effects. My chest was starting to lighten, and I could finally exhale. I worked on settling my breathing. Some of the candles had gone out during the attack. I used the remaining flames as a focal point. All was going to be fine. The one thing that bothered me was that my left shoulder kept twitching. I sighed and prepared to stand when a rattling made me freeze. The antique china cabinet was rattling as if often did when I used to run across the dining room floor, but no one was there. My next thought was there was an earthquake or the aftershocks of one from a neighboring county. But nothing else in the room was shaking, not even the walls.

My eyes darted about like those of a man deranged. What next? Were the remaining furnishings going to come to life and attack me? Was I going to be lifted to the ceiling and sprawled flat, like in the movies? I sat down, unsure of what to do. The rattling continued to the point where the vibrations from it were radiating through my ears to my skull, that they might cause my skull to shatter. I covered my ears for protection and to give myself some relief.

Before long, the rattling stopped. The thought that maybe I'd gone deaf crossed my mind, but that fear melted away as I realized I could hear the sounds the house made at night, the non-frightening ordinary ones. There was no movement except for the flickering shadows.

I sighed with some relief. Looking up toward the living room, I was met by a figure, enveloped by the dark with wildly draped thin hair, shadowed features, and sallow skin. My nerves jumped at the sudden appearance, but it didn't bring about the same reactions. My eyes adjusted to the dark, and I realized it was her.

I feared she'd ask me what I was doing and what my shouting was all about, but she didn't. She just stood there, staring with a strange expression plastered upon her face.

"Are you okay?" I asked.

No response.

She stood there, as a frightened child would, unable to move nor come up with a clear response except for the quivering of her bottom lip. I asked her again, but she just stood there.

She had to have known. I swear I could almost feel the fear pouring off of her and wrapping itself around me, around the entire room. She had been living there experiencing it, ignoring and accepting it. And I'd left her there, left her alone with it, with them.

"Please answer me," I demanded. "Are you okay? Do you... know who they are?"

Her eyes darted to me, and new sensations came over me,

tearing through my flesh and innards. My eyes started to burn, and my chest was twisted into knots. My heart made like the little metal ball in a pinball machine. I felt need and weakness, no, not weakness but innocent dependence. Hot tears tickled the pores in my face.

Not only had these spirits, these ghosts or whatever, been trapped here, but so had she; this house had become her tomb as it had for them.

"Mom, please," I heard myself say.

She was stunned for a moment, but her eyes blinked, and the expression changed. She stepped forward and clasped her arms around me. I was shaking at that moment, about to fall apart. In the dark, though, I spied a figure, the one I saw in my room. My insides almost cracked inside at that moment, and my being shattered.

She pried me away from her a bit but kept her fingers clutched around my upper arms. "Let's go," she said.

Grabbing the keyring, I turned and tumbled to the floor. A cold sensation crept close to my ankle. I looked, but nothing appeared to be there. Then, I saw it. Deep within the depths beneath the table rested the bleak outline of a formless head, bony shoulder, and a thin ancient hand. A gaunt face seemed to take shape with deep-set features. The breath in my lungs froze, unable to escape. The eyes from that face looked as though they were missing, yet they stared at me with preternatural menace. I began to gasp and fight for air.

A hushed blowing sound broke the hold the thing had over me, and the faint pulsing glow was replaced with black-ness. Out of the corner of my eye, I saw a familiar outline leaning over the table. I felt hands reaching over my shoul-ders, warm and fragile. I struggled to my feet, she helping me the best she could. We skidded to the front door, holding tightly to each other, keys jingling as we went. Once we were on the porch, I swung around, fingers reaching for the door, finding it, and giving it a yank. The door closed with a boom. I frantically locked it.

She was next to me the entire time, keeping close. We were in this together. We hurried to the safety of the truck's cabin, locking ourselves inside. Sitting there, looking about into the night, we waited to see if we were to be accompanied by something, one of them. I could finally breathe, taking in all the air I needed. It felt and tasted good, the best air I had since before I had made the journey to that godforsaken place.

I looked at her, sitting there in the passenger seat. She was taking a breath, too; her cheeks glistened with fresh tears. No longer was there the look of empty feeling and uncertainty. Understanding, hope, relief, and love replaced them. We embraced each other and sat there for a long while. She was free. We both were. All was silent and still.

DARKNESS DESCENDS

JASON WHITE

S omething in my gut told me that breaking into Mr. Carden's house with Frankie that night was going to be a big mistake. The house stood like a black void against the silvery moon-stained sky. My skin crawled as though invisible eyes scanned every inch of me. This wasn't far from the truth. Like a rectangular skull, the house leered at Frankie and me, the house's windows on the second floor gaping like cavernous eyes.

Frankie shifted beside me as I dug the lock picks out from my pocket.

"Let's get this over with," he said. "You're not about to chicken out on me, are you?"

My throat felt dry. My voice would break if I tried to speak, so I just shook my head. Why would I back out now? Had I ever backed out on him before?

I couldn't blame him for his suspicion; this wasn't your typical break and enter job. Old Mr. Carden's place was the house indigenous to Angus that most children avoided. Even adults detoured across the street whenever walking past. The house had haunted my own thoughts since I was a kid. It still gives me nightmares, and there I was, about to break in.

I worked my tongue around the sandpaper innards of my mouth, trying to work up some saliva.

"Let's just make it quick," I said, once I had succeeded. My plan was to get good and drunk when we were done, hopefully enough to black out the entire experience. I wanted nothing to do with Mr. Carden or his house. My only hope was that the black cloud he kept over the town for as long as my parents could remember would finally come to an end.

But somehow I knew that it wouldn't be that easy, that Mr. Carden and whatever evil he possessed couldn't be killed.

Calm down, I told myself. I was working myself up into a panic. If I had known how right my instincts were, however, I probably would have run away screaming, with or without my best friend. And then things wouldn't have turned out so...so painful.

So horrible.

On the other hand, if I had run I'd probably be dead along with everyone else.

❧

I don't mean to sound melodramatic. Right now, I'm sitting alone in the apartment above the Angus Laundromat I used to share with Frankie. My skin is covered with painful protrusions that can only be described as boils, except they are black and swollen and hurt like a bitch, even when I sit unmoving. They alone make me want to put a bullet through my brain. Even if I were courageous enough to do such a thing, I cannot allow myself. I've got to get this down on paper first. The world must know what went on that night in Carden's house; they have to know what happened to Angus.

The boils itch and explode without my having to touch

them. Their substance sprays, black and shiny across my skin, and if I don't clean it right away it hardens into rock within seconds.

I wish I were simply insane. Instead I've got this knowledge, this goddamned memory that I can never erase. I fear I don't have much time.

It hurts so much to move. Even the simple task of writing is agony!

Too bad for me that I have to keep backtracking to get the story right.

❦

OFFICER TRUDY, ANGUS'S ONLY FULLTIME COP, approached Frankie after the sixth child in one year went missing. I wasn't there for the conversation, but the look in Frankie's eyes afterwards made the hair on the back of my neck stand at attention.

"Finally, something's being done about old Carden's place," he said to me. "And we're the ones who are going to do it."

His smile was wolfish. I had never seen him so happy.

Everyone in town knew what happened to the kids who went missing. It wasn't hard to figure out. If this were any other town, the police would be hunting a prowler of the human variety. Although suit-wearing out-of-towners did search for such an individual, everyone who actually lived here knew the truth: the suits' investigation would lead to nothing.

The old man who lived on 318 Maple Drive appeared normal on the outside. His name was Mr. Carden. He wore a plain cardigan and a Fedora when seen around town. At the grocery store we all noticed he would buy more food than any old man could possibly eat. He walked with a cane, hunchbacked. Nobody spoke to him and he spoke to nobody. He hated everyone and everyone hated him right back.

Although he looked normal, he wasn't. Most felt that the man just wasn't human, even though they never voiced it. My own mother, for example, used to mutter how "That old man was just as old as he is now when I was a child." Children went missing from town all the time. Adults too. The missing kids were often last seen playing somewhere near his house. The adults, often the missing kid's hysterical parents, were usually last seen storming the property calling the name of their son or daughter.

We all should have learned to stay off the old man's property. For some reason, no one ever did.

This year something changed. Kids and adults used to go missing once, maybe twice every few years. Now, suddenly, six disappeared in one year. Little Melanie Malone, who lived down the street, was the last one to go. Her father was a good friend of mine. Frankie and I used to go to his place for beers on Friday nights to watch the Blue Jays baseball game. Melanie often hung around, bugging Frankie and me to play with her. I didn't mind. She had the bluest eyes I'd ever seen, like shallow Caribbean waters. Eventually, Sal would yell at her to go bug her mother, and she would leave.

The suits arrived soon after she disappeared. They'd drive by Carden's house every day as though they couldn't see the place. I had no doubt that everything in their investigation would lead them to that house. Yet, as far as I could tell, they never once questioned Mr. Carden.

I suppose I should explain a little. I've had a slight obsession about Carden and his house for some time now. My mother used the place, like some secret nightmare, to frighten me into obedience. How could I have turned out any differently? Frankie and I live on Maple Street. We could see the old bastard's house from our apartment's living room window, where I often found myself, pretending to read a book, but really just sitting and watching.

Most fellow villagers were obsessed with the place, too. They were also afraid of it. How could they not be?

"You're not going to chicken out on me, are you?" Frankie had asked me on that night before we entered the house. It was his way of admitting his own anxiety. The fear lay within the intensity of his eyes. He never could have broken into that house alone. But he also would never have admitted that.

I nodded, though I wasn't sure if I was telling the truth. We stepped onto the property, up the front porch steps. The wood bent and groaned under our weight. I inhaled deeply to try and steady my hands, then bent over the front door.

Smart thieves always check the door before picking it. Otherwise, you could get caught wondering why your lock picks don't work. This time was different, though. I knew that Carden's door was unlocked. What reason would he have to lock up?

I was right. The solid oak door creaked slowly open, reminding me of old black and white horror films, in which the proverbial haunted house's doors opened and closed all on their own. Frankie turned off the flashlight, and we stepped inside, closing the door softly behind us so as not to disturb the old man; with all the lights off as they were, we figured Carden was asleep.

The corrupt smell hit us right away. Like decayed road kill. Along with something chemical. My eyes watered. Right then, I knew that we had to get out of there. Something bad was going to happen if we didn't. I mean, hadn't everyone who'd gotten this far in the last fifty years gone missing? We were crazy to think that we were somehow immune.

I opened my mouth to voice my wants and fears to Frankie when he turned the flashlight back on and stepped forward. "I can't see a thing in here," he said as way of explanation, and then he moved toward a threshold I assumed led into the kitchen.

I stopped.

Frankie hadn't seen it or he would have stopped too.

On the wall beside the kitchen entrance protruded a massive, tumorous bulge. I couldn't tell if all the spider webs held it up, or if it grew out of the wall itself. Finally, Frankie noticed it and took a step back.

"Jesus," he whispered. "What the fuck's that?"

The flashlight wholly illuminated it now. Its surface was black and dry and fleshy. It pulsated along its sides as though it breathed. The beam moved, and to my utter horror, more of the things appeared to our right, in the living room. On chairs and a couch rested more, all the same black skin and spider webs, planted upon the walls as though gravity meant nothing to them.

A wet splashing in the rhythm of a drunkard's walk came from the kitchen. Frankie stepped backward, crushing my toes. Then he froze, solid as a statue. The flashlight beam moved to the kitchen threshold.

It took everything inside me not to scream. The thing moved with the grace of a dying animal, but it had no head and no real arms or legs. It walked on four stumps of muscle and bone wrapped in pink human-like skin, hoisting up a small, torso-like body. Its muscles knotted and relaxed as it moved through the threshold, sloth-like, toward the living room.

Laughter filled the room—deep, malicious, and amused. My heart filled with a dread I'd never felt before. Frankie must have felt the same horror, because we both screamed and tried to get out the door we had entered.

But the doorknob wouldn't budge no matter how hard we turned or kicked at it.

The house had us trapped. We were about to become one of Mr. Carden's missing.

I MET FRANKIE AT THE BEGINNING OF THE SECOND GRADE after his parents moved here from a neighboring town. I remember the day clearly. We were all lined up for the first day of school outside our classroom and this funny looking kid I'd never seen before stood behind me. He stared at me with sunken eyes and a pale face. He looked mean, but too small to be a threat.

Entering a classroom for the first day of school always fascinated me. Where would everyone sit? Would the desk and seating arrangement remain throughout the year? Sometimes the desks were organized into groups of four or six; sometimes they were single file. At the beginning of the second grade, this was nothing more than a curiosity, but when the teacher finally let us in, I noticed that desks were paired into three aisles.

I'm not sure how, it certainly wasn't intentional, but Frankie and I ended up sitting beside each other near the back of the classroom. I can't speak for Frankie—we've never talked about it—but I chose that spot for the window. I was smarter than most my classmates at the time. The teachers had wanted me to skip a few grades, but after a lot of foot stomping, screaming until I could barely speak, my parents looking like they hadn't slept in a week, they let me remain in regular rotation.

Just because I was smart didn't mean I wanted to learn. I already knew everything the teachers tried to cram down everyone's throat. Waiting for all the others to catch up was boring.

So, a window seat was just fine. It would become a habit throughout my school career.

What the teachers did not know, however, was the catalyst this would create. Frankie looked at me that morning as he sat down, the sunlight making him squint.

"The fuck you staring at?" he said.

That's all it took, and I laughed. It seemed like Frankie had always been there. He laughed, too. Nothing changed between us in the years to come.

We grew to be best friends, no matter how often the teachers tried to separate us. Our interests in deviance grew as well. Toilets exploded during our reign. The weak shivered inside the length of our shadows. It didn't take long for our inclinations to leak outside the school grounds as well.

Enter Constable Trudy, Angus's only cop. I don't know how many times I sat in the back of his cruiser, listening to lectures about the future and my place in it if I continued vandalizing and shoplifting. And later, when he had finally given up, I endured the silences as he escorted me to and from Juvie hall.

So it had surprised me when he approached Frankie about old Carden's place. In retrospect, it shouldn't have. Trudy knew that the old man was behind the missing children. We all did. But he also knew that he couldn't do anything about it. He had no proof. If he went all vigilante on the old man, his career and life would be ruined.

I can't imagine what they'd do a cop in jail. Trudy might be an asshole, but he only did what he believed in. I have nothing against him. I wouldn't want to see the man suffer that way.

I doubt he has the same respect for me. He knew the history of the house, after all, and he still wanted to send us in there. Despite this, I could see his point of view. He could take out two birds with one stone, so to speak. If he were lucky, he'd get rid of the Frankie and Greg team along with the town's evil secret. Offering us the freedom to fuck with Carden and his home was like offering candy to a hungry child.

And we sucked the offer up until it was dry.

Even now, as I sit here in my window seat, the boils causing me constant pain, I can't hate Trudy. We're the same beast; we just wear different uniforms. Still, I try to picture Trudy in that house with that thing crawling across the floor. And the laughter that bled from the walls. I can picture his tanned face going white, his eyes like mangos sticking out of his skull. I laugh. Despite the pain, I laugh, because he would not have survived.

Hell, I'm surprised I did.

But it was close.

Back in Cardin's nightmare house, the laughter faded to a hum and Frankie and I got our nerve back. Frankie shrugged, as though he hadn't screamed like a little girl only minutes ago. "Let's finish the job," he said.

Only one place remained for us to go. We headed up the staircase. Thankfully, the four-stumped thing was no longer in sight. However, more of the cocoon-like bulges stuck out of the walls along the way up, some of them lying on the stairs. We took wide steps around them. Despite my best efforts, my fingers grazed one. Although the exterior was tough, it felt as fleshy as it looked. And it was warm.

Shivering, I yanked my hand away and unsheathed the hunting knife strapped to my belt. Why hadn't I pulled it before? Frankie noted my move and did the same.

The second floor was a single hallway with five more rooms. The low drawl of laughter picked up again. This time we could tell where it was coming from. We headed in the laughter's direction with only Frankie's flashlight to lead the way. The cocoon-like pods were everywhere. I was afraid one would burst.

I was afraid of what would come out.

I didn't want to know, but that didn't matter as I would see it happen soon enough. When we made it to the room from where the laughter came, Frankie shone the flashlight in. We saw him. Old Mr. Carden. He sat on a chair in the corner of his bedroom. Fat cocoons perched on the bed beside him. Suddenly the room filled with light. I jumped. Frankie had flipped on the ceiling light, but I wish he hadn't.

A black and grey funnel jittered in the corner above Carden. Its thick fleshy mass, covered in spider webs, flowed down the wall and attached to the old man's head. It pumped like a heart. My immediate thought was that it breathed dark thoughts into the man's skull. He smiled and laughed, his skin black as the midnight sky, his teeth white. Whenever I'd seen him at the grocery, buying all that food, he'd been pale as death, his teeth yellow. This blackness was a fluid thing; it flowed from the tube down into his face.

The laughter died and his eyes opened—two black holes with a glint of white.

"You humans are so boring," he said. He licked his lips, his tongue a grey mass of dead flesh. "So predictable. I grow weary of this. I'm empty and nothing fills the void anymore."

The cocoon, perched on the wall by the light switch, burst open in a frenzy of shell and wings. The wings fluttered, black with tiny, white dots. They grabbed Frankie, enfolding him within their grasp. He tried to scream, but the wings muffled the sound. The wings tightened; their carnivorous fabric distorted his face. His gaping mouth twitched. He struggled to get loose. I stabbed them with my knife, but they were too strong, my blade worthless.

I redoubled my efforts as Frankie's outlined face and chest began to dissolve. His screams faded. His struggling slowed until he lay still and flat on the floor. A greenish smoking slime bubbled on the floor by his feet. His legs fell off sideways, slopping in the puddle.

The stench of that chemical smell, some perversion of sulfur and ammonia, stifled my screams. I covered my nose with the top of my shirt and hacked, trying to get the smell out of my throat and sinuses.

The old man laughed, still attached to the wall. He watched me with those dead, black eyes, his smile the stiff rictus of a corpse.

"And to think I was going to let both of you go," he said, and chuckled.

A giant set of wings grew on the wall where Frankie had died. Between them, the fat body of a moth or butterfly. I blinked. It had a face! Two little eyes, the color of Caribbean oceans, looked around the room and then settled on me. Oh Jesus! Was that little Melanie Malone's smile? The wings twitched as though about to take flight, but the Melanie thing remained on the wall.

The old man continued, "You and your people are no longer entertaining." He said the word 'people' as though it tasted sour on his tongue. "It's time for me to up the ante, play this game a little more...drastically."

"What the hell are you?" I said, and realized that I knelt before him. Tears welled in my eyes. My whole body trembled with cold and fear and anguish. My chest ached as though someone had stabbed me and left me to die.

"I was here before your kind crawled out of the oceans, boy," the thing said. "And I'll be here when you are gone. Your puny brain cannot conceive of my true existence without breaking into a million little pieces. I am old. I'm tired. I've built an army over the years, and soon I will witness the destruction of your town. Call it a test. The world shall be next!" Again it laughed. It sounded insane.

He leaned closer to me and said, "You'll make a fine soldier."

Without thinking, I was up on my feet and running at him. I sliced my knife through the fat appendage attached to the creature's head. I slashed again. Once more and I severed it completely. A black substance spewed from it and it from the ragged stump, sprayed everything, including me, as it thrashed through the air.

Mr. Carden screamed in agony and fell forward. I landed on his back and reached around. Was this going to work? I acted on instinct. I slid the knife into his throat until the blade scraped against his spine, my fingers sticky from its hot, black blood. The light from the ceiling blinked, and then burned out and I was in the dark. I kept hacking until the head finally came free, and in a moment of pure insanity, I held it up by the remaining flaps of skin. I carried it to the window to look at the dead creature's face in the moonlight.

The creature's eyes found mine. It opened its mouth wide and sprayed hot tar into my face. I dropped the head, swiping at my burning nostrils and eyes. The stench of sulfur and ammonia was suffocating. I stumbled out of the room and down the hall to the top of the steps. My vision went black. The shit he had sprayed on my face spread throughout my body. I could no longer walk. I fell to my knees, then my side. I lay there panting, trying to breathe, but oblivion soon took me.

I WAS A FOOL TO THINK THAT I COULD HAVE DEFEATED whatever Mr. Carden is. I often sit here, taking a small break from writing this account, and wonder what he is. Some form of Earth spirit incarnate? Was he even older than that? Had he visited other towns and villages throughout history? Other planets?

It's useless to think of such things. Doing so only furthers the itch inside my skull. I know I'm insane, but there's something else that's seriously wrong with me.

I awoke the next morning on Mr. Carden's front lawn, confused and hungrier than I'd ever been. Carden's blood still covered me. Whatever he'd spat at me still stuck. But I didn't care. I went home, headed for the fridge, guzzled down an entire carton of milk. I took a spoon and ate a jar of peanut butter and washed it down with raw hamburger. I then fell to the floor in agony. I could barely tell if I was still hungry or overfull.

When I felt better I crawled over to my chair. I looked out the window, and to my horror, there was Mr. Carden, standing between our homes. He was alive and looked human again! His skin pale, his teeth yellow. His hand trembled as he waved at me. He motioned to his dilapidated house, and all the windows burst at the same time. From the house's innards, massive moths flew into the sky. They swarmed, formed a storm cloud, and swooped down like a great darkness descending to destroy everything in its path. They folded their wings around people walking down the street, dissolving them where they stood. They smashed through the windows and doors of people's houses. They rammed cars, rolling them onto their tops.

For over a day chaos reigned. For some reason, they left me alone. I think I now know why, because as it settled down out there, my body grew golf ball-size boils, and I continued to eat as much as I could. It felt as though I could never fill the hole.

The boils burst without my touching them. The draining mucous is black and hardens almost immediately. I am in constant pain. Pain that pot, liquor, and pills no longer muffle. I can't think straight. I can barely move, so I sit in front of the window and watch the empty streets and write this down. Mr. Carden is out there somewhere, no doubt spitting that substance into survivors' faces so that they can change into what I've become.

Somebody must find these words someday. They need to know what they're up against.

Outside, giant black moths hang in trees, on telephone poles, on the sides of houses. Every so often I hear the screams of some unfortunate, who had remained hidden until then. I should've eaten a bullet long before now. But hope can be as crippling as despair. I'm not even sure if I could hold the gun up that long. Holding this pen upright takes all my energy.

Really, it's either kill myself or become one of those things.

I think that they're waiting for me to turn into one of them before moving on to the next town.

I can't let that happen.

I won't!

AT THE END OF THE ROPE

CAMERON CHANEY

I was nine years old when Henry died. Teddy was eleven. Henry was my ten-year-old chocolate lab and Teddy was my big brother. It sounds like it should be the other way around, but it wasn't. Best not get them confused.

I remember standing at the edge of Henry's doggy pin, a bag of kibble dangling from one hand, Teddy at my side. It was raining that morning, a lot. The ground was liquid. Swallowed me up deep into the earth's belly as I stared at what used to be my dog. Any other day, Henry would have heard the back door of the farmhouse swing open, springing from his slumber to meet us at the gate. Wiggly butt, tappy paws. Today, he just slept, unmoving in the shelter of his doghouse.

My brother and I didn't have to say anything. We knew it right away. I wasn't crying about it, but my big brother hugged me anyway, real super tight. That's when I realized Teddy was the one crying, his tears joining the raindrops on my shoulder. I squeezed him tight, told him everything was gonna be okay, just as he had always done for me.

Later that afternoon, when the rain had stopped and the mosquitoes communed on anyone who dared enter their domain, Teddy and I wrapped Henry in one of Dad's plastic tarps, dragged him out into the woods bordering our property. There was this spot deep in the forest we liked to visit when school was out, a clearing barren of any and all foliage. Just a giant, perfectly round dirt patch surrounded by greenery. The older I get, the harder it is to remember why we liked it there so much, but I suppose the clearing did have a magical quality to it. Maybe you just had to be young enough to notice how different the air felt there, how the days seemed to crawl on all fours, lasting hours longer than possible.

Or maybe it was because of the doghouse.

Sun-bleached, paint-chipped and in need of repair, the doghouse sat abandoned at the center of the clearing. Teddy and I never questioned the existence of the doghouse, just thought it was a ripe place for Henry to rest as we played in the sun. I think Henry liked knowing where we were at, knowing his kids weren't hurt. He was our protector, after all. Good ol' Henry, always looking out for us.

The doghouse was where we left him. Together, Teddy and I pushed Henry's body inside where we could still see him and where he could see us. That's where he stayed the rest of the summer, watching as we played tag or had tea parties or hunted for boggarts in the trees. We tried to keep our distance because of the smell—it was dang bad—but it gave us piece of mind knowing Henry was still with us.

Teddy never let me go out into the woods alone, insisting on playing with me just in case Margaret Morton and her friends were to come tromping through the trees. Those kids were mean as all get-out and liked to call me bad names when Teddy wasn't around so he kept me close, would chase them away with a big stick if they were brave enough to show their ugly faces. "I don't take none of that bullshit," he said. "And you shouldn't neither." But I was way too small to stick up for myself, and he knew it. That's why he didn't leave me home alone with Daddy either, especially after Henry died. It was all on my poor brother to protect me now.

The flowers were my idea. I began swiping packets of seeds from Ms. Tammy's greenhouse down the road so we could plant them around the doghouse, all over the clearing. Many kinds of flowers, by the thousands. Come August, the clearing was no longer a clearing at all but a beautiful garden paradise all in tribute to our Henry. It wasn't much of a paradise for Teddy though. At the end of each day, when the sun had set and the fireflies lit the forest ablaze, Teddy's eyes would look like Mama's after Daddy was through yelling at her: hydrant red and bursting at the bolts.

"Why you crying?" I asked him one time.

"I ain't. I feel like my head's gonna pop," Teddy replied, scrunching his eyes shut real tight. "And my throat hurts. I had to sleep in the rocking chair last night 'cause I couldn't breathe."

"You tell Mama?" I said, staring at the snot bubble in his nose.

"Course not. If Mama thinks I'm sick, she'll make me stay in bed all summer and you'll have no one to plant flowers with. Don't say nothin' to Mama, Abigail. Nothin'. Promise."

I did.

The next day, as my big brother and I were playing in our new garden—Henry's decaying body watching from the doghouse—Teddy began to choke. He raised his hands to his throat. His eyeballs looked like they were gonna plop out of their sockets. I remembered what he'd said the previous night, about his head feeling like it was gonna pop. I backed away from him as he gasped for air, scared he was gonna explode all over me.

Instead, he just collapsed into the flowers in slow motion, or at least that's how I remember it.

I'd like to say I practiced CPR on him, pulled that gasp of life from his lungs like they do in the movies, but I was a terrified ten-year-old girl and Autumncrow Elementary school sure didn't teach such things. Instead, I ran. I ran and ran all the way home and by the time I told someone—I can't even remember who—it was already too late. The heroes showed up at the forest garden to find a dead Teddy, bloodshot eyes staring straight up at the clouds as if searching for zoo animals.

They said it was the flowers, or at least one kind of them, that he had some kind of allergic reaction, making his throat shrink till he couldn't breathe no more. Making him die. But I didn't like to think it was the flowers, so I didn't. Instead, I told myself Teddy just missed Henry a whole bunch, wanted to be with him in Heaven so bad he made his own throat close up just by thinking about it. This thought made me feel lots better, knowing my two favorites were up in the sky, playing fetch and racecars and maybe even planting a garden for me since I was the one all alone now.

The couple weeks following Teddy's death are hazy to me, but I do recall asking Mama why we had to bury Teddy in the cemetery. "Maybe we can dig him up and put him in the doghouse with Henry instead," I suggested. This made Mama cry a lot, sent her running to the bedroom while Daddy smacked me across the face a few times.

I didn't say nothing more about that idea 'cause I was embarrassed. If I thought about it too much, my face would start hurting again, then I would become super small and sink into a dark place in my belly. No one could find me in that place, and I couldn't feel stuff there either. Just a tingly feeling all around, in my scalp and in my chest and in my bones. Tingling, but nothing more.

Daddy must have realized I didn't have anyone to protect me during those days because he started hitting me more often, about trivial things, like if I left my socks on the living room rug or used the bathroom without turning the fan on. His blows got stronger by the day, and so did Mama's neglect.

Her drinking got heavier after Teddy died and she spent most of her days in bed, probably because she was exhausted from staying up all night, sobbing. Sometimes, it didn't sound like crying at all, but laughter echoing up and down the halls. Hysterical laughter. More than once, I thought she was in my bedroom with me, giggle-crying in a dark corner, but I was too scared to come out from underneath my comforter, too scared of what I'd see. What if Mama's tears glowed in the dark? What if I would see her misty eyes staring at me from the shadows?

—It wasn't long before I found myself in the woods again. Even though it was strange not having Teddy or Henry there —Daddy must have taken my dog's body to the cemetery too since the doghouse was now empty—I got used to the quiet, preferring it to the noise parents make when they hate each other. I spent as much time tending to my garden as possible and talking to the fairies. Those showed up soon after Teddy's passing, told me they were too shy to introduce themselves when he was around. They kept me company, made me feel less alone.

Sadly, my days spent in the garden were short-lived.

One crisp September day—a Saturday, I believe— Margaret Morton and her team found me in the woods caring for the pumpkins I'd planted back in July.

"Jesus Christ, you're still here?"

That was Margaret. I yelped in surprise, shaken by the unexpected company, and nearly tripped over a vine. Margaret and her six friends filed out of the trees and stepped inside the circle as if they belonged there. Some held their hands on their hips while others crossed their arms, posing the way all tough kids do.

"You must be one weird bitch to be coming out here, with your brother dying here and all," Margaret said. "What the hell you doing anyway?"

"Gardening," I whispered.

Margaret scoffed and so did the rest of them, following suit. "You do realize those flowers is what killed Teddy, right?" she spat. "Your stupid little garden killed your brother."

I looked down at my yellow rain boots and saw a fairy peeking out from behind a pumpkin. She was crying.

Margaret Morton shook her head and looked around the garden, at the lilies and roses and marigolds and tulips. At the doghouse.

A ghastly grin spread across her face.

"You know why that doghouse is here, right?" she asked.

I looked up from my boots, looked back down. "No," I answered, wanting desperately for Teddy to come running out of the trees, swinging a baseball bat at Margaret Morton's head and crack it open like an egg.

Margaret leered, shared a look with her friends. "Did y'all hear that? She really doesn't know." Slowly, the large girl lifted her knees, stepping over the flowers and half-grown pumpkins, closing in while her friends stayed behind. When she reached me, she placed her hands on my shoulders and spun me around so I was facing the doghouse.

"That there," she said, pointing, "is the home of a hellhound."

"A what?" I asked.

"You telling me you ain't never heard of a hellhound?" Margaret asked.

I shook my head.

"Ever been to church?" she pressed.

"Mama and Daddy don't like church," I replied.

Margaret breathed a laugh through her nose. "Well, you're

in for a world of trouble then, Abigail Greenwood, because even the devil has pets.

"See, a man once summoned a hellhound here. He built this doghouse and used black magic to call on it, and it came. It came to drag the man's enemies kickin' and screamin' to hell. And once a hell portal is opened, it can't be closed. I'm surprised it ain't come out of there and dragged you to hell already since you killed your. . ."

She paused. The wind had started to pick up, tossing the tree limbs above like balloons at a birthday party. Clouds were rolling in too, ashen and threatening to crack.

"Well," Margaret said, staring up at the sky. "I suppose it ain't none of my business. The Bible says not to judge, lest you be judged yourself, so I better keep my mouth shut."

Margaret returned to her friends, adding, "I'd be careful out here if I was you. You wouldn't want to be swallowed up." With that, the group ran off into the trees, in the direction of town.

I was so transfixed by the doghouse—the "hell portal"—that I may have stood in that same spot for ten minutes or more, unconcerned with the coming storm.

A bajillion thoughts ran through my head. Had Teddy known about the doghouse? Surely he woulda told me if he did, forbidden me from ever going out there with or without him. And Henry, he spent so much time in that doghouse even when he was alive that he would have noticed if something was wrong; if a hellhound lived beneath his paws.

Yes, it did spring to mind that maybe Margaret Morton was telling stories, trying to scare the weird ten-year-old girl who liked to play alone in the forest, but that thought didn't last long. Because staring at me from the doghouse, peering out from the pitch-dark blackness inside were eyes. Two beady red eyes.

I couldn't help it, I started crying. Tears rolled down my

face as did the droplets that burst forth from the clouds, and I started screaming words at the thing.

"I'm sorry!" I shouted. "I'm so sorry! I didn't mean it. I swear I didn't. I didn't mean to kill him. I just wanted flowers!"

I was sobbing, harder than I ever did in all my life, crying for my big brother, for my sweet dog, for my mama, and even for Daddy. Those mean kids and teachers from school. I cried for everything, but the creature inside the doghouse stared on, unblinking. Judging.

"More," I heard it say, its voice deep and rumbling like summer thunder. "More. . ."

"More?" I asked through chattering teeth, clutching my cold, wet arms in an attempt to stay warm. "More what?"

"More. . ." it repeated.

And then it was gone. Those cruel red eyes disappeared from the darkness of the doghouse, taking with it the rain and the clouds. Suddenly, the world was as it was before: sunny and calm, a beautiful September afternoon.

I quickly gathered my things—my gardening tools, my art supplies, my sopping wet copy of The Blue Fairy Book—and I ran off toward home. I didn't return to the garden clearing the rest of the summer, or the summer after, or the summer after that. Instead, I stayed home listening to Mama and Daddy, trying to be on my best behavior always. I stayed in my room a lot, thinking about Teddy and Henry and the hellhound in the woods, thinking of dark red eyes and the word "More. . ."

What had it meant, I wondered. More of what?

It was hard for me to sleep after that. I was so scared that what Margaret Morton said was true, that the hound would find me and drag me down to hell for what I did.

What I accidentally did.

I think about those days now whenever I pass by the

forest on my way to and from school, and more than that, I think about the days Teddy and I spent together, catching fireflies in the woods as Henry watched, collecting them in a jar only to pull off the lid and let them fly away, off into the treetops and into the stars, screaming "Goodbye!" at the top of our lungs. Yes . . . I think about those days as I stare into the trees, as I diverge from the path leading to Autumncrow High and descend deep into the green, the forest floor crackling like bonfire kindling beneath my feet.

"Goodbye!" I want to scream. "Goodbye!"

The woods are exactly as they were six years ago, back when I was a little girl with velvet pigtails and wayward feet, playing hide-and-seek with tiny fairies and partaking in tea parties with my other woodland friends.

I can see them now. Those very same creatures spying on me from their hiding places, peeking from hollowed tree trunks, wondering who this strange girl is, wondering why she is dragging a noose through their peaceful land.

Instead of comforting me, the fairies do what most humans do: they avert their eyes, return to their lively celebrations, allowing me to pass without further notice or concern.

They don't recognize me.

I can't blame them though. I don't recognize me either. I haven't since Teddy died. But God, I recognize them. Every wing, iris, freckle, footprint—I remember, always.

When I reach the clearing, a tear falls onto my cheek. Unlike the forest, my garden paradise is only a shadow of what it once was; all dried up, twisted and blackened like overcooked burgers at a barbeque. I don't know what I was expecting. The garden hasn't been cared for in years and, somehow, I know that if I'm unhappy, the garden will be too.

Sitting at the center of the wasteland, as it always had, is the doghouse, the only thing that hasn't changed since I'd last been here. There are no red eyes peeking out at me though, and I am old enough now to realize I may have imagined them. Still, I avert my gaze, looking away from the dilapidated old thing and finding a nice solid oak with branches that stretch out above the clearing.

This will do.

The thought is grim, but there is no other place I'd rather spend my final moments. This place, no matter how different it may look now, is home and I wish to remain here forever.

Never before have I climbed a tree, but I'd seen Teddy do it enough times I am able to replicate his movements from memory. In ten minutes, I have made it safely to a steady branch that runs parallel to the ground, a good fifteen feet above. Sliding to the center, I know if I fall while trying to ready the noose—fall and break a leg or an arm—I will simply climb back up again, ignoring the pain and trying a second, third, fourth time until the deed is done.

I get it right on the first try.

I wrap the noose around the branch, getting it nice and tight before pulling the loop over my head, fastening it around my neck. The rope is dry and prickly. It scratches my skin, giving me the ironic desire to scratch my neck; ironic because I soon won't feel anything at all. I won't feel itchy nerves or sorrow or emptiness. I won't feel trapped anymore. I want so desperately to break free, to run and take control of my life, but I am at the mercy of Mama's addiction, of Daddy's rage. This is my only way out, the only thing I know to do.

I sit on the branch, my legs dangling off the edge as I prepare to drop, to suspend my body in the air for everyone else to try and understand. But I notice something. There is movement below, a stirring at the center of the clearing.

Something is climbing out of the doghouse.

The distraction is enough to make me nearly lose my

balance. I clutch the branch to steady myself and look down at the hand reaching from the opening. Yes, a hand. For half a second, I think maybe a homeless person is hiding in there, has claimed the doghouse as shelter, but this hand isn't quite human. It is proportioned like one, but the fingers are long and obscured by thick, black fur down to daggerlike claws.

I expel a choked gasp. Chills callus over my body like a second skin.

The hand stretches further outward, followed by a skeletal, humanlike arm also completely covered in coarse hair like that of a bear. There is a smell, pungent like decayed flesh baked in the sun. It reminds me of Henry.

The fingers plunge into the earth, gaining leverage so the thing can pull, hauling a quarter of its body out of the doghouse. I see pointed ears and dark pits where eyes should be and a canine's snout, lips peeling back to reveal yellowed incisors and an ashy-gray tongue that hangs to one side as it pants into the dirt. I see a human torso beneath Kleenex-thin skin beneath patchwork fur, and I see a rope around the creature's neck, skin chaffed from the tension of being bound to the doghouse.

"Jesus. . ." I breathe.

It hears me.

The head of the beast snaps in my direction, empty eye sockets staring up at me. I freeze, holding my breath as if doing so will render me invisible. I can see now that the creature's eyes aren't exactly empty. There is something in those black pits, swimming around like bacteria under a microscope. Something red.

The color quickly fades, replaced by an eon of blackness. With that, the beast's head collapses into the dirt. Its grip on the soil loosens and its body seems to deflate. Whatever breath was in the thing whooshes out, leaving behind a motionless husk.

Is it dead?

I'm not sure, but it certainly looks so. I stay in the tree a while, waiting, staring intently at the animal, if it can be called that. Then, when I am sure the thing is asleep at the very least, I pull the noose from my neck, completely disinterested in it for the time being, and climb down from the tree.

I stand still at the base of the oak, watching for any further movement before taking a cautious step toward the creature, then another. Soon, I am only a few strides away from the doghouse, the smell of death stronger than ever.

It looks like a werewolf, I think to myself, remembering those Saturday night monster movies I sometimes saw on CRYP-TV as a kid, that strange local station I was only able to pick up if I adjusted the television antenna just right. Only this creature isn't strong and powerful like those movie monsters. It is more like a malnourished dog left tied up in the yard by its abusive owner. A deep sadness settles in my gut, a sorrow so intense I can't help but reach out and touch the creature behind one ear.

It stirs.

I pull back, falling from my crouched position onto my butt. There is a moment of regret, of thinking how stupid I am for coming near this thing, for wanting to touch it—nurture it, even. But then I remember why I'm out here in the first place. If it decides to spring up and kill me, I'll be saved the trouble of having to do so myself.

But it doesn't. Instead, it flinches at my touch as if startled, jerking its head and looking right into my eyes. It doesn't leap to its hind legs, doesn't slash my throat with its claws. It just fixes that angry glare on me, the red glow returning to its eyes, dancing about like fiery charcoal.

I recognize these eyes, but I am not scared this time. Yes,

the anger is hot and filled with hatred, but somehow, I don't believe it is anger for me, just as the anger I feel is not for it.

Minutes pass, the two of us staring at each other in silence. Then I nod in understanding and walk away, moving through the woods toward home.

A GRUMBLE. A MOAN.

I pull harder, tugging with all my weight on the plastic tarp, just like the one Teddy and I had used to drag Henry through the woods all those years ago.

Another groan breaks the silence, then a voice: "Abby. . .?"

Daddy is waking up.

I am no more than two minutes away from the forest clearing. Close. So, so close.

"Abigail?" he says again, his voice firmer. "Abigail, what are you doing?"

I ignore him, try focusing my attention on getting to the clearing before he gains strength. Only thirty minutes ago, I had taken a cast iron skillet to the back of his head while he sat in his recliner, drinking a Budweiser and watching live politics on the TV. I thought I'd hit him hard enough to put him out for hours, but here he was already coming to.

My heart races.

"Jesus Christ, my head!" Daddy shouts. "Ow! What happened to my head?"

Don't stop, I tell myself, feet digging into the muddy forest floor. My fingers are cramping up from clenching the tarp, but my knees hurt worse, burning from exertion.

Daddy props himself up on his elbows and glances around. "What the fuck are you doing?" he demands, darting forward and clamping a meaty hand around my wrist. "What the fuck have you done?"

I act impulsively. Turning around, I swing the hand of my free arm. It whistles through the fresh forest air, followed by a sharp slap as my palm strikes him across the face.

I've fantasized about this. Every day. Every single day since Teddy died, I wondered what it would be like to hit Daddy back, to make him hurt the way he's made me hurt, but I never acted on it. I knew the day I hit him would be the day he killed me. Or worse.

Today, though, was different. Today, he would hurt.

Today, Daddy would burn.

The slap takes him by shock, rocking him sideways off the tarp and onto the leaf-strewn ground. He moves his fingers to his split lip, blood already oozing to the surface.

"You hit me," he whispers. His eyes bug out of his head in befuddlement and, for a moment, he looks like a nervous pug sitting in the mud and grime. But that expression quickly turns to rage. "You hit me," he repeats. "You bitch. I'm gonna kill you!"

I do the only thing I can think to do; I run, forgetting all about the pain in my knees.

Daddy is behind me. I hear him stumbling through the trees, shouting words unintelligible to anyone but me. The words are city sewage spilling from his mouth, and not one of them is new to my ears.

The clearing is ahead, the day's remaining sunlight filtering through the top and brushing the surrounding trees with alpenglow. The luminous sight gives me a moment's peace.

I'm here. I'm home.

I burst into the clearing, not stopping until I reach the doghouse. I don't see the hellhound anywhere, but I can feel him. He's here with me, waiting in the shelter of the doghouse right now, waiting to do what he was brought here to do.

"Abigail! Get your skinny ass back here or I swear I'll put your lights out."

I twirl on my heels to see Daddy standing at the edge of the clearing. He is drenched in sweat, the fabric of his t-shirt sticking to his gut as it heaves with each furious breath.

"Come. Now," he demands.

I back away. "No," I say.

Daddy grins and takes a step forward. "Say that again."

I swallow and raise my chin in the air. "No. No more, Daddy. No more."

The man shakes his head, looks down at the ground. "You know what?" he says, stepping around the gnarled remnants of my garden. "I think I'm going to enjoy this."

He runs, sprinting toward me with his hands outstretched, a boogeyman reaching from the back of a child's closet. I turn and dart behind the doghouse, using it as a shield against the large man that somehow helped bring me into this world.

Daddy reaches the front of the doghouse, standing at the opening and leering at me over the roof. "What did you think you were going to do, huh?" he shouts. "Were ya gonna bury me out here or something? Eh?" He pulls out a pocketknife he keeps tucked in a sheath inside his pocket.

The knife. How did I forget about the knife?

"Were ya gonna try and get rid of me?" he asks, waving the blade through the air.

I peer into those buggy eyes and dig for my voice. As a young girl, I would have wet myself as I did many times when faced with this man's swinging fists. But today, I do no such thing.

"No," I reply. "I don't have to do anything."

In a flash, a clawed hand bursts forth from the doghouse,

whacking across Daddy's shins in a spray of red. Daddy screams, a raspy wail that booms through the forest sending nesting birds fleeing for the skies.

The knife flies from his hand as he falls onto his back, but his bare feet remain standing at the entrance of the doghouse.

"Oh, God!" Daddy screeches, ogling down at his legs, blood spewing from where his feet had once been. "Oh, my— No! NOOO!"

Once again, the hand of the hellhound reaches out of the doghouse, long fingers ensnaring one of the feet and dragging it inside. Daddy is too busy screaming in pain to notice, but the noises grab his attention. Floating out of the doghouse is the sound of chewing.

Daddy's shrieks crumble to a whimper as we both listen, listen to the smacking of jaws, the lapping of a tongue, and then swallowing, a deep gulp gulp gulp.

The hand extends into the light again, grabbing the other foot and bringing it inside. More sounds follow. Chomping. Crunching. Devouring.

"What's in there?" Daddy cries. "What is it?"

I can't answer. I can't even move. I stare at the scene before me in utter shock, at Daddy's bleeding legs, at the monster crawling out of the doghouse.

Daddy's screams of terror push at my temples, filling my head, as do the gulping sounds. The hound rises onto its hind legs, towering several feet above both my father and me. It tilts its head back. In its open mouth, I can see Daddy's toes for a split-second before they disappear, sliding down the beast's throat.

Gulp gulp gulp.

Daddy is trying to escape. He is on his belly now, pulling himself away with his arms, dragging what's left of his legs behind him.

He doesn't get far.

I put my hands to my mouth, wanting to cover my eyes but feeling as though I shouldn't.

No, Abby. You started this. Now you must watch.

So, I do. I watch as the hound's mouth opens, opens wider and wider, extending as far as possible and then extending even further. The skin breaks at the jowls, jaw detaching with an audible pop!

Deep inside the throat of this monster shines . . . a light? No. No, whatever this brightness is, it can't be called a light. The word seems too pure, wholesome. This isn't. It is a fiery red inferno that tosses and churns inside the gut of the hound, blazing into my eyes and blinding me to everything else around. It is sadness and hopelessness and pain and loss. It is agony. It is grief.

Hell, Abigail Greenwood. See it there? Hell. . .

The hound stoops, dropping onto all fours and scooping the bloody stumps of my father's legs into its widened mouth. Daddy cries out in surprise, stopping his army crawl and turning to look down at the thing as it begins to devour him whole, gulping, swallowing.

"GAAAHHHHH—" Daddy cries.

He flips onto his back, sits up, and pounds his fists against the hound's snout. It doesn't seem to notice. It continues to consume the man, pulling him deeper and deeper until half his body is lost inside. The hound bites down once it reaches my father's midriff, chomping hard, reminding me of that scene in Jaws when Robert Shaw is bit in half by the great white. Except, the blood that spews from Daddy's mouth isn't bright red like in the movies. It is darker, almost black in color.

Losing his fight, Daddy flops onto his back, staring dazedly up at the clouds—Zoo animals . . . Zoo animals . . . — allowing himself to be swallowed by the hound. He doesn't scream anymore, doesn't even flinch as he is inhaled deep into the hound's gut, into the bowels of the earth.

And then there is silence.

Once again, the hound stands to its hind legs and turns, glaring down at me with fire and malice. It is no longer sick, no longer weak and starving for souls. It has eaten, and I am the one who fed it.

It steps toward me, bringing its shoulders back and looming taller than ever.

Tall. So tall.

As the power returns to its bones, it gently strokes the rope around its neck—the rope still binding it to the doghouse—and fastens those soulless eyes on mine.

"More. . ." it says.

A whimper leaves my throat. Me . . . It wants to eat me. . .

A chill surrounds me, filling my bones clear down to the marrow. My teeth chatter and tears fill my eyes as I realize for the first time in years that I don't want to die.

Oh, Jesus, I don't want to die. . .

The beast raises one gnarled finger to its side, pointing it like a dagger ready to slash me from ear to ear. I close my eyes, bracing for an impact, waiting for the inevitable slice that will render me immobile, bleeding out as I am swallowed whole just like my father.

But the blow never comes.

I open my eyes one by one, seeing the hellhound still standing before me, seeing that single finger still outstretched, pointing down at Daddy's pocketknife on the ground.

I look at the knife. I look at the rope.

Then I understand. More.

I meet the creature's eyes, dread settling in my gut. It wants me to set it free. It'll let me live—live—if I cut the rope and let it run free.

I hesitate, thinking about all the people in town who would be put in danger, all the people in Autumncrow that could be hunted down, devoured.

I think of the teachers at my high school, of my classmates . . . I think of their hurtful words.

I think of Mama, of her neglect, of all the times she turned her back on me as a child while Daddy beat me.

I think of everyone, of every ounce of pain I have endured over the years.

I meet the hound's eyes.

More.

I pick the pocketknife off the ground and slice the rope, cutting it through in a single slash. The hellhound wastes no time. It turns, braces itself on all fours, then runs off into the woods, swallowed by the thicket. I am left in its wake, trembling in the sun's final rays.

I'm alive, I think. I'm alive.

I look to my left and see a noose swinging from a tree. It is the same one I had placed there myself only a short while ago, but it is foreign to me now, put there by someone else.

Some movement to my right catches my eye. I glance down and see something green rising up from the ground between thorny vines and brambles. I draw closer, crouching low and watching as the thing—the stem—begins to bud before my eyes, opening up and revealing bright, yellow pedals.

A tulip.

Flowers are sprouting all around me now, pushing through the soil and bursting open like fireworks in the night. Reds, blues, purples, greens—my garden is coming alive.

I can't help it, I start laughing, laughing so hard that tears spill down my cheeks. Those laughs turn to sobs, which turns to laughter and back again, over and over as I watch the forest garden become anew in the settling twilight.

For a moment, I think I can see Teddy and Henry standing together at the edge of the clearing, side-by-side in the shadows, staring at me forlornly. My smile falters as I stare back, raising my palm in the air and giving them an unsure wave. But just like that, they are gone, and I wonder if they were really there to begin with.

A familiar sadness fills my head, a tingling on my scalp and in my bones. I stay with it for a moment, feeling those waves come and eventually go.

The smile soon returns to my face and I gaze off into the trees, in the direction of town.

Yes, I think, more.

More, indeed.

ABOUT THE AUTHORS

KEVIN DAVID ANDERSON'S DEBUT NOVEL IS THE CULT zombie romp, *Night of the Living Trekkies* and his latest book is the horror/comedy *.Midnight Men* Anderson's short stories have appeared in many publications including the British Fantasy Award-winning quarterly *Murky Depths*, and the Bram Stoker nominated anthology *The Beauty of Death*. For more information go to KevinDavidAnderson.com and be sure to check out **Kevin David Anderson's** YouTube channel.

CAMERON CHANEY IS A HORROR NERD. WHEN HE'S NOT writing scary stories or filming videos (or battling the forces of evil), He can be found in his private library, curled up in his reading chair with a cup of tea and a good book. You can follow Cameron's adventures in horror on Instagram and Twitter (@bookmovieguy), and on Facebook (@Library-MacabreBooks). Cameron's YouTube channel, **Library Macabre** will keep you up at night.

DANE COBAIN (HIGH WYCOMBE, UK) IS A PUBLISHED author, freelance writer and (occasional) poet and musician. When he's not working on his next release, he can be found reading and reviewing books for his BookTube channel, **Dane Reads**, and his award-winning book blog, SocialBook-shelves.com. His releases include No Rest for the Wicked (supernatural thriller), Eyes Like Lighthouses When the Boats Come Home (poetry) Former.ly (literary fiction), Social

Paranoia (non-fiction) and Come On Up to the House (horror), as well as and Driven and The Tower Hill Terror in the Leipfold quirky cosy detective series. Find and follow him at www.danecobain.com.

JAMES FLYNN IS THE AUTHOR OF TWO BOOKS, 'Conservation' and 'The Edge of Insanity'. His work is often described as eerie and disturbing. When he's not scribbling on bits of paper to create stories, he scribbles on bits of paper to create drawings. James resides in Vietnam. All of his accumulated work can be found at JamesFlynn.org. James can also be found on YouTube at **Artist James Flynn**.

MIHALIS GEORGOSTATHIS IS A NATIVE GREEK CURRENTLY living in Athens (where his story takes place). He writes horror, dark fantasy, and science fiction, and speaks about them on his YouTube Channel **The Nihilist Geek**.

NICHOLAS GRAY IS AN ASPIRING HORROR AUTHOR WHO got his start writing creepypastas for narrators on YouTube and has had his work featured on the official creepypasta website. Born with a TBI (Traumatic Brain Injury) he was told he wouldn't read, write, talk, or be able to tie his shoes. Gray is also a Cancer survivor, suffering from stage 3B Hodgkin's Lymphoma back in 2012. He has since been "cured," and is living a good life with his family in his home state of Michigan. Find him on YouTube at **Spooky Noodles.**

. . .

E.D. Lewis GREW UP IN THE AMERICAN MIDWEST. During his adolescence, he developed a love for storytelling and wanted to craft stories from his imagination and share them with others one day. Shortly after college he met and fell in love with his partner, who is both loving and supportive. Today, they still reside in the Midwest. He is the author of *The Curse of Rydge House: A Gothic Novel*, as well as an erotic short story entitled *Alone with the Professor*. E.D. Lewis can be found on platforms such as Instagram, Twitter, Wattpad, and his YouTube channel, **E.D. Lewis Reviews**.

Andrew Lyall LIVES IN THE SOUTH OF ENGLAND WITH two dogs and a very understanding fiancée. He spent his teenaged years growing up in the village of Crowthorne, the setting for his story, and more of the details in that tale than you might expect are true. You can find him discussing all things horror on Youtube at **Grumpy Andrew's Horror House** and tweeting horror on Twitter @grumpyandrew

Marie McWilliams HAILS FROM NORTHERN IRELAND. Her writing has been featured in various anthologies and book subscription boxes and her first novel 'Broken Mirrors' is available now on Amazon. You can find Marie on Instagram, TikTok and on YouTube at **Marie McWilliams** where she shares her love of Horror.

Lydia Peever'S DEBUT NOVEL, *Nightface*, WAS published in 2011. Her short stories have appeared in *Postscripts To Darkness*, *Dark Moon Digest*, *For When The Veil Drops*, *Memento Mori*, *The Wicked Library*, and two collections, *Pray Lied Eve 1* and *Pray Lied Eve 2*. Alongside writing horror, she is also a web designer and public servant from Northern Ontario, Canada, who currently lives in Ottawa. In her spare time, she updates the new releases section of the Horror Writers Association website, co-hosts a podcast called *Splatterpictures Dead Air,* and talks horror books on Youtube at **Typical Books**.

KEN POIRIER IS A LOVER OF STORIES. HE CHOOSES TO express those stories in many ways, from writing, to performing, to creating video games, films, and more. He is a graduate of Indiana University, Indiana River State College, and the Greater Hartford Academy of the Arts. He has been publishing as a freelance columnist since 2008. His first book, The Bear Wife, was published in 2015 with MeTime Publishing. Ken has last been seen traveling the United States with his mechanical typewriter, working on the latest novel in his fantasy-horror series, **Fake Tattoos**. You can always check out his website, kenpoirier.com, or get in touch with him on Wattpad or Goodreads. You'll find Ken on YouTube at **theking4mayor**.

R. SAINT CLAIRE IS AN AUTHOR OF ADULT AND YOUNG adult horror and suspense fiction with a background in theater and filmmaking. Honors include the Wattys shortlist, winner of the Dazed for Horror film festival for best screenplay, and a Webby honoree for her 2009 web series, Gemini Rising. Check out Regina and her alter ego, Batilda Belfry, at **Regina's Haunted Library** and on her blog RSaint-Claire.com

. . .

RYAN STROUD IS AN EDUCATOR FROM ATLANTA, GEORGIA. Before his journey into shaping young minds, he spent many years as a Public Affairs/Journalist in the U.S. Army. In his spare time, when he's not grading papers or writing, he loves to go camping with his wife and kids, play with his dogs and cats, and coach soccer. Check out Ryan's YouTube channel, **Coach Stroud's What to Read While Quarantined**.

MICHAEL TAYLOR HAS A LIFELONG APPETITE FOR READING and writing. He earned BA/MA in English at Canterbury Christ Church University, lectured in Victorian and Gothic literature before taking up a role teaching secondary English wishing to shape young readers' minds. Now he happily manages a coffee shop (in a cinema!) while reading, writing and updating his YouTube channel, **It's Mikey's Mind**, in his spare time.

D.L. TILLERY WAS HOMESCHOOLED FROM A YOUNG AGE and also attended college online. Her poetry was first published when she was nineteen. Since then, she has written for the Gothic magazine, Carpe Nocturne. Now in her 30's, she has coined the title "The Mistress of Horror" and hosts weekly episodes on her YouTube Channel under **Author D.L. Tillery**. She is currently working on her debut "Caliostro," a supernatural horror novel series. D.L. was born and raised in the state of Maryland, where she currently resides with her 4-year-old daughter, two brothers, and mother. The message she loves to leave for all her readers is to "Stay Scared."

. . .

Matt Wall is a writer and BookTuber. He lives in the middle of nowhere in Southern California with his family and two dogs. Find out more at www.ihatemattwall.com You'll find him discussing books and more at his YouTube channel, **Paperback Junky**.

Jason White is a writer and BookTuber from the frozen lands of Ontario, Canada. On his YouTube channel, **Jason's Weird Reads**, he likes to talk about the books he reads and records top ten videos of his favorite horror novels. He is the author of over 20 short stories, published in various magazines and anthologies, and the now out of print novel, The Haunted Country. You can buy his first collection, Isolation, at Amazon.

Cam Wolfe grew up in that spider infested island down under, Australia. Being born to a father who loved telling people stories, and a mother who loved reading them, gave him a passion for writing since he could string a sentence together. He is a fan of almost every genre, but there's a special place in his heart for the most epic of Fantasy, and the grimmest of Horror. You can find Cam on Youtube at **Page Nomad**, where he makes videos about reading and writing.

CJ Wright has always had an interest in writing and horror for as long as he can remember, but it wasn't until 2000 that he decided to try his hand at writing a novel. Once he had finished the first draft, he kept going to see how far he could go with following his dream. In 2003 his first novel, Ritual of Blood, was published, and so far, he's published eight novels and a collection of short stories. He was born in Birmingham, England, and has lived in the town of Droitwich Spa, where his story in this anthology is set, most of his life. Follow CJ's reviews and discussions on his YouTube channel, **CJ Wright's Books and Horror**.

AFTERWORD

Thank you for reading Local Haunts. If you enjoyed your journey here, please consider leaving a review on Amazon and Goodreads. Also, feel free to send me an email at exlibrisregina@gmail.com I would love to hear your thoughts about the book and your experiences on BookTube. Who knows? This anthology may be the start of a fun and scary tradition.

R. Saint Claire (Editor and Contributor)

Printed in Great Britain
by Amazon

47846861R00182